MW01253305

S.P. Hozy

If Only To Say Goodbye

NDE Publishing
2005

If Only To Say Goodbye

By S.P. Hozy

Edited by Myrna Riback

Cover and title page illustrations by François Thisdale © 2005

© 2005 by S.P. Hozy

© 2005 by NDE Publishing

Elena Mazour, Publisher

NDE Publishing

15-30 Wertheim Court

Richmond Hill, ON L4B 1B9

tel: 905-731-1288

toll free: 800-675-1263

fax: 905-731-5744

e-mail: info@ndepublishing.com

url: www.ndepublishing.com

Library and Archives Canada Cataloguing in Publication

Hozy, Penny, 1947-

　　　　If only to say goodbye : a mystery novel / by S.P. Hozy.
ISBN 1-55321-109-X

　　　　I. Title.
PS8615.O99I35 2005　　　　C813'.6　　　　C2005-901142-4

Printed in Canada

NDE Publishing is a trademark of NDE Canada Corp.

For Sylvia and Gerry

Enjoy... again!

S.P. Hozy

If Only To Say Goodbye

S.P. Hozy

Penny

NDE Publishing
2005

"I suppose sooner or later in the life of everyone comes a moment of trial. We all of us have our particular devil who rides us and torments us, and we must give battle in the end."
Daphne Du Maurier, *Rebecca*

Chapter One

On May 15, 1976, Joanna Reynolds was reading the section on the Snake personality in a book on Chinese astrology when the doorbell rang. Her husband Franklin was born in the Year of the Snake and she had been struck by the uncanny accuracy of the book's description of his personality. It said he was "self-reliant" and had a "profound sense of responsibility." The book told Joanna that the Snake was a reflective individual and an enigma who did not always communicate well with those closest to him. The Franklin Joanna knew could be demanding and distrustful of others but also soft-spoken and diplomatic when he had to be. The book also said his life would end in triumph or in tragedy, dictated by his past actions.

She was contemplating the meaning of Karma in her husband's life, and how sixteen years of marriage and Franklin's powerful personality had shaped their life together, when the doorbell rang. She opened the door to find a man over six feet tall with broad shoulders and a square face standing there. His moustache was thick and black and the square-cut, flat style of his gray-flecked hair made him all the more intimidating. His gray suit was well cut but well worn and he wore a white shirt and dark blue tie. He showed her some identification and introduced himself as Peter Morgan from the State Department. She invited him in.

"Mrs. Reynolds, I'm afraid I have some bad news for you." Peter Morgan's bulk looked out of place on Joanna's white, satin brocade sofa. "Your husband has drowned in an accident in Thailand."

Her first reaction to the news was amazement. Not grief, or sadness, but a kind of reverberating shock at the coincidental aptness of the words she had just been reading. She stared at Peter Morgan with her mouth open. All she could think was, God isn't supposed to play dice with the universe. Peter Morgan started to stammer an apology but Joanna didn't wait to hear it. Her stomach was churning like a washing machine and she ran from the room and threw up into the toilet in the downstairs powder room.

When she returned, Peter Morgan offered to make her some tea, but she declined. He asked if she would prefer some brandy and she told him to help himself but that she didn't want anything. She sat down in her rose-colored wing chair, wishing none of this were happening.

"I'm so sorry, Mrs. Reynolds," he said, attempting to comfort her. "I wish I could tell you there was some mistake, but there's no doubt that the deceased is Franklin Reynolds." He told her Franklin's body had been found washed up on the beach at Pattaya, a resort town less than a hundred miles from Bangkok. He said Franklin was wearing swimming trunks and the only mark on him was a bump on his forehead. The cause of death listed as drowning.

She didn't doubt that the Thai police had identified the body correctly. Franklin was a high-profile American who had been in Thailand for the past nine months as head of Americans Aid Refugees. When the war in Vietnam had ended, he was appointed by a Senate committee formed to solve the Vietnamese refugee problem. After the fall of Saigon and the sudden departure of the Americans, boatloads of Vietnamese fleeing the communists became an embarrassment to the American government. People all over the world saw their desperate faces daily on television as they fled across the border into Thailand. The camps set up for them by the Thai government became a nightmare. Most of the refugees were ill, famished and exhausted and their babies were dying in the unsanitary, crowded conditions. The wait was interminable and many seemed doomed to a life in limbo, unwanted and hopeless.

Peter Morgan stayed until he was sure she would be all right by herself. Joanna ended up making tea for both of them and they sat at the kitchen table talking about life and death for a couple of hours. She was glad he was there and that he was doing most of the talking. His wife had died suddenly two years before and he seemed to know the right things to say. As he spoke, Joanna was aware that he may have wondered why she didn't cry. She didn't know why herself, except that it seemed as if they were talking about somebody else's life. It was like watching a disaster on the six o'clock news. Somebody else's tragedy. He offered to call someone to stay with her but she told him she needed to be alone for a while. She needed time to think.

After Peter Morgan left, Joanna went out into the back garden and examined every tree, bush and plant. She pulled a few weeds, inhaled the familiar fragrance of the purple lilacs and watered the lawn. She and Franklin had lived in this same house in the suburb of Oak Park just west of Chicago all their married life. The house had been built in 1913 by the architect Vernon S. Watson. It was a proud house of cream stucco with clean geometric lines and understated detailing that foreshadowed the Art Deco movement. Joanna loved the stained glass panes that topped the second-floor bedroom windows and the slightly arched lintel over the front door.

They had landscapers and gardeners to maintain the grounds, but Joanna had always been the one who decided what should be planted and she took pride in the garden's oriental simplicity. It was elegant without being ascetic. Each bush and flower, every tree, had a rightness and importance about it. The total effect was one of quiet serenity. She always felt peaceful here, not surrounded by unanswered questions or dilemmas, but filled with a sense of knowing. And she believed Franklin had felt that as well. He liked to spend time in the garden when he was at home. It seemed to refresh him. The garden was the "safety zone" in their marriage, a place where they could be together – because theirs had become a marriage based on separateness and separation. She and Franklin had never had children, more by accident than design. The garden was one of the few things they still shared.

They had not shared each other's lives for some years and she was used to being alone. Now it was difficult to accept Franklin's absence as anything but normal. She accepted Franklin's long absences and learned to cherish her privacy, telling herself their arrangement gave her a great deal of freedom. She wasn't jealous by nature and didn't pry into other people's secrets – not even her own husband's. She believed that whatever Franklin wanted her to know, he had told her. The bills were always paid on time and there was very little of a mundane nature that couldn't be taken care of by picking up the phone or hiring someone. Joanna was solitary and bookish by nature and, anyway, Franklin didn't seem to want her to be part of his public life.

He had been the perfect choice to head Americans Aid Refugees. He was a high-profile mover and shaker who could get things done with a few phone calls and a few words in the right ears. He'd been doing this kind of thing for over a decade. In 1964, he had been part of Lyndon Johnson's anti-poverty drive. He was asked to oversee the presidential election in Saigon in 1967. Then in 1968, he was part of the delegation to the Paris Peace Talks with the North Vietnamese.

That was the first time Joanna had asked to go along on one of his trips. But Franklin had bluntly told her he didn't want her there. She had hidden her disappointment; he was so adamantly against her going that she didn't even ask his reasons. She just assumed it would be inappropriate for her to go. But he wouldn't let her go with him to Helsinki in 1969 where he was attending the SALT talks, or to China and Moscow in 1972 where he was part of Nixon's protocol team. There were other trips to places like Turkey, Panama and Athens, but she wasn't allowed to go on those either. All these disappointments now came crowding back on Joanna.

In the early years of their marriage Joanna tried to be the right kind of wife to the son of a wealthy, respected Chicago family. Franklin's family owned Reynolds Medical Instruments and were established society people. Joanna's upbringing had been very different. Her father had died when she was four and her mother took the insurance money and put it into a small hairdressing salon on the main street of Aurora, Illinois. Her hard work and determination put Joanna through the University of Chicago where she graduated with a degree in literature. After school, Joanna took her skills to the public library and was hired as a clerk whose job it was to sort and shelve books, stamp them out, check them in and direct people to the washrooms. That was in 1956. The Eisenhower administration was in charge, Grace Kelly married the Prince of Monaco and Elvis Presley sang "You Ain't Nothin' But A Hound Dog." Life was pretty good. By the time she met Franklin, three years later, Joanna had worked her way up to assistant librarian – literature – and got to go to department meetings, answer reference questions from readers and help kids with their homework. She enjoyed her work, even though a lot of it was routine and repetitive, because it was cloistered and familiar and made her feel useful.

She met Franklin at the library's opening of a new history wing that had been sponsored by his family. Franklin's father was a history buff and had bequeathed his entire library, plus a substantial cash gift, toward the new wing. At first, Franklin was attracted to Joanna's quietness. He said he felt peaceful whenever she was around. He wasn't looking for excitement; he already had plenty of that in his life as a junior partner in one of the city's more prominent law firms. Even in those days Franklin was a crusader. He was a rich man's son with a conscience. He took up causes the way some people picked up stray animals. Housing for the poor. Medical care for the elderly. He loved to tell her about his victories and Joanna loved to listen. She couldn't help but be fascinated by the handsome and charismatic Franklin.

It was the attraction of opposites in so many ways. He was tall and patrician, with dark hair and surprisingly blue eyes that seemed to stare into her soul when he talked about his dreams and ambitions. He trusted her because she wasn't flighty or a gossip like a lot of the society girls he met. Joanna had an intelligence and depth of character that Franklin found appealing. She wasn't a beauty, but that meant she wasn't vain, either. She had warm brown eyes and wore her sandy-colored hair short and brushed back from her face, accentuating its perfect oval shape. Her best feature, Franklin said. They made a handsome couple when she wore high heels and a little makeup to hide her freckles. Franklin liked it when she wore high heels. He told her it improved her posture because she had a tendency to slouch.

They got married in 1960. His family didn't dislike Joanna but they didn't consider it a match made in society heaven either. She wasn't what they'd had in mind for Franklin, but she grew on them the same way she'd grown on Franklin. They were talkers and she was a listener. They acted and she watched. She had good manners and wasn't bad looking. Franklin's sisters taught her how to dress and put on makeup and shake hands with important people. Joanna was an able, if unspectacular, pupil and she was what Franklin wanted. Franklin, as the favorite son, usually got what he wanted.

Joanna spent a long time in the garden that day. In a way, she was just passing time, giving herself a chance to catch up with the bad news. She knew the unanswered questions that were not there in the garden would still be in the house, or in other people's minds or in Thailand on a beach somewhere. When the sun hit the lower half of the western sky, its redness caught her eye and she went into the house. It was early June and the evenings were still chilly. She wasn't hungry even though she hadn't eaten all day, but she made a sandwich and poured herself a drink – an ounce of gin with four ounces of tonic water over ice. Joanna liked to drink gin in the summer and she usually added a slice of lime or lemon. She wandered around the house, knowing she should call people to inform them of Franklin's death, but she didn't feel like talking to anybody.

Before going to bed, Joanna picked up the book on Chinese horoscopes she had been reading earlier in the day. She re-read the chapter on the Boar personality to see what it said about her. She read the words "honesty," "simplicity" and "fortitude." It said she was gallant, sturdy and courageous. The Boar hates conflict and confrontation, it said. He's a genial and accommodating fellow who always gives his opponent the benefit of the doubt. Then she looked up the section on the marriage combination between a Snake husband and a Boar wife. "He is mysterious, worldly and profound. She is unaffected, trusting and ingenuous. Their dia-metrically opposed personalities cannot promise either of them much joy."

Now Franklin was dead, drowned according to the police report, while swimming from the beach or off the side of a boat. They hadn't been able to determine which. The part she didn't understand, and that she hadn't mentioned to Peter Morgan because Franklin didn't like her to talk about it, was that Franklin never swam a stroke in his life. He was deathly afraid of the water and didn't like going on boats. As far as she knew, he didn't even own a bathing suit. Joanna finally fell into an uneasy sleep, won-dering if anything in the last sixteen years had happened the way she thought it had.

Chapter Two

Joanna woke up the next morning just before eight. It was later than she was used to sleeping, but she still had difficulty waking up. She felt as if she were emerging from a black pit and it took her a few minutes to remember the events of the previous day. She felt disoriented and wasn't sure whether she had dreamed the news of Franklin's death or it had really happened. She didn't seem to be feeling the sense of grief and loss she thought she should be feeling. She had woken to a lovely June morning but she had not woken up to reality. She felt vaguely depressed, the way she might feel if she were getting the flu. The feeling clung to her like wet clothing.

She didn't usually drink coffee first thing in the morning but she went straight to the kitchen and made a pot, strong and black, and drank it on an empty stomach, knowing she would probably regret it later. Then she began to feel guilty that she had not yet contacted Franklin's family, hoarding the news as if it were hers alone. She decided to talk to Claire, Franklin's older sister, before telling anyone else. She was closest to Claire, who was her friend as well as her sister-in-law. She didn't want to tell Claire over the phone so it meant she would have to get dressed and drive the five or so miles to Claire's home.

Joanna stood under the shower for a full ten minutes wondering if she was going to feel half-dead for the rest of her life. She put on a pale green, knit dress with a soft leather belt. It was comfortable and familiar and she always wore it with the gold necklace Franklin had given her for their tenth anniversary. She felt overly concerned with what to wear, but she knew it was her way of keeping her inner self and her outer self together. She didn't want to fall apart.

Were things going to be very different from now on, she wondered? Over the years she had come to accept Franklin's absences as normal. After it became apparent he didn't want her traveling with him, Joanna had started taking courses at the university. She studied philosophy, sociology, anthropology, world religion, anything that took her fancy. She even dabbled in astrology, learned to knit, thought about joining a quilting group but didn't and took some courses in drawing and painting. She discovered she had a modest talent, but mostly she liked to be occupied in solitary pursuits that forced her to concentrate and focus her mind. She told herself she liked being alone. She could garden in the summer and read and study during the winter. She had a few friends that she went out to dinner with occasionally and once in a while they would go to New York for a couple of days to do some shopping and see a show.

And now, all of a sudden, it was 1976, she was forty years old and Franklin was dead, drowned apparently while swimming in Thailand. Except, in all the years she'd know him, Franklin never went swimming. The few times they'd taken a vacation together, he'd refused to go to the Caribbean or any place that involved boats. "I don't like the water," he said, "and I can't swim. It's not my idea of a holiday." So they'd gone to London and Rome instead. Yet, according to the report, Franklin's body had been found washed up on the beach at Pattaya. How was she going to tell Claire?

When she backed the car out of the garage, she saw that the day was clear and sunny and the birds were singing their heads off. It seemed in such bad taste. She drove the familiar route to Claire's Oak Park home, still not knowing what she would say to her. She allowed her mind to be distracted by the beautiful homes that had been built around the turn of the century by some of America's most illustrious architects. You couldn't drive through Oak Park without thinking about architecture, she thought. She had always loved the drive along Chicago Avenue and then down Forest, where some of Frank Lloyd Wright's earliest Prairie Style homes had been built. Her favorite was the Thomas House built in 1901. She loved its precise lines, its elegantly arched entrance and the leaded glass windows with beaded moldings. Before they were married, she and Franklin often drove through this stately, tree-lined neighborhood, imagining what it would be like to live in one of those magnificent homes.

"Who do you want?" she remembered him saying. "Frank Lloyd Wright? E.E. Roberts? Vernon S. Watson? Take your pick. Your wish shall be my command."

"Frank Lloyd Wright," she'd said. "Definitely."

"Are you sure? You know when Wright built a house he didn't let the owners change a thing. He designed the interiors and the furniture and they had to live with his choices. Could you put up with such tyranny?"

"Well, Wright's dead now, isn't he?"

"Only just. I wouldn't put it past him to find a way to show his displeasure. His ghost is probably listening to us right now."

"Who would you choose, then?" she asked.

"I'm partial to Wright myself, but I'm only heir to a small fortune, not a large one, so we might have to be practical – at least for now. I think Van Bergen might suit us. He's unpretentious, like you, and I like that."

Joanna swallowed hard to hold back the tears. I'm still unpretentious, she thought. At least that hasn't changed.

She made a left onto Lake Street and drove past the Unity Temple, taking in its bold, cubist lines. Built to last, she thought. A temple in the true sense of the word. She liked the idea that the modernism of the twentieth century had found its expression in this corner of the world. Even Ernest Hemingway had been born in Oak Park. She felt anchored here. Safe. It was a solid place, sure of itself and proud of its uniqueness. She turned onto Claire's street and felt her heart lurch. She was here to tell Franklin's sister that he was dead. She realized she hadn't called ahead and it hadn't even occurred to her that Claire might not be home. She pulled into the driveway, trying to decide what to do if no one was there. When Claire came to the door Joanna was both surprised and relieved. Her face must have reflected both emotions.

"What's wrong?" were the first words out of her sister-in-law's mouth.

On meeting her, many people found Claire austere and even intimidating, but she was by nature reserved and quite shy. To mask her shyness, she adopted a persona that was cool and distant. Joanna was a bit like that herself and always thought of Claire as her spiritual sister. Claire was ten years older than Joanna and had a graceful maturity that Joanna envied. She seemed to move with time, not against it. She was what some people called an "old soul." She was intelligent and kind and Joanna trusted her. Many times in the past Joanna had relied on her wisdom.

She made Claire sit down and poured them both a Scotch, even though it was only ten o'clock in the morning. She saw that Claire, clearly alarmed by her strange behavior, sensed something must be terribly wrong, so Joanna said, simply, "It's Franklin. He's dead. Drowned in Thailand."

The color drained from Claire's face. "Are they absolutely certain it was Franklin?"

"Yes, they're sure. It wouldn't be that difficult to identify someone as well known as Franklin. He's been in Bangkok for nearly nine months. There must be a whole network of people he was involved with."

"But you know he never goes near the water." Claire's hand was shaking as she picked up her glass.

"I know. That puzzled me too. But the man from the State Department assured me the Thai police did a thorough investigation. I thought maybe Franklin had finally made up his mind to overcome his phobia. You know if he decides to do something, he does it with absolute determination."

"I suppose it's possible," Claire said. "Franklin has always been so stubborn and secretive. He might do something like that and never say a word about it." Her eyes filled with tears as she said the words, but she blinked them away and took another sip of her Scotch.

"Franklin never talked about why he was so afraid of the water and I got the impression it was one of those taboo subjects, so I never asked," Joanna said. She wanted Claire to remind her of the man she had married and to help her understand what was happening.

Claire looked down at her hands and carefully examined the rings that adorned her long, slender fingers. She was looking back to a day in her childhood that had affected her deeply. "When we were children," she said, "we had a summer home on Lake Michigan. We were all taught to swim very early on, but Franklin was still too young and he hadn't learned yet." She told Joanna that Franklin and their sister Ina had been building sand castles under the supposedly watchful eye of their nurse. Maybe the nurse looked away for only an instant; maybe she dozed off for a few seconds in the hot sun. In any case, she didn't notice Ina run into the water with a bucket full of sand in one hand and a shovel in the other.

"Her own momentum must have overtaken her," said Claire. "I don't know how else it could have happened. She may have hit her head with the bucket when she fell and got her eyes and mouth full of water and sand. Before anyone even noticed, she was dead. Franklin probably thought Ina was trying to swim. He didn't know she was dying. The hysterical scene that followed frightened him so badly that he refused to go near the water ever again. The lake had been so calm. It gave no warning of what was to come, yet, in an instant, it took away Ina's life. My mother just kept screaming, 'My baby's dead! My baby's dead!' We children had never experienced such a feeling of utter helplessness."

Franklin had never mentioned the episode to Joanna. She knew he had a sister who died young but the family never discussed it. They were all bred to be careful and discreet, and not to talk about themselves or their feelings. Joanna knew it was hard for Claire to tell the story even after all those years.

"I guess you'll need to contact Franklin's lawyer," Claire finally said, steering the conversation in a more practical direction. It was all right to talk about lawyers at a time like this.

"I'm sure everything's in order," said Joanna. "But I will have to call Ed and let him know what's happened. To tell you the truth, I'm not sure what I should do. The State Department said they'd notify me when Franklin's body was being shipped home."

Neither of them could grasp the finality of the situation. There was nothing to look at, no evidence of a death. No body to confirm their worst fears. They were both used to Franklin being away for long periods of time, but, if he were dead, surely they would feel some sense of loss. Finally, Claire asked what kind of service Joanna intended to have. Had Franklin and she ever discussed their wishes on the subject? Had they purchased cemetery plots?

"He once mentioned that he wanted to be cremated and his ashes buried in the garden," Joanna said. "I assume there will be instructions in his will." Claire was trying to keep Joanna's mind on mundane matters, away from the unanswered questions that neither of them wanted to think about.

They made up lists of people to be contacted and kept to practical matters. Although Joanna didn't discuss the details with Claire, she knew Franklin had left her everything outright and that his net cash worth was around a million dollars. Even though the Reynolds family no longer owned the controlling interest in the business, they lived comfortably on the interest earned from investments.

Joanna went into the den and phoned Ed Lauder, Franklin's lawyer. Ed was genuinely upset by the news. He and Franklin had been friends for close to fifteen years.

"I'll have to contact Franklin's office in Bangkok and ascertain whether any personal documents are being held there," he said. "I'll call the State Department and the Embassy in Bangkok to verify the arrangements and get an official death certificate." He would call, he said, and they would get together as soon as he was certain he had all the relevant papers.

While Joanna was talking to the lawyer, Claire made coffee in the kitchen. She thought back to the first time her brother had brought Joanna to meet the family. It had been such a solemn occasion, she half expected the shy young woman on Franklin's arm to turn and flee. They had always expected Franklin to choose someone who was confident and outgoing, a woman who would be a partner in his active life. But instead he had chosen a quiet, passive girl who worked at the library. Her mother was a hairdresser or something and, even though she was well educated, Joanna seemed unable to converse comfortably with Franklin's family and friends. She always took her cue from him and was silent and approving, or critical and disapproving, depending on whatever opinion Franklin expressed. It was almost as if she had no personality of her own, thought Claire. She was to learn otherwise over the years. She soon became quite fond of Joanna and learned to enjoy her quiet company. There was substance to Joanna, she discovered, although she lacked any sense of style. But style could be learned and Joanna was an apt pupil. She wanted to please Franklin and did what she believed she had to do to earn his approval.

Claire often wondered why Franklin had been attracted to and married Joanna. It seemed to reveal something about him that none of them had been aware of. Franklin was the baby of the family and, after Ina died, they had all spoiled and indulged him. He quickly learned how to get what he wanted, but it wasn't that difficult. He didn't have to fight for his place in the family or demand attention. All he had to say was, "I want," and whatever it was he wanted became his. He grew up confident and sure of himself. He never doubted his ability to achieve his goals or his innate power to persuade others of the rightness of his ideas. Yet he had chosen as his wife someone who was submissive and agreeable, not someone who would challenge him or try to control him. In fact, it was Franklin who tried to control Joanna. In time, Claire came to understand that, although Franklin controlled Joanna's outer life, how she lived and who she saw, even what she wore, he was never able to control her inner life. Joanna lived her true life in her mind. She read voraciously and was always learning about things. She was curious but she lacked the experience of life. Franklin always seemed to stand between Joanna and life, as if his experience was enough for both of them. The one thing Claire feared was that with Franklin gone, Joanna would retreat further into herself and the life she lived in her imagination.

"Joanna," Claire said, when she had poured their coffee, "whatever you do, don't brood. Don't let yourself slide. It's just too easy. When Robert died, I couldn't think of a reason to keep going. He left me well off, no loose ends, but the bottom line was he left me. And even though there were times when our life together was difficult, he was too much a part of me to want to carry on without him. I felt I had no right to be alive."

Claire's marriage to Robert Fletcher had been tumultuous and marred by scandal. Robert had been married for ten years to a woman of good family and connections who was a few years older than he was. They had two children and an apparently solid marriage. He had a good position and an assured future as an executive vice-president with the Reynolds family firm. Then he met Claire. She was nearly twenty years his junior and in her last year at university. She was a serious student and was planning to do post-graduate work at the Sorbonne in Paris. But when Robert Fletcher left his society wife and two children to be with her, she was called a "home wrecker." Their relationship began under a heavy cloud of shame from which it never entirely recovered.

They went to France to try and escape the smell of scandal that followed them wherever they went, but came back after a year because they didn't want to live in Europe. They tried to settle into quiet obscurity. Robert was reinstated as a Reynolds executive in an attempt to save face and they assumed an air of "normalcy" that bound them in a conspiracy of sorts for the rest of their married life. There would be no going back, no admission of error or bad judgment. Their marriage became a bunker, sheltering them from the world outside. They had no children of their own and it was many years before Robert's children acknowledged Claire's right to exist and use the Fletcher name. Since Robert's death five years ago, Claire had become more reclusive, attending only Reynolds family functions. She was close to her brother Donald and her sister Irene and their children. But Robert's children still considered her an intruder.

When Joanna got home from Claire's she checked the mailbox. There were a few bills and fliers, but while she was sorting through them she came across a letter addressed to her in Franklin's hand-writing. Her hands shook as she tore open the envelope. The letter was written on blue airmail paper and dated nearly three weeks earlier.

"Dear Joanna," it said, "I've been trying to write this letter all day. I have a lot to tell you, but I can't say any of it in a letter. Things have not gone as I planned and I need to get away from here and sort this mess out. I've been negligent in my financial affairs and made a few unwise business decisions that have left us rather badly off. I will be coming home as soon as I can extricate myself from my responsibilities here. Please respect my confidence and don't speak of this to anyone. Forgive me for being stupid. I feel I've let us both down. F."

Chapter Three

What was going on? The man she knew to be terrified of the water had drowned; and the man who was always scrupulously careful about financial matters had made a few unwise decisions and left them "rather badly off." Living without Franklin somewhere in her life was going to be an adjustment, but living without Franklin's money was not a prospect Joanna had even considered. She had always assumed she'd be financially secure. Now she realized she might be facing the kind of life she was totally unprepared for. She'd married Franklin a few years after finishing college and, except for her brief stint at the library, she had no marketable skills or experience. She had only a little money of her own – some unspectacular bonds left to her by her mother that she kept more out of sentiment than financial benefit – and their household goods, some of them fairly valuable but none of which she wanted to part with.

What if Franklin had left a pile of debts? She might not even end up with the house. Was she going to be a penniless widow forced to scrape by on a pittance? Would she have to declare bankruptcy? Joanna started to cry and hated herself for it. "You're so selfish," she sobbed. "You're not crying for your dead husband or the end of your marriage, but for yourself, because you've lost your life of ease." She felt confused and afraid. Things like this didn't happen to people like them. What was she going to do?

"You bastard," she shouted to the empty room, "you didn't share things with me when you were alive. You didn't tell me things. You wouldn't let me travel with you. And now you've left me nothing. How dare you! How dare you leave me like this!"

Joanna cried out her anger for a good hour before acknowledging that she was angry with a dead person. What was the point? The damage had been done. It was left to her to pick up the pieces and carry on with her life. But she couldn't help feeling betrayed and cheated and powerless, and she knew those feelings weren't going to go away in a few hours or a few days. She wanted to talk to someone who wouldn't judge her or expect her to put on a brave face.

Since her mother's death nine years earlier, Joanna's grandparents were the people who cared about her most in the world. During her parents' brief but stormy marriage, they had provided the only stability in Joanna's life. In the years after her father's death, while her mother struggled to establish her beauty parlor and worked long hours to keep it going, her grandparents were the people Joanna went home to. They fed her and watched over her and put up with her childish tantrums until her mother came and tucked her in at night.

Joanna's grandfather had been a master carpenter and built a cozy two-room basement apartment for his daughter and granddaughter, using odds and ends left over from other jobs, creating a patchwork of pine, oak and cedar. Joanna could still be transported back to her childhood by the scent of a cedar closet or a freshly cut pine board. Now they were both well into their eighties, a little more careful than they had been in their seventies but still relishing each day and enjoying each other's company. Joanna remembered reading somewhere that people who shared the same sense of humor usually had the most enduring marriages. She believed her grandparents had remained friends all through their married life because they laughed at the same things and generally agreed with each other about the things that mattered. Although they were different on the outside – her grandmother was soft and sweet and a little sentimental; her grandfather gruff, even a little harsh at times – on the inside they were the same.

Her grandparents had accepted the fact that she and Franklin had been leading separate lives for some time because Franklin was important. "After all," her grandmother once said, "you can't say no to senators and congressmen when they think you're the best man for the job."

Good old Grams, thought Joanna as she pulled into the driveway of their immaculate bungalow, she had been half in love with Franklin. He had charmed her the first time Joanna brought him to meet her and Gramps. Joanna had never seen that side of Franklin before. He had eaten oatmeal cookies and drank tea from a china cup with just the right balance of good manners and down-home friendliness. With her grandfather he was formal and reserved and he had treated her mother with polite respect. He called her Mrs. Clark and behaved like the perfect gentleman caller, which he was. Franklin seemed to know how to draw the best out of everyone. People trusted him and believed he wouldn't let them down.

Joanna locked the car and walked up to the porch, still not knowing exactly what she was going to say to her grandparents. Even as the solid brass knocker hit the carved oak door – her grandfather's handiwork – she was like an actor without a script, hoping she would do the right thing when the moment came. Joanna heard her grandmother's slow, even steps behind the door and saw the door open. When she saw her grandmother's slightly stooped, thin frame, that familiar inquiring look in her eyes and the stray, wiry gray curls that had escaped her careful attempts to pull them back, Joanna burst into tears.

"Joanna, my dear child, what's the matter? What's happened?" Joanna couldn't seem to stop sobbing even though she knew she was upsetting her grandmother. "Owen!" her grandmother called to the back of the house. "Come here quickly! Something's happened to Joanna."

Joanna heard her grandfather's leather slippers on the hardwood floor as she tried taking deep breaths to slow down her convulsive sobbing. "I'm sorry, I'm sorry," she said, gulping. "Franklin's dead. He drowned in Thailand."

Her grandparents led her gently across the worn, flowered carpet to the still sturdy, wood-framed sofa her grandfather had built over forty years ago. She could hear their voices, one on top of the other, trying to comfort her as the three of them sat down, Joanna in the middle, each of them holding one of her hands.

"Dear child, dear child," said her grandmother, "how dreadful for you. Owen, get the girl some of that pear brandy. She needs something to warm her up."

Slowly, Joanna began to feel calmer and started to tell her grandparents about the man from the State Department coming to the house and what little information she had about Franklin's death.

"They claim it was an accident, that he drowned while swimming." She didn't mention Franklin's letter or any of the problems it raised.

"How dreadful," said Grams, wiping her eyes on one of the tissues that she always tucked into the sleeve of her sweater. "I'm going to miss him," she sighed. "You know, it almost makes you believe what they say, that only the good die young."

Joanna heard a barely audible grunt from her grandfather as he leaned forward to pour a little more brandy into her glass. "What about Lyle?" he said. "That would seem to disprove the theory, wouldn't it?"

"Now Owen," Grams said to him, a note of warning in her voice. "This is not the time to bring that up."

There was no love lost between Joanna's grandparents and her father, though she never heard the specific reasons for this. Her father was a car salesman – used cars – and they believed their beautiful young daughter had thrown her life away on the fast-talking, slick young man from Grand Rapids. Slick. That was the word her grandfather always used to describe him. "He was slick. Didn't trust him as far as I could spit."

But Joanna never heard any of this until after her mother died. Then they had felt the need to talk about her and her life. Joanna never even knew whether her parents had loved each other. She was only four years old when her father was killed while out on a test drive in one of the used cars he was trying to sell to a college student. The brakes had failed and both her father and the student had died instantly. After that, he was never mentioned and, for a long time, Joanna kept expecting him to walk through the door of her grandparents' house and say, "Come on kiddo, we're going home." Her only real memory of him was how the light used to shine on his straight, slicked-back hair.

"Come into the kitchen, dear," she heard her grandmother saying. "You need to eat something. You're white as a sheet." Joanna tried to protest but knew her grandmother was right. The brandy, on top of the scotch and the coffee she'd drunk at Claire's, had left a burning sensation at the bottom of her stomach. Her grandmother started to heat up some cream of chicken soup – made with milk, not water – and Joanna sliced some of the fresh home-made bread they had been buying for years from Bernstein's Bakery. She felt herself starting to slow down, like someone coming home after a hard day's work in the hot sun. They sat around the maple table on chairs her grandfather had built and ate the soup and bread, talking quietly about the past and about Franklin.

"Who would ever have thought my daughter and granddaughter would both be left widows and me still married to the same man for over sixty years," Grams said, looking at Joanna sadly. "When you married Franklin I thought it was the most wonderful thing in the world. Now she's set, I told myself, set for life. She'll never know poverty or unhappiness again. Maybe I jinxed it then and there.

You should never say things like that, not even to yourself. Sure as God made cherry pits, your words'll come back to haunt you."

"Don't be an old fool," Gramps said gently. "You know it doesn't happen that way. If this is what Joanna's life was meant to be, then she'll have to live with it. At least you were partly right, though. She won't know poverty."

Joanna couldn't bring herself to tell them about Franklin's letter. She didn't even know if she would still have her home or any money at all. Her grandparents had told Joanna when she married Franklin that, if anything happened, she'd always have a home with them. The Depression had been hard on them but they had managed to hold onto their small house and didn't hesitate to take Joanna and her mother into their home after her father died in 1939. They respected their daughter's privacy by building her and Joanna the small apartment, but they were never more than a word away. Joanna knew they would not hesitate to take her back if that's what she wanted.

"If only Franklin had let me go to Thailand with him maybe things wouldn't have turned out this way."

"Now don't you start being foolish like your grandmother," said Gramps. "What's happened has happened and you've got to accept it."

"Oh, Owen, don't be hard," her grandmother said. "I'm sure Joanna knows that well enough. Child, do you remember when Franklin came back from Japan the time they sent him on that fact-finding mission? He brought me back a pearl inside an oyster shell. And he said to me, 'Do you know what this oyster shell represents for me, Grams? It's this beautiful home that you and Gramps have built. And inside is a beautiful, perfect pearl and that's Joanna. Now every time you look at this oyster shell you'll know I haven't taken Joanna away from you. She's as much a part of your home as this pearl is a part of this oyster.' I still have that oyster shell and I think of Franklin every time I look at it. And of you, my dear, because you are the perfect pearl at the center of our life."

They cried a little more and then her grandparents made Joanna lie down for a while and she fell asleep under a handmade quilt. When she woke up, her grandmother had cooked a chicken and they ate it with mashed potatoes and carrots. Joanna still felt a little dazed and, though they tried to persuade her to stay, she wanted to go home and be alone for a while. They hugged and kissed and her grandmother wrapped up the leftover chicken and made Joanna take it home. "You won't feel like cooking," she said, "and I know you'll forget to eat."

On the drive home, Joanna tried to concentrate on the traffic instead of her thoughts but she kept thinking about the pearl in the oyster, a small, private episode between Franklin and her grandmother that she'd never known about. There were so many sides to Franklin's nature that she hadn't known – partly because he hadn't let her. To her he was a husband and provider and she became the kind of wife he wanted. Franklin made the rules and Joanna lived by them. What had she missed by not being a bigger part of his life?

Chapter Four

Carrying on with her life meant calling people and notifying various institutions of Franklin's death. Most of the people Franklin and Joanna were involved with socially were acquaintances through Franklin's former law practice and the various philanthropic causes he had embraced – the Chicago Symphony, the Art Institute, the Institute of Technology and the Museum of Science and Industry – people with whom she had only a passing relationship. Ed Lauder advised Joanna to call the bank and the insurance company that held a policy on Franklin's life. When she spoke to them they told her Franklin had stopped making payments and had cashed in the policy three months earlier. She was past being surprised at this point. She responded with a numb "I see" and hung up.

She couldn't stop thinking about Franklin's letter and what it might mean for her future. It was the last thing she thought about before she went to sleep at night and the first thing on her mind when she woke up. She hated not knowing where she stood and she hated the fear that paralyzed her when she thought about it. Should she just put the house on the market and prepare for the worst? Maybe she should start looking for a job. She found herself reading the want ads in the newspaper and becoming completely overwhelmed by the prospect of having to go to work. She had no idea where to start. She needed to talk to someone she trusted.

The only person Joanna felt comfortable confiding in was Fay Wright, her best friend since college. They had been roommates and the connection had lasted even though they had very different personalities. They each seemed to find something in the other that kept them balanced. When Joanna retreated too far into herself, Fay pulled her back into the real world. When Fay got too far away from herself, Joanna reeled her in and reminded her to stay grounded. And because they didn't see each other often or talk every day, the relationship worked.

Fay had made a disastrous marriage right after school that left her so burned she never wanted to marry again. "At least not without a great deal of money in the bank – preferably his," she said shortly after her divorce. She had gone on to become head buyer for a chain of women's clothing stores and lived alone in a fashionable condominium on the lakeshore. When Joanna told her she was marrying Franklin, Fay said she had made an excellent choice. "I figure the first time you marry for the bedroom, the second time for the bank. Looks like you've scored on both counts the first time, Joanna." Fay could always make her laugh. Joanna called Fay's office hoping they'd know where she was and was surprised and relieved when they put her right through.

"Joanna!" she heard Fay's pack-a-day voice crack. "To what do I owe the pleasure? It's not my birthday is it?" She hadn't called Fay in over a month and Fay always used the excuse that she worked long hours and traveled a lot not to call her. She figured Joanna was the one with the time so she should do the calling.

"I was hoping to catch you for dinner," Joanna said, trying to sound casual and serious at the same time. "I've had some bad news, Fay. Franklin's dead. He died in an accident in Thailand." Fay stopped breathing for a second while she tried to absorb what Joanna had said.

"Are you sure?"

"Yes, I'm sure. It was the State Department that informed me. I'd really like to see you if you can spare the time."

"Don't move," Fay said, clearly in control again. "I'm on my way over."

Fay arrived within half an hour, smelling of cigarettes and expensive perfume, and hugged Joanna as she came through the door. "You poor darling," she said, leading Joanna into the living room and sitting her down on the silk brocade sofa. "How are you taking it? Are you going to be all right?"

Joanna told her she had known for a couple of days now and was still getting used to the idea. She said she had talked to Franklin's sister and his lawyer and had been to see her grandparents.

"How on earth did it happen?" Fay asked, slipping her shoes off and reaching into her handbag for a pack of cigarettes.

"They claim it was a drowning accident," Joanna said, telling her what little she knew.

"Franklin didn't have accidents. He was too smart and too careful."

"Everybody has accidents, Fay. I admit I was surprised that he had been swimming – Franklin never liked the water. But he is, I mean was, in a tropical country and maybe he decided to take it up."

"Well I think it stinks," Fay said, blowing smoke through her nose. "What kind of an investigation did they have?"

"According to the man from the State Department, there was a police investigation and they found no evidence of foul play or anything suspicious. They thought at first he might have fallen off the side of a boat, but there was no record of a boat anywhere in the vicinity and no witnesses. So they concluded he must have drowned while swimming. It was an accident."

"Do you believe it?" Fay looked straight at Joanna, demanding that she be truthful. Joanna could never lie to Fay. She wondered if it was because Fay was a redhead. She once read that some tribes in Africa killed any red-haired babies that were born, believing them to have evil spirits. Joanna thought it was probably because they could see right through you, especially the ones with green eyes. They could practically hypnotize you into telling the truth.

"Well," she said, choosing her words carefully, "I can't say I disbelieve it. But I don't understand it." She got up and walked over to the desk to find Franklin's letter. "Now you're not to breathe a word of this. I wouldn't want it getting back to his family, or anyone for that matter." She handed Fay the letter.

Fay butted out her cigarette in the Venetian glass ashtray on the coffee table and read the letter carefully. Then she read it again. "This doesn't sound like Franklin," she said.

"I know. I didn't know what to think when I read it. What do you think it means? Do you think he was depressed and …"

"Franklin depressed?" Fay got up to pour herself a Scotch. Joanna nodded when Fay held up the bottle and she poured her one too. "Franklin was never depressed a minute in his life. Let me tell you something about guys like Franklin. They have enormous egos that feed on the gratitude of other people. That's how things get done in this world, by people like Franklin. They derive a terrific sense of power from doing good. Franklin liked having people depend on him. He was driven by it. The only thing that would depress him is if the world suddenly stopped needing people like him. And that's not likely to happen."

"You make it sound more like a vice than a virtue. You know Franklin did a tremendous number of important and valuable things for his community and for his country. He was selfless. He didn't just write checks, he gave his time and energy to raising money and helping people. That's the reason he was asked to go to Thailand and head up that organization in the first place."

"I don't mean to be hard, Joanna. And I'm not saying that

Franklin wasn't a good man. He did a lot of good things. I'm just saying that Franklin was a man of action, not of consequences. I'm sure whatever momentary lapse of judgment he might have had over finances wouldn't make him go into a depression. He was more resilient than that."

Isn't it interesting, thought Joanna. Fay saw Franklin as a man driven by ego and I saw him as a sensitive, caring person committed to improving conditions for everyone. Did we each see only what we wanted to see? Or was Franklin all the things she thought he was and all the things I thought he was wrapped up in one complex human being?

Joanna hadn't yet made a public announcement about Franklin's death, waiting until the plans were complete for a memorial service. But when she turned on the six o'clock news at Fay's request, she discovered the press had already been informed. "Franklin J. Reynolds," the announcer said, "head of Americans Aid Refugees in Bangkok, Thailand, has died as the result of an accident. The American government made the announcement after notifying Mr. Reynolds's family …" Joanna didn't wait to hear the rest. She ran to the phone and took the receiver off the hook, knowing the Chicago papers would be after her for some comment or a tearful photograph.

Assuming the news had only just come over the wire, Joanna knew they were already madly digging in the files for Franklin's obit. She knew they had the obituaries of prominent people at the ready and would be rushing it into the next edition. She figured they would track her down eventually and she even contemplated slipping out of town for a few days until the fuss was over.

"Well, no dinner out for us tonight, my friend," said Fay, coming into the kitchen in her stocking feet. "If I were you I'd stay out of sight for a few days and say 'no comment' to the butcher, the baker and the candlestick maker."

Joanna found the leftover chicken her grandmother had given her and pulled some salad fixings out of the fridge. Fay was right, she thought, I should just lay low for a few days. After all, she reasoned, there wasn't a hint of scandal surrounding Franklin and, without some kind of smell to keep them sniffing, the press would quickly lose interest.

By the time Fay left, much later that night after a lot of talk and a lot of wine, Joanna was feeling like she had a better grip on things. Fay always had that effect on her. Just when she was starting to doubt her own version of reality, Fay would come along and give hers in very specific terms. Somehow that always helped Joanna get lined up again, more because she thought Fay was wrong than because she thought she was right. Fay made her defend her ideas and that would clarify them for Joanna, as well as for Fay. Interestingly, by the time Fay hugged her, said goodnight and promised she would call soon, she had half conceded that Franklin's death could have been an accident. But Joanna had a nagging feeling in the back of her mind that it wasn't. She was pretty sure Franklin had killed himself, and that it had something to do with losing the money.

Chapter Five

Joanna spent the next few days dealing with letters and phone calls of condolence from Franklin's associates. She wasn't ungrateful. In fact, it helped to pass the time and, in this enforced activity, she found a certain comfort. By keeping busy she didn't have to think about how Franklin had died or about what had happened to the money. That would have to wait until later.

One day she spent nearly an entire morning staring at Franklin's suits hanging in the closet. She counted the belts and ties that hung from racks made for hanging belts and ties. She felt the soft leathers and smooth silks and smelled the lingering scent of the cologne Franklin liked to wear. She opened the drawers in his dresser and looked at the stacks of perfectly folded expensive shirts that he always bought by the dozen. It made her think of Gatsby, who had also come to a bad end. But Gatsby had not felt entitled the way Franklin had. Gatsby was bewildered and filled with doubts. For Gatsby there had been wonder at his great good fortune mixed with his desperate desire to impress Daisy. But he had "an extraordinary gift for hope," she remembered. "Gatsby believed in the green light, the orgiastic future that year by year recedes before us." Had Franklin also believed in the "green light"? Was that what had driven him to accomplish so much? Had he seen the future receding and known that his life would be short?

She refused to talk to the press and Franklin's death soon became "old news." Ed Lauder phoned before the week was out. "Joanna," he said, "I have to ask how you want to deal with the issue of Franklin's body. You can either have it shipped back here for burial or he can be cremated in Thailand and the ashes shipped. I'm sorry, but you have to make that decision."

She knew Franklin would want cremation. He would be horrified at the thought of his body being shipped halfway around the world, the indignity of it, and the fact that it all came down to paperwork and rubber stamps. But it meant she would never see him again. She wouldn't be able to look at his face, see the bump on his head, know for sure that he was dead.

"Cremation," she told Ed. "It's what Franklin would want."

"Is it what you want, Joanna? He can be cremated here, if you prefer."

"No, Ed. I think it's better this way."

Ed agreed and it gave her some comfort to hear him say, "I know it's what I would want, Joanna."

That night she had a dream about Franklin. He was sitting behind a large desk, stamping pieces of paper with a rubber stamp. His movements were measured and methodical and the only sound was the heavy thud of the rubber stamp – whomp, whomp, whomp. Then she heard the faint sound of a woman's voice repeatedly calling his name, "Franklin," until she realized it was her voice and she was desperately trying to get his attention. She was somewhere on the other side of the desk but she might as well have been a thousand miles away. He didn't look up from his task or even acknowledge that he could hear her. In the dream she could feel her anxiety rising. It was imperative that she get his attention. "Franklin," she said. "Franklin!" She must have spoken his name aloud because she was suddenly awake, her heart beating furiously and a feeling of terror gripping her so strongly she couldn't breathe. No! she thought and inhaled with a gasp, choking on her own saliva. She rolled over on her side and tried to catch her breath. Finally the choking stopped and she fell onto her back, breathing deeply to calm herself. This must be what it feels like to suffocate, she thought.

Eventually, she began to sleep through the night because she went to bed so exhausted. Claire was a great help as well. She called daily and spent hours helping Joanna compose and write notes and this helped keep the anxiety at bay. Joanna didn't tell her that she was afraid Franklin might have left her without a cent. Even though she considered Claire to be a close friend, she was still Franklin's sister and Joanna didn't want pity or charity from his family. She would figure out a way of dealing with the problem in due time. But first of all there were certain formalities that had to be taken care of, certain ceremonies to be performed.

The most difficult of these was the public memorial service Joanna arranged with Claire's help, two weeks after the news of Franklin's death. It was held at the largest Episcopalian church in downtown Chicago and no less than three hundred people showed up to pay their respects. Limousine after limousine pulled up in front of the church and disgorged solemn-faced people dressed in black who greeted each other with a nod as they entered the church. There were business people, investment bankers, philanthropists and politicians, representatives from local, state and national spheres of power. Some had flown in from Washington and a few had even come from Europe. They had come to acknowledge the loss of one of their own and to reflect on the righteousness of their lives.

For two hours, in eulogy after eulogy, they sang Franklin's praises as a fine man and a humanitarian. He would be sorely missed, they said, not just by his friends and family, but by a world in which there were too few men like him. Franklin Reynolds, a man born to privilege, had sought, not to further fill his own coffers, but to enrich the lives of those born into a world of pain and suffering. Psalms were read and hymns were sung. Prayers were murmured; amens repeated. The words rang in Joanna's ears as she tried to hold onto the memories of the Franklin she had fallen in love with and thought she had understood. How little she seemed to know of the public Franklin in this crowd of his colleagues and associates. She just wanted it to be over so she could go home and immerse herself in a good book and forget for a while.

As they filed out of the church, people whose faces were familiar but whose names she couldn't remember came up to her to offer their condolences. She absorbed their words like a sponge until she thought she would explode. "We're so sorry for your loss," they said. "It's a great loss for the community." "It's a great loss for the country." "He'll be missed." None of them said, "How are you holding up?" "Are you going to be all right?" "Can we do anything for you?" "Do you miss him?" But Joanna didn't notice. She was used to Franklin being the center of attention; she was used to being invisible.

Claire came over to her when nearly everyone had gone. She looked taller and thinner in her black Chanel suit with the black and white braid around the edges of the jacket. It set off the whiteness of her hair and her pale, powdered skin. The familiar scent of Arpège hung in the air around her.

"Well," said Claire, "that's over, thank God. I thought they'd never stop droning. I can't seem to think of my younger brother in terms of public service and humanitarianism. To me he's still the kid who put frogs in my bed and embarrassed me in front of my friends by behaving like a stupid jackass."

Claire stopped talking suddenly and Joanna saw she was on the verge of crying. My God, she's one of the few people who loved him for himself, Joanna thought, not for what he became or seemed to become. Where in all this, Joanna wondered, was the Franklin she had married? Hadn't they once been in love and enjoyed being together? How had they let that slip away? Maybe I allowed too much space to come between us, mistaking it for trust and thinking it was about freedom and independence, not boredom and indifference. Had she been content to let him move away from her? Why hadn't she fought to keep them closer? Why hadn't he?

"Come on," she said to Claire. "We both need a drink."

They drove back to her house where she had arranged a private reception for family and friends and managed to get there just ahead of everyone else. Franklin's brother Donald, his wife Margaret and their two sons, and his other sister Irene, her husband Lloyd and their daughter Randi were the first to arrive. A couple of Joanna's friends from the university stopped by and one of her girlfriends from the library came with her husband. The house soon filled with people – family members, neighbors, and a few colleagues from his law firm that Franklin and Joanna occasionally socialized with. Some dabbed at moist eyes and a few uncomfortably cleared their throats, but the atmosphere was one of affection and respect. This had been Franklin's home and they had come to honor his memory and to acknowledge their loss. This is the real funeral, thought Joanna. These are the people who cared about Franklin. These are the people who will miss him in their lives.

Joanna caught sight of Fay, looking elegant and severe. She was dressed from head to toe in black with her brazen red hair pulled back as tightly as possible as if to remind her to keep her personality in check as well. Joanna knew Fay hated occasions like this and thought they were the worst form of hypocrisy.

"My God," said Fay, pulling her aside, "if this had been an election year we could have gotten Franklin elected President, dead or alive."

"Fay!" Joanna whispered, only half horrified. She had a point.

"Well, you know what they say, Joanna. 'You can fool some of the people all of the time.' And that's enough to get you elected in this country." When Fay saw Joanna trying not to laugh, she pulled down the corners of her mouth and said, "Okay, okay, I'll behave. But I mean really, Joanna, couldn't you have found someone to say something personal about the guy? You'd have thought they were unveiling a statue rather than bidding fond farewell to a friend."

"I know," said Joanna, trying to keep out of earshot of the others. "But all those people wanted to speak. I couldn't very well refuse. Besides, I think Franklin would have liked it."

"Oh, I'm sure he would have," said Fay, giving Joanna a look that said, So what does that tell you about him?

Joanna kissed the air beside her friend's cheek and said, "Thanks for coming anyway, you old bag."

Fay took hold of Joanna's upper arms and looked into her eyes. "Are you going to be all right?"

"I think so."

"You know where I am. I'm never more than a phone call away if you need me."

"I know. And thanks."

Just then Joanna's neighbors, Nick and Natalie Firchuk, came over and Fay slipped away to get herself a drink.

"How are you Joanna? We're so very, very sorry."

"Hello Natalie, Nick. Thanks so much for coming."

Natalie took Joanna's hand in both of hers and started rubbing it as if it were ice cold. "It was such a wonderful service. You must be very proud of Franklin. His loss will be felt for a long time." Natalie and Nick hadn't really known Franklin all that well. They had lived next door to the Reynolds' for four years and Franklin hadn't been around much. But they never missed mentioning that they had seen his name in the paper or had heard about him on the news.

Nick made his living in the construction business and he and Natalie seemed always to be doing some kind of renovation or improvement to their home and inviting Joanna over to see it. Natalie was a consummate homemaker and during the past week had been coming over almost daily with some kind of casserole or salad for her to eat.

"You've been so good to me, Natalie, I'll never be able to thank you enough."

"Listen, you just take care of yourself and don't hesitate to call us if you need anything." Natalie squeezed Joanna's hand to emphasize her sincerity.

"Anything," said Nick. "We mean it."

"Thanks Nick," said Joanna, retrieving her hand from Natalie and reaching over to shake his. "I know you do. And I appreciate it."

Joanna excused herself when she saw Franklin's nephew, his brother's son Herbert, standing off in a corner by himself. He seemed genuinely distressed by the whole situation. Of all Franklin's nieces and nephews, Herbert had been closest to his often-absent uncle. He had truly admired Franklin's public persona and would hear no criticism of it. Not that Joanna ever heard any, but Herbert gave the impression that he would punch someone for even suggesting that Franklin had been anything less than perfect. Joanna could see he was tense and unhappy. He kept clenching and unclenching his fists in a way that made her want to comfort him, but warned her not to get too close.

"Herbert," she said when she got near enough for him to hear her, "I know you'll miss your Uncle Franklin. He thought very highly of you and spoke so enthusiastically about your future." Herbert's jaw muscles relaxed slightly, but his hands remained clenched at his sides.

"There's a first edition of Morison & Commanger's *Growth of the American Republic* in the library that I know he would want you to have. Why don't you go in there and find it. It has a tooled leather binding and he prized it highly. It was his father's, you know."

"Thank you, Aunt Joanna," he said, as softly as she'd ever heard him speak. He turned and went into the library, shutting the door behind him. When he emerged an hour or so later, book in hand, he seemed comforted, or perhaps a little more resigned. His grief was genuine and Joanna was grateful, for Franklin's sake and for her own.

Imagine, she thought, a man dies and no one seems to feel much for him. Was there really a Franklin J. Reynolds or was he just someone pieced together by the press and the various stories told about him? She was becoming less and less sure of her own memories.

Her grandparents were seated together on a sofa and as she walked toward them they moved apart so she could sit between them.

"How are you, dear?" her grandmother asked, her voice and her eyes filled with concern. "Are you holding up all right?"

"Yes, I'm fine Grams."

"You were always such a serious child, Joanna, always feeling responsible for everyone. Your grandfather and I used to despair of your ever having any fun in life, losing your father, then your mother. And now Franklin. You know you're more dear to us than anything in the world. And, God willing, it'll be a long time before He boots you upstairs. So try not to think of this as the end of the world. I know it feels like that right now, but you've got to live for yourself. That's what Franklin would want."

Joanna's meeting with Franklin's lawyer Ed Lauder served to further confuse her and plant more questions in her mind. Ed had received the ashes and all of Franklin's personal papers and files two days earlier. Franklin's staff had packed them immediately and shipped them air freight, government priority, within days of his death. His instructions were clear: Ed Lauder was his lawyer and Chief Executor of his will and estate and, in any emergency, disaster, or in case of his disappearance and/or death, Lauder was to be sent any personal papers that were not considered government property. Once clearance had been received, they had been forwarded immediately.

Ed had aged since the last time she'd seen him. A heavy-set man, his appearance belied the fact that he was both a natural athlete and a good dancer. He had always had dark pouches under his eyes and now they seemed darker. An uncharacteristic heaviness of spirit served to exaggerate their puffiness.

He sighed as he took her hand and said, "Joanna, how have you been?"

"I'm all right, Ed. But I'm sure what you're going to tell me won't make things any easier."

He looked surprised but didn't comment. Joanna hadn't told him about Franklin's letter, hoping that she would learn what had really happened when Ed received the papers from Franklin's personal files. She assumed the explanation would be there. Ed walked around behind his desk and sat down rather heavily in his high-backed leather chair. He wasn't a very tall man and the back of the chair extended about a foot above the top of his head. Joanna sat facing him and prepared herself for the worst.

"Well, Joanna, I don't know why you'd say that. Franklin has left you very well off." He looked up at her and Joanna held her breath. "According to his last will, he's left you everything and according to this document, his estate is substantial."

"When was it dated?" she asked, already knowing the answer and realizing she would have to show Ed the letter. They would have to begin untangling Franklin's affairs without benefit of documentation.

"Ironically, the will is dated only three days before his body was discovered. He must have written it just before he went to Pattaya. Joanna, I've been checking. It appears Franklin's left you something in the neighborhood of three million dollars."

Chapter Six

Once again, Joanna was faced with the confusing inconsistency of Franklin's last days. Her husband, who was terrified of the water, had drowned. He was scrupulous about his financial affairs, but wrote to her three weeks before his death to say he'd left them "rather badly off." And then, just before he died, he wrote a will leaving her three million dollars. She couldn't even open her mouth. Joanna let her disbelieving eyes wander over the polished wood and worn leathers of Ed's office and didn't say a word. She looked at Ed and he looked back at her, his gaze steady but puzzled.

"Joanna," he said, "you look as if you don't believe me. I know it's probably a lot more than you expected – and quite frankly I don't know where it came from. I checked with Franklin's broker and he told me Franklin liquidated everything three months ago, giving no indication of what he intended to do with the money. He cashed in about a million dollars in assets and, by God, Joanna, there's three million in cash sitting in a Swiss numbered account, free and clear. I've checked. Didn't he tell you anything?"

When she found her voice, Joanna told him about Franklin's letter and showed it to him. Ed verified that it was Franklin's handwriting and looked as baffled as she felt.

"Ed, I don't know what's going on. Was Franklin involved in something he didn't want us to know about? You don't lose a million dollars one day and end up with three million the next. I don't know what to do. I'm starting to wonder what the last few weeks of his life must have been like."

For Joanna, the mystery of Franklin's life had become increasingly tied to her feelings about her own life and what had really been happening during the last sixteen years. Had she been wrong about everything? Had none of it happened the way she thought it had?

"Well, Joanna," Ed's words broke into her thoughts, "I don't know how to advise you at this point. I suggest you take things as they are, or as they appear to be, and eventually the facts might become clear. These things have a way of working themselves out."

"But how, Ed? You know as well as I do that none of this makes sense. Franklin must have been involved in something very unusual to have turned one million dollars into three in less than three weeks."

"Joanna, I suggest you leave it alone. It's been nearly a month since he died and nothing's been said, no one's come forward. Franklin probably saw a chance to speculate on something he needed to deal with in cash. You know how they are over there. Maybe it was gems or something. Strictly cash. I'm not saying it was a smart thing to do, but he probably saw it as a sure thing and decided to go for it. Then, at one point, he thought he'd lost everything and so he wrote to you. The next thing he knows, it comes through, he puts the money in a Swiss bank and, before he can notify you, he dies."

Joanna was shaking her head and twisting the plain gold band she still wore on her left hand. "It just doesn't sound like him, Ed. It's just not like him."

"I know you're confused. He's left you with some unanswered

questions. But I'm telling you, the money is free and clear. There are no strings, no loose ends."

"Yes there are, Ed. There are loose ends and I don't like it. It's not like Franklin. He wouldn't do those things, and he especially wouldn't drown. I'd almost feel better if he'd shot himself or something. Then it would somehow fit. If he'd done something he regretted, Franklin might kill himself to save face. If he feared exposure, he might do that."

"Are you suggesting Franklin committed suicide?" Ed's face reflected his total disbelief at the possibility.

"I don't know what I'm suggesting, Ed. At first it seemed like the only explanation. But if Franklin wanted to commit suicide, why would he choose drowning? He *never* went near the water. He didn't even own a bathing suit. I'm really beginning to think I never knew Franklin at all."

"Don't say that, Joanna. You were married to him for a long time. He couldn't have been a stranger. Look, maybe he did drown himself. At least then it would look like an accident. Then he would spare you the shame and the consequences. In a way it would be a lot neater. Right?" She nodded. It did kind of make sense. "Don't torture yourself, Joanna. There's a perfectly logical explanation for all of this. We just haven't found it yet. Besides, what are you going to do? Go to Bangkok and start snooping around? You can't do that. You'll just have to wait and assume the reason for things will become clear in time."

Joanna took a deep breath and looked at Ed's concerned face. "I guess you're right, Ed. There isn't anything I can do."

He was relieved when she said that and proceeded in an efficient manner to fill her in on the details of the bank account and what she would have to do to claim the money.

"It would be a lot faster and simpler if you could go to Zurich. Besides, the trip might do you good. Force you to think about other things. Take your mind off your troubles. Do you think you could manage it?"

Maybe Ed was right, she thought. Maybe she was just being paranoid, overzealous. Was she feeling guilty for not having been a better wife? She should have been relieved that Franklin hadn't left her broke. Instead, she was confused and upset. Joanna couldn't stop wondering about what had happened to Franklin in those last few months. Was his death in some way linked to the three million dollars? Had he killed himself in order to avoid some unpleasant or shameful discovery? There were too many questions she couldn't answer. There had to be an explanation and she needed to know it.

"Joanna," said Ed, with an uncharacteristic sternness, "stop thinking. Stop wondering. Go home. Plan your trip. Book a flight, buy some clothes, keep busy. Don't brood about it. If I find out anything, I'll let you know immediately."

She needed a good strong dose of Fay's philosophy of life and called her office from a pay phone in the lobby of Ed's building. She had to wait on hold for quite a long time but she didn't mind because she hadn't expected to find Fay in at all. When Fay finally came on the line, Joanna told her she was downtown and asked if she had time for dinner. Fay said she was leaving for New York that night on a buying trip but suggested they meet out by the airport. She would get the latest flight she could so they'd have a few hours.

Joanna spent the rest of the afternoon shopping on State Street. She didn't really enjoy shopping at the boutique-style shops on Michigan Avenue and preferred wandering around the old-fashioned department stores like Marshall Field's and Carson Pirie Scott. It was easier and cheaper. She didn't understand why anyone would spend more money for something just because they could afford to. Besides, she never tired of looking at the iridescent splendor of the Marshall Field's Tiffany-glassed, domed ceiling and the intricacy of the iron scrollwork on the doors at Carson Pirie Scott, which had recently been designated a Chicago landmark. She considered its architect, Louis Sullivan, to be a genius and a visionary. If she had to endure the drudgery of shopping, at least it could be a cultural experience of sorts.

She eventually bought two summer-weight cotton dresses, one with sleeves, one with a jacket; three loose-fitting skirts, one with buttons down the front and pockets; an embroidered, peasant-style blouse that was on sale; two sleeveless tops and three cotton T-shirts. Then she bought shoes: thin-soled sandals with little heels, sturdier sandals with thicker straps for walking, some slip-ons and a pair of canvas espadrilles, also on sale. She took only one fifteen-minute break and had a banana muffin and some coffee. After half an hour of intense deliberation, she bought a nylon flight bag and matching carry-on in a caramel color with dark brown trim. She got her car out of the parking lot, picked up her parcels and headed home. She just had time to take a quick shower, change her clothes and get to the airport hotel where she had agreed to meet Fay.

Fay had said she might be a few minutes late so Joanna went on up to the revolving restaurant that sat on top of the twenty-six-storey hotel. The table was ready so she sat down and ordered herself a gin and tonic. While she waited, Joanna thought about what she was going to tell Fay. She knew she could trust her with the information about the three million dollars. Fay knew more about the world of finance than Joanna did and if she thought it sounded all right then maybe Joanna would stop worrying about it. On the other hand, Fay could be so unpredictable she might convince Joanna that Franklin had stolen the money and then where would she be? When Joanna saw Fay talking to the maitre d', she raised her hand to get her attention. Fay was wearing a green, two-piece travel suit in a soft knit with a beige knit top that flattered her creamy complexion. Joanna had always envied Fay's sense of style and her flair for "occasion" dressing. Even as a poor college student Fay always managed to put together exactly the right outfit for any event.

"Well," she said, sinking into the plush velvet-covered chair opposite Joanna, "this is going to be so nice. To actually sit down to a meal for a change. I've been so busy the last couple of weeks the only things I've eaten have come in cardboard boxes or wrapped in paper. But enough of my pathetic existence, what have you been up to?"

Joanna told her that Franklin's papers and his ashes had arrived and that she'd finally had a meeting with his lawyer. Once Fay had a drink in her hand Joanna told her about the money in the Swiss bank account.

Fay's eyebrows went up about an inch and she took a long, slow sip of her drink. "My, my," she said softly, "how clever of him." She started to shake her head and chuckle and Joanna finally said, "What do you think it means? Is it possible to make that kind of money so fast?"

"Oh it's possible," said Fay, lighting a cigarette, "if you're in the right place at the right time. I mean, anything's possible Joanna. Anything."

"But don't you think it's a little out of character for Franklin? I mean you said yourself that he was a very careful man." Joanna desperately wanted Fay to tell her it was a normal occurrence for people to triple their money. That it happened every day.

"Well, yes that's true," Fay agreed, clearly thinking it over. "I guess he must have believed it was a sure thing and decided to grab it."

"That's what Ed Lauder said."

Fay saw the look of doubt on Joanna's face and knew what she wanted to hear. "Life is full of surprises, Joanna," she said, "and this is one of the nicer ones. Why can't you just be glad? Take the money and run. God knows you've earned it."

"What's that supposed to mean?" At that moment the waiter came to take their order so she had to wait to hear Fay's response.

Joanna ordered the medallions of veal with a mixed salad, dressing on the side. Her appetite was slowly coming back and she had started to eat because she was hungry, not just because she thought she should. Fay ordered rack of lamb with the watercress soup to start.

When the waiter left, Joanna asked her again. "What do you mean, I've earned it?"

"Well," said Fay, choosing her words carefully, "I mean, it can't have been a picnic being married to Franklin all those years. He wasn't exactly an ideal husband."

"Yes he was," said Joanna, without thinking. "I mean, he wasn't perfect, of course not, nobody is. But he was good to me and we had a beautiful home and an interesting life."

"He had an interesting life," Fay corrected her. "You stayed home and played doormat."

"I wasn't a doormat. Franklin didn't want me going on those trips with him and so I made my own life. I took courses. I studied. I like my life." But her voice cracked as she said it.

The waiter brought a bottle of wine, opened it and poured some in Fay's glass. Joanna watched her as she tasted the wine. "Nice," she said.

"Look, Joanna, I don't want to be judgmental. We live our lives very differently and who am I to say whether my life is more interesting than yours, or anybody's for that matter? It's just that I don't understand why you stayed married to Franklin when you weren't sharing his life. And vice versa, I should add."

"I was secure," Joanna said, after thinking it over for a minute. She didn't want to get defensive and end up talking in black-and-white terms with Fay. She was interested in exploring the gray areas, but Fay was implying her whole life had been gray.

"Secure? That's all? Were you happy? Stimulated? Sexually satisfied? Optimistic about the future?"

"No. Are you?"

Fay laughed and nearly spilled her wine down the front of her sweater. "No," she said, "but I have had an orgasm in the last six months."

"Fay!" Joanna said, looking around to make sure no one had heard. She should have known better than to be surprised by anything Fay said. "What's that got to do with anything? I like my life. So what if it isn't full of surprises, or orgasms," she whispered. "Not everyone wants to live in the fast lane."

"That's true, but most people want to put their foot on the

accelerator once in a while. You're only forty years old, Joanna. I know we used to think that was middle-aged, but it's not. For some people that's when life starts getting interesting. Maybe you're a late bloomer."

"I don't want to be a late bloomer," Joanna said as the waiter brought their appetizers. "I want life to be the way it was."

"It can't be. Everything's changed. You're a rich widow in the prime of your life. Doesn't that excite you at all?"

Joanna poured some dressing on her salad and started to eat it. She thought for a bit and said, "No, it depresses me."

"What depresses you about it?" Fay asked, adding pepper to her soup. "The money?"

"Well, yes. I'd like to know where it came from and how Franklin got it. It's really bothering me."

"Why? Do you think he stole it?"

"I hope not. But it throws everything off balance. It makes me think I didn't know anything about him, about what he was doing before he died. And I don't like not knowing."

"That's not all that's bothering you, is it? It's not just about Franklin and the money."

Good old Fay, Joanna thought. She was prying her open like a steamed clam. "No, it's not just about Franklin and the money. It's about me and my whole life. Or at least the last sixteen years of it. I'm having trouble connecting with reality. I don't know what's real anymore. I think I'm mad at Franklin for letting me down, or betraying me. Or fooling me, maybe. I don't know, but …"

"Franklin didn't betray you, Joanna. He just didn't follow the rules of the game you invented to make everything work."

"I didn't make the rules, Fay. He did."

"Joanna, you've been living in a bubble for a long time. When Franklin shut you out of his world, you created a nice neat world of your own so you wouldn't have to confront your own anger."

"I wasn't angry, Fay. I was just hurt."

"Just hurt? Listen to yourself, Joanna. *Just* hurt? I'd have been furious with him and I think you were too. Only you couldn't deal with it. So you buried it."

"Too much information," Joanna said, putting her hand up to stop Fay. It was an old way they had of slowing things down if either of them didn't like what she was hearing. Joanna was usually the one to invoke it, although she had caught Fay a few times about her smoking and working too hard. But this was different. They weren't talking details anymore. They were talking the big picture. Fay sighed and poured more wine into their glasses as Joanna told her about Ed Lauder's suggestion that she go to Zurich, travel around a bit.

"I think it's a great idea," said Fay, finishing her soup. "It's just what you need. A change of scene, some new clothes. Meet some new people."

The waiter brought their entrees and, as always, they each gave the other a taste of what they had ordered. "I already bought the clothes," said Joanna, watching Fay for her reaction.

Fay's head shot up in surprise. "Does that mean you're going?"

"Well, I still have to get a passport and everything, but I'm thinking about it. Do you really think it'll help?"

"Oh yes," she said, taking a big gulp of wine. "It'll do you the world of good. And while you're over there you should go to Paris and Rome and …"

"What about Bangkok?" Joanna interrupted, surprising both Fay and herself. She had no idea why she'd said it.

"Why Bangkok?" Fay asked, a worried look coming over her face.

"Well, maybe it would be interesting to go there and talk to some of the people who knew Franklin."

"I don't think that's a good idea. I think you should get on with your life and try and forget Franklin. I don't mean forget him, but put that life behind you and find your own way. You can do anything you want now. You have time, you have money and you're still young enough, and attractive – very attractive, in fact. Don't sell yourself short."

"So you don't think I should go to Bangkok?"

"No, I don't. Not by yourself, that's for sure. Look, Joanna, Franklin just got lucky with the money, like winning the lottery. He also got unlucky and died, but that's a fact, just like the money, and it's not going to go away. I say cut your losses and enjoy the money."

Joanna sighed, finished her meal and Fay asked for the dessert menu. They usually shared a dessert and this time it was Fay's turn to choose. She chose chocolate pecan pie. Life in the fast lane, thought Joanna.

They had time for brandy with their coffee before Fay had to catch her plane. It didn't seem to bother her that Franklin's holdings had tripled overnight and that he had left them in cash, in a Swiss bank account, and then died in an inexplicable drowning accident. She thought it was Joanna's great good fortune to be rich and free. She thought Joanna would be wasting more of her life if she tried to find out why any of it had happened. Fay knew Franklin was capable of turning a blind eye and making a fast deal if it presented itself. He was an opportunist, after all.

"Move on," said Fay. "Don't look back."

Fay believed that if Joanna started to look back and analyze the details of her life with Franklin it might paralyze her emotionally and leave her with nothing but a handful of ashes. But how could she tell her friend that she had spent sixteen years with the wrong man? Because that's what Fay believed. Franklin had not been the partner Joanna needed. He had not allowed her to be the person she might have been. He had been controlling and inflexible in almost every aspect of their life together. If Franklin didn't like something, Joanna changed it. And Joanna always defended him whenever Fay tried to point it out.

In college Joanna had been a "square," but she had a sense of fun that was occasionally revealed when she allowed herself to relax and feel safe in the company of friends. Fay had watched that spark be extinguished during Joanna's years with Franklin. She had recognized Franklin's need to control right away and had seen her friend succumb to his smooth charm almost immediately. Had Joanna been so insecure that she'd been willing to hand over her life to this demanding, uncompromising man?

Fay had made the decision at the time of Joanna's marriage to step back and stay out of Franklin's way. She knew she would lose if there was ever a confrontation between them. To be honest, she didn't want to lose the small piece of Joanna that was hers. She valued Joanna for her kindness and her steadiness. Joanna gave her lots of room to be herself and Fay knew where she stood with her. Joanna was like a beacon that Fay could always find. But now Joanna seemed rudderless, without purpose or direction. Where had this sudden desire to go to Bangkok come from? Fay saw it as a step backward into the past, but she knew if the idea became fixed in Joanna's mind she wouldn't be able to talk her out of it. Fay could see Joanna falling either way now that Franklin was gone. Either she would slide back into a memory of things as they never were and be Franklin's widow forever or she would move forward and discover the person she was meant to become. The trouble was, Fay didn't know whether to push or pull.

They took the elevator down to the underground parking and Joanna drove Fay to O'Hare. During the short ride, Fay wrote down the names of hotels in Zurich, Geneva, Paris and Rome. "Go to Europe and enjoy yourself," she said as she got out of the car. "All this other stuff will stop bothering you sooner than you think. Why make things more complicated than they have to be? Besides, what if you don't like what you find out? What are you going to do, give the money back?"

Joanna laughed and Fay was gone, but just before she was out of sight Joanna caught her glancing back in her direction. Fay had an uncharacteristic frown on her face.

Chapter Seven

The next day Joanna made a reservation for Bangkok via Zurich. She gave herself a week to look after her passport and visas and spent part of the time in the library reading everything she could about the history of Thailand. She knew if she didn't keep very busy she'd lose her nerve and cancel the ticket. She'd been to Europe before, on holiday with Franklin, but she had never traveled alone. She was frightened and excited at the same time. The decision to go to Bangkok had been impulsive but she believed it was something she had to do. It was her last connection to Franklin. He had loved so many things about Thailand and his letters to her had been descriptive and intriguing. Of course, there had been things that drove him crazy too, like the fact that it took so long to get anything done. But that was Franklin. He was impatient and didn't want to stop until the job was finished. But the place he described in his letters had obviously affected him. Bangkok was hot and dirty, he said, but it vibrated with life and was the most interesting place he'd ever been. Whenever he had a chance to get out of the city he would golf or rent a car and do some sightseeing. At those times, Joanna wished she could be there with him, but she never suggested it and neither had he.

The flight to Zurich was long and uneventful. Claire drove her to the airport just to be there and, in a way, Joanna was grateful. But she felt guilty about not telling Claire she was going on to Bangkok. She hadn't told Ed Lauder or her grandparents either. They all thought she was on her way to Europe for a three-week jaunt to spend some money and get her mind off things. She knew they'd only try and talk her out of going to Thailand and she didn't want to be talked out of it. As for Fay, Joanna left a message with her secretary that she would be in Europe – no fixed address. It took all the courage she had to get on the plane. As she hugged Claire goodbye she wondered if she would ever see her again and then realized she was being morbid. Not everyone who went to Thailand ended up in jail or dead. Just some people.

Joanna had no experience traveling on her own, but she made up her mind to take things one step at a time and not panic over anything, especially minor things like airports, customs, hotels and officials. She was after information and knew the search for it would take her down a few roads where she might encounter less than friendly faces. As the plane landed at Zurich-Kloten Airport, Joanna could see the clear, glassy lake and the soft rolling hills and mountains that surrounded the city, giving it a picture-postcard perfection. Once away from the airport she was convinced she was inhaling the freshest, cleanest air in the world.

The hotel Fay had recommended was the Baur au Lac, an elegant old inn that dated back to 1844 and was the epitome of Swiss hospitality and charm. Her scribbled note had said "expensive, but a must" and as the taxi pulled into the courtyard off the Talstrasse, Joanna knew she was going to like it. It was a four-storey, cream-colored building with tall windows and sparkling white trim. Her bags were whisked away and by the time she had checked in and climbed the marble stairway to her room, her things had been unpacked and put away in drawers or hung in the closet. Where the lobby had been warm and intimate with oak and leather and antique tapestries, Joanna's room was cool and expansive, with bright sunlight pouring in the tall arched windows that gave a spectacular view of the lake and the mountains. Even though she hadn't slept much on the long overnight flight, Joanna was wide awake and too keyed up to rest. So she went back downstairs and outside for a walk through the park beside the hotel. The flowerbeds were in full bloom and the trees were so brilliantly green she almost couldn't look at them. It was early July and the height of the European summer.

Hunger finally drew her back to the hotel and she asked for an outside table in the Pavillion, facing the canal. She dined on sliced chicken breast in whisky cream sauce that was superb and drank coffee that had been made only seconds before it was served. The second cup was as fresh as the first and she thought she had died and gone to heaven. She began to feel very sleepy after lunch so she went up to her room, took a hot bath and washed her hair. She propped herself up with pillows on the king-size bed and tried to read the little guide book on the city that the hotel had provided, but within minutes she was fast asleep.

Joanna woke up slowly, thinking she had only been asleep for a few minutes. The book had fallen out of her hand and her hair had dried in uncombed clumps. When she looked at her watch she was astonished to see it was nearly eight o'clock in the evening and she had slept for almost five hours. She shouldn't have been hungry but she was, so she ordered a light meal from room service and it arrived on a trolley twenty minutes later. The salmon was grilled to perfection and the endive salad was crisp and fresh. The wine was a little fruity for her taste so she made a mental note not to order it again. As before, the coffee was perfect and the apple tart was rich and sweet. She curled up on the bed again and finished the novel she had been reading on the plane. She didn't think once about the folks back home or her own bed and took it as a sign that she was going to enjoy traveling on her own.

Joanna went to the Credit Suisse Bank first thing the next morning. The money was there all right, just as Ed had said. Clear and unencumbered. She took care of the necessary arrangements that gave her free access to the money and was impressed by the Swiss machinery that reduced a mountain of red tape to a single signature – hers. It reminded Joanna of those doors in supermarkets and hospitals – just stand on the mat and they swing open. She arranged for a letter of credit and took what she thought would be enough in cash and traveler's checks to give her easy mobility in places where real money still counted. She had only taken one credit card with her because she'd read somewhere you shouldn't carry all your cards with you in foreign countries.

The few days she spent in Zurich were taken up with expeditions to the Swiss National Museum and several of the historic churches she felt obliged to see. The twin-towered, Romanesque Grossmunster exhausted her and she spent two hours in a café drinking excellent coffee and eating Sachertorte to get her energy back. Between churches, she walked around the city trying to decide if she really liked the sparse, rather puritan look of the buildings, or was merely impressed by their longstanding virtue. She also spent some time on the Bahnhofstrasse outfitting herself for the next leg of her journey. Besides buying some loose-fitting cotton dresses, she picked up a pair of good sturdy walking shoes. To test them out she went on a half-day, beginner's hiking expedition that left her in an agony of aches and pains – muscles, bones, everything – so she spent two hours in a hot tub and then crawled straight into bed. So much for stamina.

She wanted to travel light while she was in Thailand. She knew it would be hot and she didn't want to be dragging around a bunch of stuff. As she packed her nylon flight bag and prepared for the trip, Joanna began to feel the first real signs of apprehension. Not just nervousness at traveling alone, or not knowing what to eat or how to speak the language, but fear. She wondered if what she was doing could be dangerous. She hadn't allowed herself to think about it too much before because she was certain she wouldn't have got as far as a hotel room in Zurich. But as the realization that her next move would take her into a scary unknown started to hit her, she got that sinking feeling of dread in the pit of her stomach that soldiers must get on the eve of battle.

She forced herself to push it back and wouldn't let herself say, "Take the money and run," as Fay had suggested. She wouldn't allow herself to make noble excuses for why she was going to go ahead, but she told herself she had to make the attempt. Not knowing what Franklin had been up to and whether it had led to his death would bother her for the rest of her life. Besides, she reasoned, if things started getting tough, she could always get a plane out. I've got money and an American passport, she thought. What can they do to me?

Joanna resisted the impulse to phone her grandparents and tell them what she was really planning to do. It would only upset them, she told herself. The less they knew, the better. She remembered the time when she was only about five or six years old, when she and her mother went into Chicago to see the circus. Her mother's purse was stolen with all her money and identification. Fortunately, Joanna's grandfather had stuffed five dollars into her little purse for a treat and that got them home on the bus. Her mother was very flustered by the incident and all the way back to Aurora she kept telling Joanna not to say a word about the robbery to her grandparents. "It will only upset them," she said. "The less they know the better." Her grandmother was right when she said Joanna always felt responsible for everyone. She had learned that lesson early and never forgot it.

Nothing she had read prepared Joanna for Bangkok. The deceptive coolness and modernity of Don Muang Airport lulled her with a sense of Western familiarity. Her flight arrived at mid-day and, regardless of the fact that she had been traveling for over twelve hours, the bustle of busy people in a daylight setting revived her and fooled her into thinking she wasn't tired.

One step out of the airport, though, and she realized she was in a very hot place. She felt as if she had just opened the wrong door and stepped into the sauna at the Sports Club. The brilliant sunlight momentarily blinded her and she almost turned around and walked back into the building. She rummaged in her shoulder bag for her Christian Dior sunglasses – one of the temptations of the Bahnhofstrasse she hadn't been able to resist – and covered her scrunched-up eyes. They began to focus on a small man of delicate build with skin the color of cream with a drop of coffee in it who smiled at her broadly and bowed her toward the open door of his cab.

The drive to the Oriental Hotel – she had selected it because she knew that Joseph Conrad, Somerset Maugham and Graham Greene had stayed there – took considerably longer than she expected. What the guidebooks described as charming, vital and exciting was suddenly translating as traffic-choked, chaotic and deafeningly noisy. The cab driver pointed out some landmarks – the Royal Sports Club on the right and Lumphini Park on her left – but she was already deep in the throes of culture shock brought on by a series of contradictions her eyes were seeing but her brain wasn't registering. Ancient temples sat next to modern office towers; saffron-clad Buddhist monks moved silently alongside sleek Mercedes-Benz sedans; extravagantly colored flowering bushes sprang from the black muck of slow-moving canals. She could only respond by bobbing her head and smiling fatuously.

When the driver deposited her at her hotel she saw that it was indeed on the banks of the Chao Phraya River – a fact that had registered on her brain from the travel agent's description. As she walked through the doors into the ornately decorated, marble-walled lobby, Joanna entered another phase of culture shock. She had an impression of occidental/oriental opulence bathed in a golden light emanating from high-hanging teak lamps carved in the shape of temple bells. The gleaming white marble floors were covered with soft, sand-colored oriental carpets; square glass and brass tables held oval-shaped brass and glass lamps that cast a warm milky glow. She was in an air-conditioned fantasyland, being checked in and taken to her room with a care and efficiency she had not known since her mother had given up tucking her in at night.

Once in her teak-furnished, silk-paneled room, Joanna gazed at but didn't really see the river outside her window, took a couple of strides over to the bed, kicked off her shoes and lay down on top of the blankets. When she woke up it was dark, but she could still hear the ever-present hum of traffic and the toot-toot of car horns. She looked at her watch and saw it was 7:39. It took her a minute to remember that she had re-set her watch on the plane and that this was in fact local time.

She showered in the white marble bathroom, changed into one of the crumpled cotton dresses that she had so carefully packed in Zurich and went downstairs looking for a restaurant. She was not keen to go out into the Bangkok night and risk getting lost, kidnapped or mugged and could have stayed in her room and devoured the platter of fresh tropical fruit put there by the silent, unseen hotel staff. But she knew if she resorted to room service on her first day in town, she might never pluck up the courage to leave the sumptuous Oriental. So she settled on the less scary but still adventurous course of checking out Lord Jim's, the hotel's celebrated seafood buffet.

Conrad's *Lord Jim* had always been one of Joanna's favorite novels and had fired her imagination with its densely atmospheric descriptions of hot, sultry climes and exotic adventures. She had been thrilled by the thought of sinister goings-on in sweltering jungles, where tropical fruits rotted on the vine, predatory animals watched silently from behind huge fronds of jungle fern and a sense of mystery always hung in the air like a woman's perfume. As she entered Lord Jim's restaurant on her first night in Bangkok, Joanna wasn't sure whether her imagination would be able to stand the test of reality.

The simulated ship's décor was a bit sleek on the surface, but the dim lights and her fuzzy head permitted the illusion of nine-teenth-century adventure. She ordered a gin sling to keep the thing going. She knew the Singapore Sling had been invented at Raffles' Hotel in Singapore and she was the Oriental in Bangkok, but somehow it was all right because Conrad had stayed there too.

Joanna surveyed the interesting mix of people around her and noted a definite inclination toward international banking types. Then she surveyed the seafood banquet spread out before her and forgot about the people. She sampled tiny clams and shrimp, put back a few mussels and a succulent crab claw and finished off with the better part of a red snapper that came garnished with hot chili peppers, scallions, coriander and pungent ginger root. Her taste buds soared in a frenzy of flavors and sensations and cleared her travel-weary brain in an instant. She suddenly wanted someone to be there with her so she could say to them, "Isn't this magnificent?" In the middle of all the mixed messages she was getting from Bangkok, the Oriental Hotel, Lord Jim's and the red snapper, she found herself missing Franklin and missing Fay and missing the rose-colored wing chair in her living room. Instead of reading it in a book, she was actually there, experiencing it. Yet somehow, it wasn't enough.

She signed the bill and wandered back up to her room for a nightcap and to think about what she would do the next day. She didn't have a clue where to begin, she had no plan of action, so she considered the alternatives. Her first instinct was to go to the American Embassy and start asking questions. There must be some kind of report on the investigation of Franklin's death. There had to be someone who could tell her what had happened after they discovered his body.

Joanna was reluctant to go to the Thai police until she had spo-ken to someone at the Embassy. She hoped they would advise her on how to handle the situation discreetly and without ruffling any feathers. What she wanted was information. She didn't want to raise hell in a foreign country; it would serve no purpose to be thrown out for creating an international incident. She thought that once she had the names of a few of Franklin's associates she could arrange to meet them and talk privately about his life and work in Bangkok. She didn't want to barge into the offices of Americans Aid Refugees, but she considered it legitimate for the grieving widow to have tea with her late husband's former associates.

Resolved to take the thing one step at a time and see where it led her, she finished her brandy and prepared for bed. She discovered that the invisible hotel staff had unpacked her crushed belongings and they now hung immaculately pressed in an enormous closet that would probably house a family of four in some parts of the city. The only other sign of a visit was a single pink orchid left on her pillow. She settled into the king-size bed with a copy of Maugham's *Collected Short Stories From The South Seas* that she had brought along to ease her into a reality that was beyond anything in her experience. Nothing in her real life had prepared her for what lay ahead.

Chapter Eight

Joanna woke early the next morning to a clear cloudless sky that hinted at the impending heat of the day. She dressed comfortably but somewhat formally for her visit to the Embassy, in a sleeveless cotton dress topped with a matching jacket. She put on low-heeled sandals and packed her handbag with a map, a guidebook, pencil and notebook and her Somerset Maugham stories in case she got stuck waiting somewhere.

It was still early when she finished her breakfast so she decided to take a stroll through the gardens surrounding the hotel before hailing a cab to the Embassy. The grounds were resplendent with tall palms and dense shrubs and filled with a variety of exotic flowers that she promised herself she would learn the names of before she left Thailand. She came across the original part of the hotel, a two-storied structure with a distinctly Victorian style that was now called the Authors' Residence and housed the suites named for those famous writers who had once stayed there.

Venturing out onto the street in front of the hotel, she saw that she was in a neighborhood of elegant hotels, embassies and shops that catered to a clientele of tourists from North America and Europe who were prepared to buy anything from handmade artifacts to sapphires and silks. Adjacent to her hotel was the Oriental Plaza, a collection of respectable-looking shops with fairly respectable-looking prices.

Walking along the bank of the river, she saw that the city had been awake long before she was and was already well into its activities of commerce and survival. Food and flower vendors were set up along the riverbank and private boats, from small motorized vessels to large flat-bottomed *sampans* and high-speed longboats, were laden with the day's supplies, ready to make the rounds of the city's *khlongs* – the canals that comprised a large network of waterways that had once been the main arteries of transportation. Because of them, Bangkok was sometimes referred to as the "Venice of the East." The boats were loaded down with carefully arranged piles of fresh fruits in yellow, orange and red, vegetables tied in generous bundles of green and purple, gloriously fragrant flowers that added touches of pink and white to more yellow and orange, fresh herbs and dried spices that lent broad strokes of ochre, vermilion and gold to the palette. The catch of the day was displayed in a shimmering silvery glint that sometimes shone red or blue in the brilliant sunlight.

She wandered for about half an hour observing the Thais buying the day's essentials. She was overwhelmed by the smells of garlic, ginger and chilies frying in open-air food stalls mixed with the sweet, seductive aromas of jasmine, mimosa and roses arranged in piles or hanging from stalls groaning under their abundant load. By now it was nine o'clock and, remembering what she'd set out to do, Joanna dragged herself away from the hypnotic draw of the marketplace and signaled a cab. There was no meter so she negotiated a price and the driver agreed to take her to the Embassy for fifty *baht* – about two dollars – which seemed reasonable to her but was probably exorbitant by Thai standards.

A few minutes later they were at the American Embassy, a complex of buildings surrounded by purple bougainvillea vines, royal palms and carefully manicured lawns. She still had no idea whom she should see or what she would say. In her imagination she had always just walked in the door, asked to see the person in charge and then told him her story. She now realized that this was totally unrealistic. She walked up to what appeared to be the main building and approached the first American she saw. This happened to be a tall and expressionless young Marine standing as still as a post and sending off distinct "don't ask me" signals. Joanna asked him anyway and he nodded "yes" to her enquiry about an information desk and pointed her toward it. The floors were cool, immaculate white marble and everything about the place spelled power, efficiency and bureaucratic inscrutability. The information desk was manned by another cool young Marine and she told him she was looking for someone who could talk to her about Americans living in Bangkok. He asked to see her passport, took down her name and said someone would see her in a few moments. She took a seat along the wall and waited, mentally preparing herself for the interview.

She half expected a third Marine to appear but was pleasantly surprised when a young man wearing a suit and tie and wire-rimmed glasses came up to her and said, "Mrs. Reynolds, I'm Bruce Jackson. If you'll come this way, I think Mr. Bradshaw is the man you should talk to." She followed him through a door, down a corridor of closed doors and through another door into an anteroom that led to an office in which an unsmiling but distinguished-looking gentleman sat behind a handsome walnut desk. He appeared to be in his late forties, well groomed, with a touch of gray at the temples. He had piercing blue eyes of an almost unnatural hue that made her think of Paul Newman. He was the kind of person who would be attractive to both men and women, she thought.

"Mrs. Reynolds, this is Jonathon Bradshaw. He's in charge of

U.S. Citizens' Enquiries. He'll try to answer any questions that you have." With that, Bruce Jackson left the office, closing the door behind him.

"Sit down please, Mrs. Reynolds," said Bradshaw, gesturing to a solid-looking, leather-covered chair with wooden arms. His voice was as rich and dark as the mahogany paneling on the walls. "I understand you want to see someone about American citizens living in Bangkok. Was it someone in particular you were looking for?"

"Mr. Bradshaw," she began, careful not to seem anxious or nervous, "my husband was Franklin Reynolds of Americans Aid Refugees. He died in a drowning accident in Pattaya a few weeks ago. I would like to know something of the circumstances of his death and the details of the police investigation."

Mr. Bradshaw appeared not to react to anything she said, but she thought she caught a slight twitch in the outer corner of his left eye.

"Uh, well, yes, Mrs. Reynolds, there was a police investigation into the death of your husband at the time of the unfortunate accident and the Thai police ruled death by drowning. They could not establish that he had been on a boat and there were no witnesses. The police believe he was caught in an undertow while swimming, probably hit his head on the ocean bottom and lost consciousness. I'm very sorry."

She noticed that he hadn't asked for any files, nor did he appear to have any papers in front of him. He seemed to be familiar with the case and it was almost as if he had been expecting her. Either that or he had already answered these questions before.

"What led the police to believe he hit his head?"

"Uh, there was one bump on the head, middle of the forehead actually, that would indicate he hit the bottom with some force."

"And you say there was no sign of a boat anywhere that he could have been a passenger on?"

"No, Mrs. Reynolds, no privately owned yachts were in the vicinity at the time and your husband did not apparently rent a boat any time during his stay in Pattaya." Bradshaw was definitely uncomfortable with her questions but remained in control of the interview. She could see he wasn't going to speculate or give his opinion about what had happened to Franklin. He gently and rhythmically tapped his fingertips together – a nervous gesture, but one that clearly signaled "go away and don't ask any more questions."

"Just one more thing, Mr. Bradshaw," she said. "I wonder if you could give me the name of the Thai investigating officer who handled the case?" A long shot, she figured, but she had to have somewhere to go from here. To her surprise, Bradshaw shifted slightly in his leather-upholstered, executive swivel chair, looked her in the eye with his blue stare and said, "Panakorn, Ma'am, Chief of Police Prem Panakorn, Central Division, Pattaya Police Force."

She sensed the interview wasn't over yet, so she waited in silence for him to say the rest. He lowered his eyes and looked at his fingertips tapping against each other, then raised his eyes to hers. "Uh, Mrs. Reynolds," he began, "this is strictly a Thai police matter and I must advise you that as an American citizen you have no right to interfere with this process. The case has been thoroughly investigated and the book closed. We are satisfied with the explanation of your husband's unfortunate demise and, although I'm sure it must be difficult for you to accept, we recommend you do just that and try to put the past behind you. It will do no good to start poking the ashes at this point."

Case closed. Interview over. Well, well, she thought, you certainly do send out some strong signals, Mr. Bradshaw. She was about to ask him if he had ever been in the Marines when he stood up and said, "Good day, Mrs. Reynolds. Please enjoy your stay in Thailand. You might consider visiting some of the resort areas to the south – the beaches are stunning and the seafood is excellent. Bangkok can be very hot and unpleasant this time of the year."

"Thank you, Mr. Bradshaw. I'll consider your advice."

As she walked back down the long corridor, Joanna spotted Bruce Jackson through one of the doors at the end of the hall. He was staring at her intently as if he were trying to memorize her face.

Chapter Nine

Joanna could see she was going to get nowhere fast by talking to officials, so she decided to think about taking a more unofficial approach. She wanted to talk to some of Franklin's associates at Americans Aid Refugees but she didn't want to just walk in through the front door and start asking questions. First of all, she'd have to find out who the people to talk to were and, second, she'd have to figure out where she could talk to them without attracting too much attention.

Maybe she'd made a mistake going to the Embassy first. She had assumed that they would just tell her what they knew. In fact, Bradshaw had told her almost exactly what she thought she wanted to hear. She'd wanted him to say Franklin's death was an accident, that he hit his head on the ocean floor and drowned by accident. But she also wanted him to tell her why Franklin was in the water in the first place, why he had suddenly, at this stage of his life, put on a bathing suit and gone to the beach.

Maybe Bradshaw didn't see anything unusual about a man

drowning like that. It was unfortunate, maybe, but not unusual. Had he known about Franklin's phobia, maybe he would have been suspicious. Joanna hadn't liked the warning implicit in his speech to her. It just made her more curious. She really wanted to believe Franklin's death was an accident. She wanted to believe there was nothing more to it. And if Bradshaw had shown her a file, a report, anything, or if he had expressed his own opinion about the matter, she might have been more convinced. But she hadn't come halfway across the world to be swept under the carpet. She wanted some answers.

The heat was making her uncomfortable, or maybe it was the thinking. Anyway, she decided to explore some of the city before deciding what to do next. She needed to work out a few things, including an escalating feeling of annoyance that was starting to feel like anger. It's the heat, she thought. I'm not used to it. She took a cab back to New Road a few blocks from her hotel and started to wander. She had never experienced anything like it. She was in a world of elegant shops, embassies and hotels, surrounded by fish and fruit stalls, flowers, herbs, spices and all kinds of exotic things she couldn't begin to name. It reminded her of the farmers' markets of her childhood but much more colorful and exciting. There weren't just bargains to be had here, but entertainment, street theater, art and music. Fruits and vegetables were laid out with meticulous care, as if the vendors were competing for a display award to be handed out at the end of the day. Most of the vendors were beautiful young women who occupied themselves between customers by braiding flowers into extravagant bunches or tying herbs into neat little packages. Young children were sorting mushrooms and stacking ginger root. One old woman had arranged half a dozen heads of garlic in front of her. Joanna wondered if she was a widow and if this was how she survived.

Joanna let her nose lead her to a food stall where a young man and his wife were preparing various noodle concoctions in a well-seasoned and blackened wok. The aroma of chilies and ginger frying in hot oil and the sight of plump fresh shrimp piled high was too much for her and she pointed to the wok's contents and said "one for me please" in her best sign language. She knew Franklin would have disapproved but she decided to be fatalistic about it. If she was going to die in Thailand, it wasn't going to be of food poisoning.

Joanna sat down on a small stool at a wooden table and watched her meal being prepared. She had attempted oriental-style wok cooking a couple of times at home and each time had carefully measured and timed each stage of the procedure, being careful not to overcook anything or let it burn. What she saw before her eyes was a feat of timing and coordination that reminded her of the jugglers in the Chinese circus. In minutes a plate of steaming hot noodles and shrimp, done to perfection, was placed before her. A small round dish of what appeared to be crushed chili peppers in oil accompanied it and she carefully sprinkled a little over her noodles. She was glad she hadn't dumped the whole thing on top. The small amount she ingested burned right down her throat and had her waving for a cold beer in speechless pantomime. The beer – a Singha – was the perfect antidote and she chopsticked and sipped her way through a feast of flavors – some fiery, some tangy and some delicate – that cleared her head and left her with a warm glow at the same time.

Joanna slowly worked her way back to the Oriental, stopping several times to examine a particularly colorful display of cloth sarongs or a meticulously laid out table of household articles, toiletries or medicinal cure-alls. She scrutinized every object with the same careful attention she would have given were she purchasing a perfect diamond; even such mundane articles as kitchen sponges and sewing thread fascinated her beyond explanation. She spent hours bent over those well-ordered display tables and eventually gave in and bought a tube of Colgate toothpaste. She resisted the egg shampoo as she resisted the multi-hued sarongs, knowing in her heart they were not for her.

Joanna was damp and drowsy by the time she got back to the hotel so she took a long shower, turned down the air-conditioning and lay back on the pillows to read for a while. She woke two hours later to the phone ringing in her ear. It took her a few seconds to remember where she was and, as she picked up the phone, she wondered who on earth could be calling her here.

"Mrs. Reynolds?" The voice was deep and warm and not familiar to her.

"Yes."

"My name is Tom Thorpe, Mrs. Reynolds. We've never met but I wonder if you could give me a few minutes of your time. I'd really like to talk to you."

"What about, Mr. Thorpe?"

"It's about your husband, Mrs. Reynolds, but I'd rather not discuss it over the phone. Could you meet me downstairs in the bar in half an hour?"

Joanna debated whether she should meet this man who appeared to know her husband, or something about him. How had he found her? Was it through the embassy? They were the only people who knew she was in Bangkok. But she decided that if he had information about Franklin, she wanted to know what it was. "Okay," she said. "I'll see you there."

As she put the phone down she realized her heart was pounding and her palms were sweating. Good heavens, she thought, am I nervous at the prospect of talking to a stranger in a bar or am I afraid of what he might tell me?

Half an hour later Tom Thorpe entered the Bamboo Bar and walked towards her table with the easy grace of an athlete. He appeared to be about thirty-five and had the tall, blond good looks of a boy raised in the American mid-west. "Mrs. Reynolds," he said, extending his hand, "I'm Tom Thorpe."

"Basketball?" she asked, looking up at him. When he looked puzzled she said, "Did you used to play?"

"Oh, uh, yes. U.C.L.A. But I haven't played for a long time." He seemed a little embarrassed so she decided to let him do the talking. He ordered a beer and while they waited for it to come he asked her how she liked the hotel.

"Fine," she said. "I feel I'm in good company with the likes of Conrad and Maugham."

He smiled and agreed with her. "The city's changed a bit since their time, I'm afraid. The air's a lot more polluted and the drains are more plugged."

They chatted for a few minutes about nothing and she finally said, "Look Mr. Thorpe, I assume you're not here just to make small talk." He looked a little uncomfortable. He hadn't expected her to be so direct. Joanna made a mental note to cut down on the chili peppers. "I'm sorry. That was rude of me. Was there something in particular you wanted to see me about?"

"Mrs. Reynolds," he said, "I didn't mean to upset you. I did want to talk to you about something concerning your husband's death." He looked at her for a minute as if to gauge her reaction to this and when he saw she wasn't going to burst into tears, he continued.

"I should tell you I'm a reporter, Mrs. Reynolds, and I freelance for a number of English-language newspapers in Southeast Asia. I write a kind of people and events column. It's part of my job to keep tabs on American citizens who are staying in Thailand. When I first learned of your husband's death I was a little surprised at the circumstances. I had met him a few times and I thought it seemed, well, uncharacteristic of him to be hanging around the surf at Pattaya Beach. It also wasn't the kind of thing a man in his position should be doing, if you know what I mean. Pattaya's a real swinger's resort town. A lot of Europeans and Australians go there for a good time – water skiing, windsurfing, discos, Thai girls, drugs, you name it. Anyway, from what I knew about your husband, it didn't seem like his kind of place. I knew he spent the occasional weekend golfing at the Siam Country Club in Pattaya, but that's a long way from where he was found. And he usually went with three or four other guys, so what was he doing swimming alone in the ocean? There's a pool at the country club. I started asking a few questions, mainly to satisfy my own curiosity, at first, and maybe because everyone was being so cool about the whole thing, you know, pretending it hadn't happened. It just didn't sit right with me.

"A lot of Americans live in Bangkok and they tend to hang around the same circles. I belong to the golf club here, partly because I like to golf, but mainly because it's a handy place to meet people and talk to them. Anyway, I started casually asking a few people what they thought of the accident and mostly they were reluctant to say anything. A few said, 'Too bad, he was a nice guy.' But most of them just shook their heads and shrugged their shoulders as if to say, 'Don't ask me, I don't know anything about it.' A couple of the women were a little more willing to talk, however. And more than one mentioned that your husband never went near the water and refused all invitations to go boating or swimming. They suspected he didn't like the water and, maybe, was even afraid of it. I find women are generally pretty good at picking up on men's fears."

Joanna thought she was dreaming, listening to someone she didn't know talk about people she didn't know talking about her husband. "Yes," she said, "Franklin had a phobia about the water."

"That made me even more suspicious," he continued, "so I kept asking questions. There didn't seem to be much of an investigation going on and nobody at the embassy was saying much. That bothered me, too. He was an American citizen, after all, and a prominent one at that. You'd think they'd be hollering their heads off for an investigation. But nothing. Just death by drowning. Accident. Period. It smelled like a cover-up to me. I was told in no uncertain terms by the embassy people to stop asking questions. That henchman of Jonathon Bradshaw's – what's his name? – Jackson? – he made it pretty plain that this was a hands-off affair. The Thai police were handling it and their conclusion was that it had been an accident."

"So why are you telling me this, Mr. Thorpe?"

"Call me Tom, please. I'm telling you because it bugs me to be brushed off without any explanation and because if you're here to find out what really happened to your husband, maybe I can help you."

"You could just be paranoid, Tom. I can see why the embassy wouldn't want a reporter asking a lot of uncomfortable questions. What makes you think there's a cover-up?"

"I can understand the need for a certain amount of, shall we say, discretion when it comes to highly sensitive national interests. But the diplomatic corps is the most gossip-ridden, backbiting, kiss-and-tell establishment in the world. Not only do they know each other's business, but they also know who's sleeping with whom at every other embassy in town.

"Where your husband's death was concerned, Mrs. Reynolds, there was very definitely a cover-up going on. A conspiracy of silence, if you will, and the orders were being issued from pretty high up. I'm certain of it."

Joanna didn't say anything for a few minutes while she thought about what he had said. The circumstances of Franklin's death had been eating away at her from the beginning, but she hadn't been thinking about embassy cover-ups or government involvement of any kind. She had only thought in terms of what Franklin might have been involved in, and even then she hadn't allowed herself to speculate too much.

"There's one other thing I think you should know before you decide to go ahead." He seemed distinctly uncomfortable and his eyes did a quick tour of the room before he looked at her again. "Mrs. Reynolds, I believe your husband was murdered."

There it was. Tom Thorpe had finally put a name to all the nagging doubts, all the unformed questions that had been floating just beyond her reach. Murder. Joanna's hand shook as she lifted her brandy snifter and took a large gulp. The burning in her throat brought tears to her eyes and she was suddenly taking deep breaths that sounded like sobs. Tom was signaling the waiter to bring another round of drinks and handing her a cocktail napkin and glass of water at the same time.

"I'm all right," she said. "Really. I'm all right."

"I'm sorry. I'm really sorry. It's just that I've lived with the idea for so long now, I didn't think that … you mean it never occurred to you he might have been killed?"

"Well, I guess I … I'm not sure what I thought. I was afraid he might have committed suicide."

"Suicide?" Tom said, as if the idea had never occurred to him. "Why would you think that?"

"My husband was a very proud man, Tom." Joanna was beginning to get her composure back. "Something might have happened that upset or depressed him. I don't know. I just couldn't believe he drowned accidentally." She wasn't about to tell him about the Swiss bank account. She didn't know this man or what he might do with the information. "Why do you think he was … that someone …"

"There would be no reason to cover up an accident, Mrs. Reynolds. The facts would have borne up under scrutiny and I would have stopped asking questions. As for suicide, there would be no reason to hide that either, at least unofficially. I mean there would at least have been speculation, gossip. What was so peculiar about the whole thing was that nobody was saying anything."

Joanna sat back in her chair and looked hard at Tom Thorpe's handsome face. Who was this guy who had suddenly turned everything upside down on her? Why should she trust him? Why should she believe him, for that matter? She had known Franklin's death couldn't be an accident, but she hadn't allowed herself to think someone had killed him. Why would anyone want to kill Franklin? It had to have something to do with the money. If it was true, that is. Thorpe seemed convinced it was true but he didn't really have any evidence. And if it *were* true then that meant somebody had got away with it.

"What's in it for you? Are you just looking for the next big story?"

"My reasons are personal, in a way. Call it a crisis of conscience. I don't think stuff like this should be allowed to happen. The real question is, do you want to find out what happened to your husband?"

"Not at any price. I don't want to be the subject of some sensational news story. I don't want Franklin's name splashed all over the headlines."

"If there is a story, it will be about Franklin's killers."

"That may be so, but if he was killed, it must have been for a reason. Unless it's a random act of violence, I don't see how you can separate the victim from the crime. Why does someone get killed?"

"Well, they're either involved with bad people or they do bad things."

Involved with bad people? Doing bad things? It didn't sound like the Franklin she knew, but Joanna wasn't sure who Franklin was anymore. Should she trust a newspaper reporter? Would he respect her privacy if she handed him a story?

"Look," he said, sensing her reluctance, "I'll make a deal with you. If we get to the bottom of this, and if there's a story in it, I won't write it without your permission."

"And why should I take you at your word?"

"Because I'm a nice guy?"

What could she say to that? Was she going to call him a liar before he did anything to deserve it? Maybe he really was a nice guy who would keep his word. Besides, it was either trust him or go it alone.

"So what do you want me to do?" she asked.

"Well," he said, "you can't exactly go in and blow the lid off an embassy cover-up. I mean, who knows what or who is involved at this stage. But you might be able to get a few people to open up to you a bit. You know, find out who he was associated with, what he liked to do, that kind of thing."

"Where do you suggest I begin?"

"The golf club might be a good place. Your husband was a member and you could quite legitimately talk to a few people there. Start with general kinds of questions, like, how was his health, had he been working too hard. You know, wifely questions."

Joanna tried to see herself going into an unfamiliar environment and asking strangers questions about her husband. "Wifely" questions. She wasn't very comfortable meeting new people and she wasn't sure she could pull it off. It would mean playing the role of grieving widow, which she was, it was true, but not like she wanted them to think she was. Wifely concern had never played a part in her relationship with Franklin. But she could see Tom's point. It was probably the best way to go.

"All right," she said. "Can you get me in there or should I just present myself?"

"It might not be such a good idea if I took you there – I don't think we should be seen together – but how about a compromise? You show up tomorrow for a drink at the bar at, say, five o'clock and I'll be there and approach you. There's usually a fair number that drop in for a drink before dinner and I can casually introduce you to a couple of people who knew your husband. Then you're on your own."

"Okay," she said, standing up. Joanna offered him her hand and said. "I'll see what I can find out. Let's take it one step at a time."

"Tomorrow at five then, Mrs. Reynolds?"

"Tomorrow at five." Joanna suddenly felt very tired, more tired than she had felt during the last month. She walked slowly, as if she had just gained a hundred pounds, and took the elevator back up to her room. She undressed and got into bed mechanically, putting her head down on the pillow next to another fresh orchid. She reached under the pillow and found the foil-wrapped piece of chocolate she knew would be there, unwrapped it and put it in her mouth. It was warm and bittersweet as it melted on her tongue. She remembered Fay saying she didn't think it was a good idea for her to go to Bangkok. Maybe she had tried to tell her in her own way she suspected something awful might have happened to Franklin. She probably knew Joanna wouldn't believe her anyway. She would have to hear it from a total stranger.

Chapter Ten

Tom Thorpe couldn't believe his luck. Joanna Reynolds was exactly the foil he needed to get the right people to open up, and she had practically fallen into his lap. His contact at the embassy would expect payback big-time for this. Bruce Jackson liked to play both ends against the middle. He knew he was way down the food chain when it came to power and influence, but he also knew that his pal Tom Thorpe was even farther down and always scrounging for scraps. Tom knew it made Bruce feel important that he could lord it over the press guys and hand out tidbits in return for complete anonymity. And he knew Bruce would deny everything – very convincingly – if the shit ever hit the fan.

Joanna Reynolds was as corn-fed and naïve as they came. He was about to send her into a tank full of barracudas, but what did he care? He needed this story. He'd been on the "people and places" beat too long and it was now or never. If he didn't prove he had the stuff in the very near future, his career would effectively be over. He'd be stalled in neutral, going nowhere, or worse, going backwards. He'd seen it plenty of times before. Guys who were hungry when they arrived waking up five years later to find they had been sitting on the same bar stool for the last four years. Something had happened to them while they were living the life – the booze, the girls, the dope – and they had lost their edge. They weren't hungry anymore, at least not in the same way. The parade had passed them by and they had decided it wasn't worth chasing after.

It was easy to get sucked into the hedonistic life in Bangkok. It was like a big aquarium. Stuff just floated by – lovely, tempting, exotic stuff – and all you had to do was reach out and grab it. You could just float forever in a beautiful, self-contained environment where everything was plentiful and cheap. It was the effortlessness of it all that made it so appealing. Why work your butt off when one or two stories a month would keep your editor off your back and your bank account active? It was the "less is enough" philosophy and it appealed to a lot of guys.

But Tom was still just a tiny bit hungry. He thought he had one more kick at the can before it would be too late. The little bit of edge he had was still sharp because it annoyed him that a piss-ant bureaucrat like Bruce Jackson could yank his strings. Tom was tired of being nobody from nowhere. He wanted to be somebody that people would point to and say, "That's Tom Thorpe. Helluva newsman. He cracked the embassy cover-up on the Reynolds murder. Knew something was up. Wouldn't let it go." And Tom did know something was up. There was a nasty smell about this one. If he could bring this story in, his career would be made. He'd be known as a troubleshooter and a credible investigative journalist. Then the stories would come to him.

Joanna couldn't sleep. She tried taking a hot bath but that didn't work, so she lay awake for most of the night thinking about what Tom had told her. The world was a different place for her now, a darker place, less safe, less predictable. The dream world she had been wandering around in for the past month had been shattered and replaced with a colder reality than she could ever have imagined. If what Tom had told her was true, and she had no reason to doubt it, then Franklin had been killed and no one was prepared to do anything about it. She was appalled by the fact that a man of Franklin's stature and importance could be murdered and no one was demanding his killer be found and punished. No one saw fit to ask why he had been killed and, what was worse, the American government was satisfied to record a verdict of accidental death.

She felt sick to her stomach at the thought of someone taking Franklin's life. She kept seeing his body being dumped into the cold, black water. She couldn't get the image out of her mind. Finally she got up and turned on all the lights and stood at the window, staring into the Bangkok night. She remembered the Chinese astrology book she'd been reading the day she learned of Franklin's death and recalled the part about his Karma. It had said his life would end in triumph or in tragedy, dictated by his past actions. But what could Franklin have done to deserve being murdered? It just wasn't possible. Somebody must have made a mistake. A terrible mistake. She wished she'd never come here. Wished she'd never met Tom Thorpe. Wished, wished, wished that none of it had happened. She looked at the clock and saw it was after three. What was it Scott Fitzgerald had said? "In the real dark night of the soul, it's always three o'clock in the morning, day after day." A bad time to think. A bad time to make decisions. She crawled back under the covers, closed her eyes and fell asleep from sheer exhaustion.

Joanna had forgotten to turn down the air-conditioning and when she got up a few hours later the room felt frigid. She took a hot shower, dressed and went downstairs to the restaurant for something to eat. Wanting to sit on the terrace to feel the warmth of the sun, instead she felt assaulted by its glaring brightness and bothered by the smell of rot and sewage drifting up from the river. She ate without tasting the food and finally went back up to her room because she couldn't stand the noise of people and traffic all around her. She put on a sweater and tried to read magazines to pass the time until she was to meet Tom Thorpe at the golf club.

Then she took another shower because she felt dirty and changed her clothes. Finally it was time and she ordered a taxi.

The Royal Thai Golf and Country Club was located in the affluent eastern sector of the city, Bang Kapi, where most of the resident Americans lived. It spread languidly over several acres of rolling green lawns, dotted with the occasional pond and sand trap, and was tastefully landscaped with carefully planted trees, bushes and flowerbeds. The clubhouse was middle-class American suburban, low and sprawling, but with the characteristic Thai flame-tiered, pagoda-style roof plunked right in the middle to remind you where you really were. It was a little unimaginative for her taste but more than adequate for its purpose.

Once inside, Joanna took a deep breath and headed straight for the bar. She selected a small table at one end and sat down in a fan-backed wicker chair with bright green and red floral-patterned cushions. A waiter wearing black slacks and a white shirt buttoned to the neck came up and she ordered a gin sling. She took a casual look around the room and noted that there were about twenty-five people, mainly in couples or groups of three and four, sipping on a selection of drinks that varied from white wine to half pineapples filled with fresh fruit and topped with little paper umbrellas. Her gaze rested on a lone figure hunched over a drink at one end of the bar. Tom Thorpe. He had probably seen her come in but was deciding to play it cool until a few of the other regulars took notice of her.

A few minutes later, he sauntered over to her table, drink in hand, and said, "Hello. I'm Tom Thorpe. I write the social column for the local English-language paper. I haven't seen you in here before. Do you mind if I join you? Ask you a few questions?"

"Be my guest, Mr. Thorpe," she said, as casually as possible, "but I hope you don't intend to do an in-depth interview. I'm not interested in seeing my name in the papers."

Tom smiled and took a seat beside her. He leaned into the center of the table and spoke in a low voice. "We're in luck. There are a few people here who were chummy with your husband, including a few of his golf partners. I suggest you try and talk to their wives as well."

He nodded toward a couple seated close to the center of the room and said, "That's Arthur and Ellen Roberts. He's with A.A.R., fairly close associate of your husband's. They used to socialize a bit. I'll introduce you to them in a few minutes. See that foursome near the potted palm? Both men are with Amstar Oil. Used to golf with him fairly regularly.

"There's one other person here I think it would be worth your while to talk to. See that fellow over there, sitting by himself in the corner? That's Fred Hendricks. Usually drinks alone, doesn't socialize much. Pretty morose guy. His wife Ruth was your husband's secretary at A.A.R. You won't ever see her around here, but you should try and meet her. She'd probably know better than anybody what your husband's schedule was like, whom he met, whom he liked and didn't like."

Joanna noticed that Fred Hendricks never lifted his eyes from his drink and seemed to be examining it as if it were some object of great interest. He appeared to be a shy, unhappy man. She decided to tackle the Roberts' first and asked Tom to introduce her to them.

"Okay," he said. "But after that, I'm gone. It should look strictly courteous, especially at this stage. Call me later at this number." He pushed a small card across the table with just a phone number written on it. Joanna quickly slipped it into her purse. Tom finished the rest of his beer and they both stood up and walked over to the Roberts' table.

Arthur Roberts looked up and said, "Hello, Thorpe. How are things in the newspaper business?"

Tom chuckled and said, "Fine. Just fine. Uh, I'd like you to meet someone, Art. This is Joanna Reynolds, Franklin's, uh, widow. She's touring this part of the world and I thought I'd get first dibs on her impressions of Bangkok."

Art Roberts stood up, revealing his full height – about six-foot-four – and took Joanna's hand in his rather large paw. "Mrs. Reynolds," he said, "I'm so sorry about what's happened. Your husband was a friend of mine as well as a colleague at A.A.R. We miss him very much." It was an awkward moment but before she could reply he turned to the very thin, elegantly dressed woman beside him and said, "This is my wife, Ellen."

Joanna nodded to Ellen who nodded back with a look of sympathetic understanding in her eyes that held just a hint of better-you-than-me, honey. Joanna thought Ellen seemed less than pleased to meet her.

"Won't you join us for a drink, Mrs. Reynolds?" It was Art Roberts, sounding a little uncomfortable but courteous nonetheless. "What about you, Tom?"

"Oh, no thanks, Art. I've got to be going. Supposed to meet Bill Walters for a game of squash." Tom excused himself, saying, "Nice to have met you, Mrs. Reynolds" and left.

"Please," said Ellen Roberts, "join us for a drink."

"Thank you," Joanna said, sitting down. "And, please, call me Joanna." Roberts smiled at her and signaled for another round of drinks.

"It must have been quite a shock for you to learn that Franklin had died, so far away and all." Ellen was making an honest effort to be decent and Joanna gave her credit for not taking the coward's way and ignoring the issue altogether. In fact, Ellen was doing her a favor, whether she realized it or not.

"Yes, it was," she said. "You know, it makes it very much harder to accept. I mean, I was used to Franklin being away for long periods of time. I have to keep reminding myself that he isn't coming back. That's one of the reasons I decided to come here. I thought maybe it would help me believe that it really happened." Joanna was getting better at the direct approach.

"I can't tell you how upset we all were when it happened, Joanna," said Art. "I've known Franklin for nearly three years and I never knew a man I respected more. He had a way of getting things done that almost no one else could match. And believe me, in this part of the world, that's something. I've been out here for a long time. Retired from the service after the war ended and managed to get a string of consulting jobs to keep me comfortable. I'd met Franklin several times during his previous trips here and when he asked me to come aboard at A.A.R., I accepted. We worked very closely during the last nine months of his life. I don't think we'll be able to replace him."

"I'm sorry to hear that," said Joanna. "Franklin was so deeply involved in this project, it meant so much to him. I'd hate to see it flounder now that he's not around."

"Well, the program will carry on. Something like this has its own limits in a way. We would hope that in time the problem will cease to exist. That's the ultimate aim of any project of this nature. In the meantime, it's a thankless task. We're condemned on all sides – sometimes for not doing enough and other times for doing too much!"

"It must have been frustrating for Franklin at times. Did he seem to you to be taking care of himself? I mean, did he ever take time to relax, get away from the pressure?"

"Well, he did occasionally make trips up north to the hill country to get away from the heat. He was never much for the sun and the beach."

"Yes, I know. That's why I was a little surprised that he drowned. Franklin really didn't enjoy the water. I thought maybe he had decided to take up swimming or boating since he came here, you know, to relax."

"I know, that puzzled me too," said Art. "I had never known Franklin to go near the water, but he occasionally spent a weekend at the Siam Country Club in Pattaya. The golfing there is excellent – one of the best clubs in Asia. In fact, we had a golf weekend there just about six weeks before he died."

"Yes, I remember that," said Ellen. "You wouldn't let me come. Said it was a 'boys only' weekend."

"I guess we'll never really know what made him do it – go swimming, I mean," said Joanna. "I hate to think of him being alone, though. Do you know if he was by himself on that trip?"

"Well, let's put it this way," said Art. "I don't know of anyone who went down there with him and, if someone was with him, they're not saying. And, as for the newspaper reports, there's no account of anyone else being along. Another one of life's mysteries, I'm afraid."

"I don't mean to ask so many questions," said Joanna self-consciously. "I didn't come here to conduct an investigation. I just need to convince myself this has really happened."

"We understand, Joanna," said Ellen. "It's not something that's easily explained. We may never know what happened or why it happened. You know, when you live in the East you learn to accept things that can't be explained. It's harder for us Americans because we've been taught to question everything. We really believe there are answers. But over here the attitude is different. This may have been the only time your husband went to the beach in his life. And it turned out to be the wrong time. It just happened."

It just happened, thought Joanna. And so did the three million dollars sitting in a Zurich bank.

Art Roberts cleared his throat uncomfortably and said, "Joanna, I think what Ellen means is, accidents happen, sometimes for no reason and sometimes through no one's fault. Listen, we're having some people over tomorrow night, just for a few drinks. I'll be manning the barbecue. Why don't you come along? Have a little fun."

Joanna caught the look that flashed from Ellen Roberts's eyes to her husband. It was as clear as if her lips had formed the words "bad idea." If Joanna had contemplated refusing, it was only for an instant. Nothing was going to keep her from that little backyard get-together.

"That's very thoughtful of you, Art," said Joanna. "I'd love to come."

"Good," said Art. "Then it's settled. We'll have our driver pick you up. Where are you staying?"

"I'm at the Oriental. It's really very pleasant." She smiled at Ellen and Ellen smiled back.

"Good. Eight o'clock then," said Art. "Well, I'm afraid we have to be going, Joanna. So we'll look forward to seeing you tomorrow."

"Good night," said Ellen.

"Good night. And thanks for everything."

They smiled as they left and Joanna sat at the table for quite a while after the Roberts' left, nursing her gin sling and wondering what their conversation would be on the way home. She wondered if she was attaching too much importance to some of the things that had been said and imagining subtleties where none existed. They had been distinctly uncomfortable when she expressed her surprise at Franklin's having drowned. They were careful not to mention the police or the investigation although Art did mention reading the newspaper accounts. Despite what Tom had told her, she was sure there must have been a certain amount of gossip and speculation about it. She doubted that the majority of Americans living in Bangkok had accepted the "accident" with eastern serenity.

The Amstar Oil people had already left the bar but she noticed that Fred Hendricks was still concentrating on his drink and she decided to take a chance and introduce herself to him. She was determined to meet his wife and somehow Joanna doubted she would be at the Roberts' barbecue. She walked over to his table and said quietly, "Mr. Hendricks? My name is Joanna Reynolds. I wonder if I might talk to you for a few minutes. I understand your wife was my late husband's secretary at A.A.R."

He pulled his eyes away from his drink and focused them on her face. "So?" he said. "What's that to me?" She noticed he wore his hair clipped very close to his skull and she guessed he was a former Marine. His friendly manner reminded her of her experience with the two guards at the embassy the previous day. She was beginning to have it in for the Marines.

"Uh, well, I was hoping I could meet your wife and talk to her a bit about my husband and his work here. It's just I thought she might …"

"Look, if you want to talk to my wife, call her at the office. She's there every day." If looks could snarl, his would have won first prize in a national contest. Fred Hendricks was qualified to give classes in the direct approach.

"Yes, I'll do that. Sorry to have bothered you."

Joanna made her exit as casually as possible and took a cab back to her hotel. She had managed to get through the day on some kind of automatic pilot but she had been suspicious of everyone and had felt downright hostile toward Ellen Roberts. It was as if, by what he told her, Tom Thorpe had peeled back a layer of skin and now she was raw, exposed and vulnerable, without protection or defenses. She would have to pull herself together if she wanted to get to the bottom of things. And she was just beginning to realize how important it was to get to the bottom of things. If nobody else in the world wanted to know, she wanted to know. If nobody else in the world would help her, she would help herself. She knew that she had to find out if Franklin had been murdered, and why, before she would be able to put it behind her and get on with her life.

When she got to the hotel, Joanna realized she was starving and headed straight for Lord Jim's. Working her way through some lemon grass soup and fresh crab, she thought about Fred Hendricks as she cracked open the large, brittle claws and wondered why he had been so rude to her when he didn't even know her. Had she just caught him on a bad day or did he really have a lousy personality? As soon as she was finished eating, she ordered a pot of tea sent up to her room and went upstairs to phone Thorpe.

He answered the phone after the first ring and Joanna got the impression he'd been waiting for her call. "Well?" he asked anxiously, "did you find out anything?"

"Not much," she said, "but Roberts did say he was surprised that Franklin was in the water when he died. Then both of them tried to blow me off – is that the expression? – with an 'accidents will happen' speech that I think I've heard somewhere before."

"Yeah, that's the expression all right," said Tom and she could hear him frowning over the phone. She told him about the invitation to the Roberts' place for drinks and barbecue.

"Are you going?"

"Sure," she said. "Why not? Besides, I got the distinct impression the Dragon Lady didn't want me to come. So how could I possibly refuse?"

Tom laughed and she knew he was laughing as much out of surprise at what she'd said as the humor of it. She was a little surprised herself. It wasn't like her. But these were unusual circumstances and maybe they called for unusual responses.

"Look," he said, "be careful. Try not to arouse suspicion at this stage. Believe me, if they think you're snooping around, even if it is your business, they'll avoid you like the plague."

"Okay. I'll play it cool. I guess I've got time to open a few doors and see who walks through. I'll let you know if anything interesting happens."

Chapter Eleven

Joanna was up early the next morning and took a walk through the grounds of the hotel before the heat of the sun became too oppressive. She wasn't in the mood for sightseeing or shopping, and writing letters was out of the question because everyone at home thought she was in Europe. She desperately wanted to talk to Fay or Claire but of course that was out of the question too. She couldn't tell them she was in Bangkok; it would only worry them. And even if she could find a way of letting them know, she couldn't possibly tell them what she had learned about Franklin. As far as she was concerned there was still no proof. If she was ever going to tell them about it, she wanted to be able to tell them the whole story.

Joanna didn't feel like being around people so she picked up the *Herald Tribune* and the latest issues of *Time* and *Newsweek* and went up to her room to order some tea and toast. Although she had told Tom she wanted to go to the Roberts' barbecue, the thought of dealing with more new people left her feeling a little limp. She was just finishing her second cup of tea when the telephone rang. Now what? she wondered as she crossed the room to answer it.

"Hello?"

"Hello. Is this Mrs. Reynolds?" It was a female voice, warm and pleasant with a hint of practiced charm.

"Yes. Who is this?"

"My name is Loretta Bradshaw, Mrs. Reynolds. My husband is Jonathon Bradshaw, American liaison at the embassy. I wonder if I might come up and see you for a few minutes."

"You mean this morning?" Joanna asked, immediately feeling stupid.

"Yes, if you wouldn't mind. I'm not far from your hotel and I could be there in fifteen minutes. I won't keep you long but I did want to meet you in person."

"All right," said Joanna. "I'll be happy to see you." That was a lie. She hadn't liked Mrs. Bradshaw's husband very much and hadn't been impressed with his liaison technique. But she was curious and wanted to know what his wife might have to say to her.

Loretta Bradshaw knocked on her door twenty minutes later and when Joanna saw her face she liked her immediately. Loretta was of medium height and carrying about twenty extra pounds. She carried them well, however, and wore a simple, well-cut dress and jacket in emerald green raw silk. Her well-coiffed hair was chin length and streaked with gray that she made no attempt to hide. She had a natural graciousness that put Joanna at ease as soon as she began to speak.

"My husband told me you had been to the embassy," she said, sitting on the sofa, "and I wanted to see you myself and tell you how sorry we all were at the news of your husband's death. From what Jonathon has told me of your conversation, I think he may have appeared unfeeling and I didn't want you to go away with that impression."

"It's very kind of you to say that, Mrs. Bradshaw. I must admit I had hoped to learn a little more about the circumstances of Franklin's death, but I gather from what your husband told me, there isn't much more to know."

"Unfortunately, that's true. I can't presume to know what you're going through, but I know if I were in your position I would be terribly distressed. This is not a time to be at the mercy of strangers."

"I do feel a little helpless at times. I'm not much of a traveler and it's all a bit overwhelming."

"I'm sure it is," Loretta Bradshaw said, with what sounded like genuine sympathy. "And Bangkok can be a dreadful place if you don't know anybody. I hope you'll feel free to call on me while you're here. I'd be more than happy to help in any way I can."

"Thank you," Joanna said, touched by her kindness. "I appreciate your taking the time to tell me in person."

"It's no trouble, really." She stood up and straightened her skirt. "I really must be going. I have a couple of appointments that I mustn't be late for. We're having a little soirée at home on Friday night. Just a few people. Nothing formal or official. I'd like you to come. Do you think you can make it?"

Joanna hadn't been invited to so many parties since her senior year at college, but she was happy to accept Loretta Bradshaw's invitation. She felt comfortable with her and maybe she would even learn to like her husband when she met him in an unofficial setting. She thanked Loretta for the invitation and promised to call her Loretta if she would call her Joanna. She felt as if she had made a friend, her first new friend in many years.

The rest of the day went fairly quickly after that. Joanna read some more and had a light lunch. When she woke from her nap she was a bit tense, probably because she was having mixed feelings about the barbecue and knew she would have to be on her guard. She felt lonely and vulnerable. She wasn't accustomed to wheedling information out of people and she didn't want to make any mistakes and tip her hand. Loretta Bradshaw had offered her a chance for friendship and she had instinctively trusted her. Ellen Roberts, on the other hand, had caused her to put up her guard. Tonight, on Ellen's turf, she would be playing by her rules.

The Roberts' bungalow in fashionable Bang Kapi was located behind a high, bougainvillea-covered wall, normal practice in the area to discourage burglars, squatters and beggars. In Oak Park a shrub would have been enough to ensure privacy, but here in Bangkok sterner measures were called for. The yard was spacious without being large and well kept, with flowering azalea bushes, ferns, vines and a variety of tropical plants that Joanna recognized as houseplants grown in pots in her part of the world. In the Roberts' backyard they grew in profusion and she half wondered if they kept exotic North American petunias and geraniums growing under controlled conditions in the house.

Most of the guests seemed to be there by the time Joanna arrived and Ellen Roberts took her by the arm and introduced her around. None of the names meant anything to her but they knew who she was and Joanna felt like a prize trophy being handed around for inspection. She wondered how she was expected to perform or if, in fact, she was expected not to perform. She was sure Ellen would have preferred her to behave like the perfect little widow, grateful to listen to any and all conversations without a peep. In fact, Joanna was straining to hear every word said, hoping to pick up clues conveniently dropped in her path. But the conversations Joanna heard that night were less informative than she had hoped. She wondered if her presence put a damper on the party and that's why Ellen hadn't been too excited about her coming. There were certainly things Joanna didn't know about their cozy little community and perhaps things about Franklin's part in it she was unaware of.

She was discovering that a woman who didn't accompany her husband on a lengthy stint in the East was suspect. These women were very protective of their husbands and although they were friendly to her on the surface, Joanna was getting the same subliminal messages she got from Ellen – hands off. She looked around at the selection of males, most of whom were hovering around the Texas-style brick barbecue pit that Roberts had probably built himself, drink in one hand, the other hand waving in the air as they talked about golf swings and sand traps. Joanna had difficulty being impressed. She knew that Franklin had been able to play along in these conversations with the best of them and wondered how many of these men were secretly bored to death and wished they could chuck it all and talk about the latest Bergman film or South American novel. Maybe one.

The women's conversation differed little in scope. They all sat around at the far end of the garden, drink in one hand, cigarette in the other – the women were pretty much all smokers; of the men, only about two or three smoked – and talked about their servants and their kids. A few talked about their golf game. As with the men, Joanna had the feeling that was all there was to them. They lived their husbands' lives. A house was a house; a backyard was a backyard. She got the impression living in Bangkok was more a series of inconveniences than an unusual and exciting experience. Wherever they went, these women tried to make their surroundings as American as possible and they avoided too much interaction with the members of the host society.

Joanna thought about the women in Maugham's stories and their incestuous little lives in colonial outposts. For the ones who dared venture beyond the walls of the compound, only tragedy and misfortune awaited. And here she was, an intruder and an unwanted reminder of an unpleasant episode, come to disturb the calm surface of their existence.

"So Joanna, how are you finding Bangkok? Is it what you expected?" The cheery voice belonged to someone called Peggy. Short blonde hair, cute figure, well-kept tan, with a liking for bows. Bows on her dress, bows in her hair, even her sandals had little bow ties on them.

"Well," Joanna said, considering the questions, "it's hotter than I expected and a lot more interesting."

"You must be talking about downtown. I almost never go downtown. It's too disgusting. I mean all those filthy canals and pickpockets and Lord knows what diseases you can pick up just breathing the air. I avoid it like the plague." At this point Peggy laughed at what must have been her idea of a joke and someone named Anne picked up the thread of the conversation.

"Oh come now, Peg, how can you say that. Bangkok's one of the world's most exotic cities. I have to agree with Joanna, it's a lot more interesting than I expected it to be. Although I have to admit, after two years of it, I rarely go downtown anymore either." Anne was a cool brunette with nice legs and a Texas drawl. "But tell us Joanna," she continued, "why did you choose to stay home rather than accompany your husband to Thailand?"

A somewhat awkward silence followed before Edith, who appeared to be the senior member of the group, stepped in with, "Anne, that's a very personal question. Joanna, don't pay any attention to Mrs. Nosey Parker. When they were handing out good manners she was getting a second helping of curiosity." Everyone laughed at this attempt to smooth things over but Joanna knew they all wanted to hear her answer.

"No, really, it's all right. I don't mind telling you. I had every intention of joining Franklin," she lied, "but there were a number of things I had to look after before I could come and six months became nine and well, I just never got here." They appeared to believe her but none of them was willing to take the conversation any further. "Oh, how unfortunate for you" someone murmured just as Ellen, sensing things were getting uncomfortable, offered to freshen her drink.

The talk drifted back to household chat and local gossip and Joanna drifted toward the bar to retrieve the drink Ellen had so graciously snatched from her. She watched her hand it to Art and say "Joanna needs some more gin in her drink, dear." She knew her eyes were saying, "I told you it was a mistake to invite her." Ellen had very expressive eyes.

Joanna sat in on various conversations after that but no one said a word about Franklin. In a little while, Art fired up the barbecue and produced an interesting selection of teriyaki-style chicken, beef and jumbo prawns. As luck would have it, she was sitting next to Linda Adams, whose husband was Roger Adams who had something to do with accounting at Amstar Oil. She recognized them as one of the couples Tom Thorpe had pointed out to her at the club.

Linda was a nervous, bird-like creature with fluttery mannerisms who gave the impression of having feathers rather than skin and hair. Joanna decided to pursue a conversation with her after she made some chirpy little noises about Franklin's death.

"Oh Joanna," she said, "how could you bear coming to Thailand knowing your husband had died here? I think it would be the last place I'd want to go."

"Well, I felt I had to see for myself where Franklin spent his last months. I thought maybe it would help me accept that he was dead. I was afraid I might keep expecting him to come home."

Linda looked shocked by what she'd said and Joanna wondered if she was being too honest for her. She might be the type that preferred to live in hope, possibly for years, rather than face the truth.

"But aren't you afraid you might learn something unpleasant?" Linda's eyes were wide as saucers.

"Like what?"

Linda must have realized she'd said something too suggestive and was suddenly quite nervous and uncomfortable.

"Oh, I didn't mean anything, really. I guess I was just thinking how I'd feel in your place. I mean, I'd rather not know. If Roger died suddenly in a foreign country, I'd just as soon not know the details. I guess I'm a bit of a coward."

"I'm sure there are a lot of people who feel the way you do," Joanna said. "But I'm not one of them. My mind won't rest until I'm convinced it really happened."

"You mean you don't believe Franklin's dead?" Linda spoke in a shocked whisper. Joanna could almost hear her little bird-like heart beating against her rib cage.

"No, it isn't quite that, Linda." Joanna's voice was low and confiding. "It's just that, well, Franklin died in a very uncharacteristic way. My husband was not fond of the water. I could have accepted anything more easily than drowning. A heart attack, a plane crash, even a car accident. But not drowning."

She watched Linda's reaction carefully. She was obviously uncomfortable but also more than a little excited by what Joanna had said.

"You know, there was some talk when Franklin died. I mean, I think there were some other people who were surprised he'd drowned. Not that it wasn't an accident or anything like that, but people did talk."

"Did anyone question the police report?"

"Oh no," she said quickly. "Nothing like that." Linda was getting a little breathless. "But it just seemed odd at the time."

Linda was casting uncomfortable glances across the yard as if she were looking to be rescued, so Joanna decided not to push her any further. She was sure Linda knew more than she was saying, but was not prepared to tell Joanna any more than she already had. Like most well-meaning but careless people, she had got herself in deeper than she intended and didn't know how to extricate herself.

Linda sighed with visible relief when Art Roberts came over and offered them some more teriyaki. Joanna took the opportunity to slip away and find a glass of water. The teriyaki was a bit salty and had made her thirsty. She was pouring ice water into a glass when she saw Edith, the one who had chided Anne for being too personal, coming toward her. She knew that Edith had been watching her talk to Linda Adams and wondered what she wanted to say to her.

"I'll take some of that too," she said, pointing to the pitcher of water. "I don't like salty food; it makes me swell up." Joanna laughed and poured some water into a glass for her.

"Me too. My eyes are usually puffy the next morning."

Edith drank some of the water before she spoke. "You must think we're a pretty bitchy bunch of women, the way we talk. But we're not really. It's just that most of these gals don't really like it here and would never think of coming to a place like this if it weren't for their husbands. They're naturally suspicious of any woman who lets her man out of her sight for nine months. I don't subscribe to that attitude myself. Mind you, it's not always the men who stray." She was watching Ellen Roberts tell Art they needed more ice. It sounded like a casual remark but Joanna wondered why she had made it to a stranger. "How long are you planning to be in Thailand, Joanna?"

"Well, I don't actually have a definite plan. Probably two or three weeks."

"Well, do yourself a favor and try and get out of Bangkok. The heat can make you sick at this time of year. You become nocturnal, staying indoors all day where it's air-conditioned and only coming out at night. Sort of like a vampire." She laughed at her own joke and took another sip of water. Her eyes were serious, looking at Joanna over the rim of her glass. "I hope you didn't come here looking for solace," she said, "because you won't find it. These people will not comfort you, nor will they help you. Your being here only reminds them of something they'd rather forget. Something unpleasant."

Joanna didn't say anything. Edith wasn't being unkind, just frank. She didn't want to read too much into it, but Joanna wondered if she was trying to warn her not to hang around too long. Her eyes were sympathetic but her words were not and Joanna decided not to press her luck. Her radar was telling her the crowd was just a little less than friendly. She stayed long enough to say her goodbyes, then the Roberts' driver took her back to the hotel.

She phoned Tom Thorpe and gave him her general impression of the evening. He agreed with her that it was looking more and more like people were telling less than they knew or were unwilling to say what they thought. She didn't bother telling him about her conversation with Edith because she still wasn't sure how to interpret it. Tom wanted her to talk to Ruth Hendricks, Franklin's secretary. She would know more about his activities than anyone.

Joanna went straight to bed after talking to Tom and fell asleep with thoughts of conversations and plans in her brain. She dreamed she was on a train that was hurtling along a track and she had no way of getting off. She had lost her luggage and was very concerned that she couldn't change her clothes. There seemed to be no one else on the train, but every time Joanna looked out the window she saw Thai faces looking back at her, smiling broadly and holding platters of fruit and fish and little birds on skewers for her to see.

Chapter Twelve

The next day dawned hot and clear and Joanna woke up resolved to talk to Ruth Hendricks before she tackled any more of Franklin's associates – or their wives. As Franklin's secretary, she reasoned, Ruth may have had a more down-to-earth relationship with Franklin that was based on the pragmatic realities of getting a job done rather than the carefully maneuvered social and political relationships he had at the club and the golf course. She didn't know where she got this idea but it could have been fueled by some of the detective novels she liked to read.

It didn't take Joanna long, thought, to discover that Mrs. Ruth Hendricks had been in love with her boss and that his death had left a bigger hole in her life than it had in his wife's. Her first clue was the absolute silence at the other end of the phone when Joanna introduced herself. Why isn't she breathing, she thought? I haven't even said anything yet. Joanna believed that women had a kind of radar about other women, because she knew instinctively Ruth Hendricks wasn't reacting out of a feeling of social inadequacy about saying "the right thing." She was probably staring right into the abyss, thinking to herself, This is it. I'm going under.

"Mrs. Hendricks?" Joanna said, "Are you there?"

She heard a slow, shaky exhalation. "Y-yes, Mrs. Reynolds. I'm sorry. I – you caught me by surprise." Obviously, Fred Hendricks hadn't mentioned their brief conversation at the club.

"I'm sure I did, Mrs. Hendricks. Forgive me. It never occurred to me to write and let you know I was coming." Ruth didn't respond so Joanna plunged ahead and suggested they have a drink at the hotel when Ruth finished work. She just wanted to talk to someone who knew Franklin, she said, and hoped Ruth wouldn't refuse her. Joanna felt she was in control of the situation, as if Ruth's silence were revealing more than anything she could say. Joanna was manipulating her and she responded like a fish on a hook.

"O-of course, Mrs. Reynolds. I'd be glad to see you."

"Thank you. How about the Bamboo Bar? Six o'clock?"

Ruth Hendricks was indeed staring into the abyss. Why was Franklin's wife calling her? Why did she want to meet her? Surely there was nothing Ruth could say to Joanna Reynolds that would comfort her or answer any of her questions. Was she intending to have it out with Ruth and settle some kind of score? Ruth felt a little sick. Why hadn't she just begged off? Damn, she thought. Leave me alone.

Six o'clock couldn't come soon enough for Joanna, but she spent the day browsing the western-style boutiques in the Oriental Plaza, although she was not in the mood to buy anything. The spray of jewel-colored Thai silks and ornately shaped and carved objects served only to confuse rather than entice her and she finally wandered into an air-conditioned movie theater and sat through something called *A Tattered Web*. The cool darkness surrounded her and the familiar sights and sounds of the American movie helped her organize her thoughts and remind her why she was in Bangkok.

She had always tried to keep any thoughts of Franklin's possible infidelities well back in the recesses of her mind. But sitting in the last row of a slightly shabby cinema watching a movie about illicit love and its consequences brought back an incident in her marriage that might have been one of the reasons for her moving away from Franklin into her own private world of books and solitude. They had been married about six years and Franklin was involved in one of his fundraisers for a summer camp for underprivileged kids. She was supposed to meet him in the ballroom of the Hilton to check the flower arrangements but was a few minutes early and couldn't find him. Someone said they had seen him in one of the side rooms so she went looking for him. Joanna was not a suspicious person but she had always been intuitive and sensitive to the nuances in people's emotions. She hadn't always listened to her heart, however, especially when it said things she didn't want to hear. But she'd learned, sometimes painfully, that those little messages she got were usually accurate. That day, she chose not to listen to the nuances behind Franklin's words to a pretty young campaign worker before he saw Joanna walk into the room. "You know I'd love to, honey," he said, "but I'm meeting the wife in a few minutes."

Nothing in the world could have made Joanna ask, "Love to what?" and face the consequences of Franklin's answer. She wanted to believe it had something to do with the fundraiser and so she believed it. But she had never heard Franklin use the tone of voice he used with that girl. It was like the big, bad wolf talking to Goldilocks. Franklin was a handsome man and she knew women found him attractive and charming. Some had even had the bad taste to tell her. He was what people used to call "suave" and now called charismatic. It was no surprise to her that a young woman might be flirting with a good-looking older man, but hearing Franklin's response to it gave her a stab of uncertainly about her husband.

Joanna never spoke about the incident to Franklin and she never saw the girl again but she slowly withdrew from being a part of Franklin's activities, usually making lame but plausible excuses that he didn't question. Thinking back on it all from a distance of nearly ten years, she knew it had been because she didn't want to witness any more intimate little scenes between Franklin and the young women who seemed always to be helping out at campaign headquarters and charity functions. Whatever seeds of mistrust her sixth sense had planted were plowed under and not allowed to sprout. And she had remained none the wiser by choice. Once Franklin began to travel abroad, the pattern of "don't look, don't ask" had become well established. What she didn't know couldn't hurt her.

Joanna was halfway through a gin and tonic when she spotted a woman that had to be Ruth Hendricks walking into the Bamboo Bar at six minutes past six. She had long, slender legs and shapely calves, and wore a cheap Hong Kong-made dress that unintentionally clung to her well-proportioned body. Joanna was pretty sure Ruth had been Franklin's mistress. And she knew this woman was Fred Hendricks's unhappy wife. Ruth walked straight over to her table and Joanna wondered if she had been assessing her former boss's wife with the same quick once-over.

"Mrs. Reynolds?" she asked, only slightly more self-assured than she had sounded over the phone earlier that day.

"Yes. Please sit down, Mrs. Hendricks." Joanna signaled the waiter and Ruth Hendricks ordered a drink. They looked at each other circumspectly. There was enough caution in the air between them to put on a plate and slice. Neither of them was much interested in small talk.

"Mrs. Hendricks, I came to Bangkok because I wanted to know something about the last few months of my husband's life. It's been difficult for me to come to terms with Franklin's death. I thought you might be able to help me by telling me a little about what he was doing, what he was involved in, before he died."

Ruth's preoccupation with the drink in her hand reminded Joanna of her husband's identical habit. She stared at the glass as if it were a crystal ball from which the answers to all of Joanna's questions would be forthcoming.

"Mrs. Reynolds, I'm not sure what it is you want from me and I don't know if what I can tell you will be of any help. I worked with your husband but I didn't know his friends and we didn't travel in the same social circles."

"I've met some of the people who claim to have been Franklin's friends," Joanna countered, "but I'm not so sure they are people in whom he would have confided or whom he would have trusted to any extent. I mean, if he were in any trouble or needed advice, do you think he would have gone to one of them?"

"What kind of trouble could he have been in? He was working for the U.S. government in a position of responsibility that earned him a great deal of respect from the local authorities. He had access to advice from the highest levels of administration and expertise. Arthur Roberts was his closest confidant in the organization. Between them they could handle anything that came along."

Joanna could tell by her defensive tone that Ruth Hendricks was not going to volunteer too much just-between-you-and-me information. She wanted to steer the conversation into more personal areas, but she didn't quite know how to do it without arousing Ruth's suspicion of her motives. Joanna thought that if Ruth said to her, "Look, Franklin wanted to surprise you by learning how to swim and conquering his fear of the water. He had an accident and drowned," she might have packed her bags and taken the next plane home. But that wasn't going to happen. Ruth Hendricks knew more about Franklin than she wanted Joanna to find out and Joanna suspected Ruth was pretty good at keeping secrets. She got a crazy idea she could get Ruth drunk and loosen her tongue a bit, but she noticed Ruth liked to look at her drink a lot but was in no hurry to taste it.

"Was Franklin looking after himself?" she asked, "Did he eat properly and get enough exercise?"

"Oh yes. He was very regular in his habits. He played golf frequently and even took a couple of trips up north to get away. He was always very careful about what he ate and as far as I know spent his evenings at his house reading newspapers and journals from the States. Occasionally he had dinner at the club, but mostly his houseboy Dinh looked after him and cooked his meals."

Joanna couldn't see a way of breaking into that pat answer so she didn't try. She used to send Franklin a lot of reading material that he asked her to get. Going through official channels, he said, took too long and he liked to be up-to-date on what was happening stateside and around the world. She remembered him telling her how singularly uninformed many of the expatriates were and also how surprisingly ignorant a lot of the consular and embassy people were of anything that wasn't right under their noses. They kept to themselves much as they would have back in Omaha or Scarsdale.

"Mrs. Hendricks, don't you think it was kind of odd, the way my husband died? I mean, was he in the habit of going out on boats or swimming?"

Ruth raised her eyes and looked at Joanna with a direct but troubled look. It occurred to Joanna that Ruth either doubted her motives or she doubted there was anything unusual about Franklin's death. She seemed to be trying to decide which road to take – the one straight ahead or the one that veered off into the dangerous jungle.

"No, Mrs. Reynolds," Ruth said steadily, not taking her eyes off Joanna's face, "I don't think it was odd for your husband to have drowned. There are a lot of accidents in this country. In many ways it's a dangerous place to live."

"But surely you knew," Joanna said, conscious of overstepping some boundary, "that Franklin was phobic about the water and never went near it?"

"No, Mrs. Reynolds. I didn't know. Mr. Reynolds didn't talk about himself that much. I can understand how it must have upset you. I'm sorry I can't offer an explanation that will satisfy you."

She was lying. She had to be, thought Joanna. She was so sure Ruth had been involved with Franklin she could feel it, like some electrical charge. It was there, yet she couldn't describe it, couldn't explain it. This woman knew something she didn't want Joanna to know. The only way Joanna would be able to confirm it would be to confront Ruth with some substantial piece of evidence, but she would have to be certain of the facts before she did.

"Do you think it would be possible for me to see Franklin's house and talk to his houseboy? I'd like to make sure nothing of his was left behind and I just need to see for myself that everything was taken care of."

Ruth said she understood and even offered to phone the house-boy to let him know Joanna would be coming by. She said the house was still unoccupied and the "company," as she referred to it, had kept Dinh on to prepare it for the next tenants. They were not due to arrive for another few days so everything would probably be much the way Franklin had left it.

Joanna told her how grateful she was and said she would like to go to the house around eleven the next morning. Ruth nodded and Joanna realized she was more used to taking orders than giving them. She was probably an excellent secretary but her good looks were most likely what got her the jobs. Franklin had never mentioned her in his letters.

Ruth had said all she was going to say and excused herself, leaving half her drink untouched. As she watched Ruth leave the bar, Joanna had to admit a grudging respect for her as well as a desire to know her better. She was a no-apologies sort of woman who seemed to act with conviction and did not easily betray a confidence. She could see how someone like Fred could be driven to drink by this seductively attractive but unyielding kind of woman. And she could see why Franklin would be attracted to her. It didn't occur to Joanna she might be constructing a scenario based entirely on her own imagination. Ruth Hendricks might be none of those things. She could simply be a good actress.

In the time Joanna had been in Bangkok, the known facts had not changed. Franklin was dead, his body had been found in the water off the Thai coast and she had access to three million dollars in a Swiss bank account. None of the people she had spoken to had added anything to or subtracted anything from the sum total. And only Tom Thorpe had used the word murder. The others had been politely puzzled, evasive or condescending.

Joanna went up to her room and put in a call to Tom. There was no answer so she picked up her book of Maugham stories and started to read. The story she read was called "The Letter," about a woman who murders her lover, an old friend of her husband. She lies to the police, saying he attacked her and she shot him in self-defense. Just before her trial a piece of incriminating evidence comes to light – a letter she had written to her lover on the day she killed him. She had discovered he had a Chinese mistress and was determined to confront him. The mistress now had the letter and the woman's husband either had to buy it back for ten thousand dollars or see his wife hanged. He buys the letter and gives it to her after she is acquitted, thus revealing that he knows the truth. She realizes she has lost everything, not because she has murdered a man but because she was careless enough to have written the letter and been caught.

Joanna pictured herself handing an incriminating piece of evidence to Ruth Hendricks and having everything fall neatly into place. This is what happened, she would say, and this is why. But she knew it wasn't going to be that simple. This wasn't a short story, a little moral fable with all the loose ends neatly tucked away. This was her life – what was left of it – and the uneasy truth was that she might never learn what had happened. The "letter" might already have been destroyed, the evidence consigned to the bottom of the sea along with her hopes of ever knowing the real story.

Chapter Thirteen

Joanna decided not to tell Tom she was going to Franklin's house. She wanted it to be a private visit and she wasn't really sure she was going there to find out anything. She just wanted to see where Franklin had lived. She wanted to see what it looked like and what it felt like. She wanted to understand better what his life had been like in the end and maybe she thought there would be something in the air that would remind her of him. The conversations she had been having with the people who knew him had been empty. They hadn't even drawn an outline of the man she had been married to for so many years. Franklin was already beginning to disappear into a misty haze of memory and Joanna didn't want that to happen. She wasn't finished with him yet and, even though she was pretty sure he hadn't spent a lot of time missing her, she didn't want to lay him to rest with a lot of unanswered questions. She owed herself that.

Joanna gave the cab driver the address and they agreed on a price. This time she had some help with the negotiations from the hotel doorman, a young man in white gloves who saw it as part of his responsibility to get her the best deal. She knew that the driver was going in a southeasterly direction, towards the now familiar Bang Kapi district, but she didn't pay a lot of attention to the route he took. He deposited her some twenty minutes later in front of a modest bungalow set behind a whitewashed wall that was all but hidden by masses of fuchsia bougainvillea. The house itself was white and looked immaculate in its well-cared-for surroundings. A warm, misty rain started to fall as she approached the front door and when she looked back toward the street she saw everything through a soft gray curtain of rain mixed with steam from the hot pavement.

The door was answered by a young Vietnamese man, not more than thirty, about her height and slightly built. Joanna introduced herself and he bowed and said, "Of course, Madame. I am Dinh, houseboy to Mr. Franklin. Please enter." He spoke with an accent that softened the edges of his words, as would someone who had spoken French a lot in his early years. Joanna crossed the threshold into a spacious sitting room furnished in the oriental style with a bamboo settee and lacquered tables and chests. It was decorated to the barest minimum with the occasional jade-colored figurine and dragon-patterned plate and what hung on the walls was the sort of waterfall and heron artwork she was used to seeing in Chinese restaurants. The predominant color was red, not one of Franklin's favorites. This was not the room he would have spent his evenings in.

Dinh offered her tea, which she declined, and she said she just wanted to look around if it was all right with him. "Of course, Madame," he murmured, and proceeded to show her through the rest of the house. There were two bedrooms, sparsely furnished and immaculately kept. One of the rooms was larger than the other and Joanna presumed it was the one Franklin had slept in. There was nothing to indicate that this was the case, but when she looked at Dinh he nodded his head once as if he knew what she was thinking. The last room he showed her was the library, furnished western-style with a masculine feel to it. This would have been Franklin's sitting room. The sofa was tan-colored leather, large enough to seat three people, and a darker, brown leather armchair was placed on the other side of a low coffee table facing the sofa but angled toward the center of the room. At one end was a large oak desk and leather-covered chair. There weren't many bookshelves in the room and the windows on the two outside walls were hung with dark green drapes. The floor was covered with a maroon, black and green wool Persian carpet. The room was dark and cool, aided by air-conditioning thoughtfully installed by the absent owners for the benefit of their foreign tenants. She could imagine Franklin spending quiet evenings in this room, reading his periodicals and newspapers. The room had a faint aroma of pipe tobacco and she felt an ache in her heart as she realized for the first time that Franklin really had lived in this house, that he had sat and smoked his pipe in this room. Joanna walked over to the leather armchair and sat down. When she looked up she saw that Dinh was standing in the doorway holding something in his hand. "Yes, Dinh," she said, "What is it?"

The room was very still and quiet as he crossed it and stood in front of her. He handed her a flat, rectangular object wrapped in brown paper. "I am sorry, Madame, but I find this after I send Mr. Franklin things to United States. Perhaps you will take with you." Joanna watched him turn and leave the room before she unwrapped the brown parcel. When she saw what it was, tears began to well in her eyes; they dropped onto the glass covering the photograph in her hand. It was the wedding portrait of Franklin and her that had been taken at the time of their marriage. She didn't know he'd had it with him.

Joanna cried for the first time as if her heart had been broken. She knew finally, sitting in this room, that the person she had been married to was gone forever and that the man she thought he had been never really existed. There had been another Franklin, a man she knew nothing about, who had inhabited this house and worked with Art Roberts and possibly made love to Ruth Hendricks. That

Franklin Reynolds had put three million dollars into a Swiss bank account and then drowned in a place called Pattaya.

But surely she wasn't so naïve, she reasoned, to think that a man couldn't have several personalities to help him get through the day? Maybe he needed to be one person in order to fraternize with Art Roberts and that crowd and another personality to be married to her. Why couldn't she see how simple it really was? She couldn't expect the same Franklin who shared a spacious and comfortable house with her in the suburbs of Chicago to be identical to the man who lived with a Vietnamese manservant in this small, sparsely furnished house in the suburbs of Bangkok. Surely that made sense. The man who was dealing with the aftermath of a war in Indo-China needed to be different from the man who relaxed in his own backyard. But that Franklin Reynolds, she remembered, had deliberately shut her out of his life by refusing to let her travel with him. Was it his need to control people and situations that had kept her at bay? Or had her willingness to acquiesce to his wishes contributed to their growing apart? As she dried her eyes on a piece of tissue she found in her handbag, Joanna began to think about what a miserable excuse for a human being she was. While Franklin had grown into the multi-faceted personality she was beginning to discover so many miles from home, she had settled into an insular, unadventurous life. Why hadn't she fought back? Why hadn't she demanded more of him? Of their marriage? Of life?

She was getting a headache and wanted to get out of the house and go back to the privacy of her hotel room. Too much information, she thought. She found her way to the back of the house where Dinh was sitting in the small, bright kitchen waiting for her visit to end. The rain had stopped and the sun pouring in the windows was hurting her swollen eyes. She asked Dinh to get her a taxi while she fished around in her bag for her sunglasses. He was gone for a few minutes – obviously it was not the custom to phone for a cab – so she stood and waited on the front porch until she saw a black and yellow car come round the corner and stop in front of the house. Dinh jumped out of the passenger side and opened the back door for her to get in. He had apparently made the necessary arrangements with the driver and told her how much to pay him when she got to the hotel. Ruth Hendricks must have told Dinh what hotel she was at because she did not recollect mentioning it to him. She thanked him for showing her through the house and wished him well.

"Thank you," he said. "I am so sorry." She was touched by this and believed he meant it. He signaled to the driver to go and, as they drove away from the house, she didn't look back.

When Joanna got to the hotel she went straight up to her room and ran a bath. She asked room service to bring her some tea and every magazine and newspaper they had in English. She buried herself in print and glossy pictures, not wanting to think about the real world and what was happening to her in it. There would be enough time for that later when she was feeling a little tougher. Right now she just needed to escape.

Chapter Fourteen

The informal get-together the following evening at Jonathon and Loretta Bradshaw's was not what Joanna had expected it to be. By her definition, it was a full-blown cocktail party complete with white-jacketed waiters circulating trays of drinks and hors d'oeuvres. Someone hired for the evening was playing the grand piano elegantly tucked into a corner of the very large sunken living room. At least a hundred people were there, including representatives from the various international organizations headquartered in Bangkok, the United Nations Economic Commission for Asia and the Far East, the Southeast Asia Treaty Organization and branches of the World Health Organization and the World Bank. There were also local businessmen and professionals, some Embassy people, a visiting Congressman and his wife from Ohio and a few well-connected tourists doing a tour of the Orient.

Loretta Bradshaw opened the door herself and seemed genuinely pleased that Joanna had come. "I was hoping it would be you," she said as she escorted her into the midst of the festivities

and started introducing her around. Loretta was careful to introduce her as Joanna Reynolds, making no mention that she was
Franklin's widow or that she was in Thailand for any reason other
than travel and leisure. Joanna recognized some familiar faces in the
crowd, including Ellen and Art Roberts, Linda and Roger Adams,
and even Tom Thorpe, who was, apparently, a regular at these social
events. She saw him laughing and talking easily with a number of
the guests. Loretta left her in the company of a Thai couple, Sam
and Lily Koh, while she went off to play hostess for a while.

"Don't disappear on me, Joanna," she said. "We'll have more
time to talk later."

Sam and Lily were charming and friendly and wanted to know
where she had been and what she had seen in Bangkok. Joanna
told them she had enjoyed the local marketplace and it turned out
Sam was in the import-export business and had a lot to do with
those displays of soap and toothpaste that had so intrigued her.

"Most of the stuff is manufactured here," he explained, "but we
must import a lot of the materials that are used to make it. You'd
be surprised at all the licensing agreements that must be honored.
The black market here is very extensive and bootleg items – everything from cassette tapes to designer sunglasses – are often hard to
detect and impossible to control."

Lily proceeded to explain how she had recently purchased what
she thought was an authentic Gucci bag only to discover that it
was a fake. "Mind you," she informed Joanna, "if I hadn't been
married to Sam I might never have found out and would still be so
pleased with myself for having got such a good deal."

Sam laughed and said, "She's right. I should have kept my
mouth shut. Now she says I have to get her a real Gucci bag to
make up for it. At three times the price!"

They discussed the black market a little more and Joanna eventually excused herself to wander around and watch the goings on.
She was careful to avoid Ellen Roberts and she noticed Linda
Adams was careful to avoid her. She saw Tom among a group of
guests just as he spotted her.

"I didn't expect to see you here," he said. "You didn't mention you were coming." She told him about Loretta's visit the other morning and the invitation she had extended. "I was glad to come," she told him. "Loretta seems like a person I would like to get to know."

"She's a wonderful lady," he said, nodding to someone he recognized across the room. Joanna glanced over her shoulder and realized it was Bradshaw's assistant from the embassy, Bruce Jackson. "It figures she'd do something like that," Tom was saying. "She'd be much better at the liaison job than her husband. Half the credit for his success should go to her."

"She said she wasn't too impressed with his sensitivity when he first met me," Joanna said as she deftly switched her empty glass for a full one when a white-coated waiter drifted by with champagne. "But to be fair, I probably did put him on the spot. He had to give me the official version of things. That's his job."

Just then the visiting Congressman and his wife came up. Tom said he needed a refill and excused himself. Joanna chatted with the couple for a bit about the heat and the traffic problems in the city.

"Have you traveled south at all to see the magnificent beaches this beautiful country has to offer, Mrs. Reynolds?" the Congressman asked her. Joanna told him she hadn't done that yet and he said, "Oh, you must, you really must. Edna and I have never seen anything like it. The sand is so white and the water's so blue and everything's as clean as can be. And not very crowded, you know. That's what really surprised us. You're not being stampeded by other tourists all the time." Edna nodded in agreement and Joanna told them about her conversation with the Koh's and warned them to watch out for bootleg items in the markets and shops. The Congressman looked at his wife and said, "We'll have to remember that, Edna. I don't want to end up paying duty on something that's fake."

After a while they moved on and she looked around for Tom. She spotted him deep in conversation with Bruce Jackson, although it appeared that Jackson was the one doing most of the talking. She noticed that he kept pointing his finger at Tom's chest for emphasis and that Tom appeared tense and uncomfortable. When Jackson walked away, Tom finished his drink in one swallow and then stared at the ice cubes in the bottom of the glass.

"This is really a beautiful house," Joanna said when she got close to him. "It looks like it could have been designed by Frank Lloyd Wright."

"It does, doesn't it," Tom said. His smile seemed forced, as if she'd surprised him in the middle of something, but he recovered himself quickly. "Actually, it was built in the fifties by a cousin of the King who studied architecture in the U.S. and was a great admirer of Frank Lloyd Wright. Come on, I'll show you around a bit."

Joanna snatched an hors d'oeuvre off a passing tray and stuffed it in her mouth. "Great," she said, wishing she'd taken two of the little shrimp and mushroom things.

The house consisted of a series of apparently floating islands, each a few steps higher or lower than the one before and after it. These islands were joined by long square-cut beams of wood that Tom said was probably teak. Although the property appeared level from the front, the garden in the back sloped down from the house to a patio and swimming pool that was kidney-shaped and irregular, emphasizing the angles of the house. They were leaning against the smooth wooden railing of one of the house's three balconies overlooking the pool and discussing architecture. Joanna described some of her favorite buildings in Chicago and talked a bit about the architectural history of the region. She was enjoying the cool quiet of the garden and felt comfortable for the first time since arriving in Bangkok. She hoped Tom wouldn't say anything about Franklin, enjoying his comments about the house and the party, and looking forward to talking to Loretta as soon as she could extricate herself from her other guests.

"Was that Bradshaw's assistant I saw you talking to earlier?" she asked. "You two seemed to be having a pretty serious conversation."

Tom looked uncomfortable and she wished she hadn't said any-thing. After all, it was none of her business whom Tom talked to. "I'm sorry," she said. "I didn't mean to be nosey. I was just trying to make conversation."

"It's okay," said Tom. "I was going to tell you anyway. I just wasn't sure how to broach the subject."

"What subject?" Joanna was puzzled. Had they been talking about her?

"Jackson told me Bradshaw's pissed off at both of us. He thinks we've been snooping around, asking a lot of questions."

"Well, we have," said Joanna. "But how would he know?"

"Bradshaw has his spies," said Tom. "Jackson being one of them. Nothing happens that Bruce doesn't see. And anything Bruce sees, he reports to Bradshaw. They're quite an efficient little team. Just like Nick and Nora Charles."

"Which one's Nora?" Joanna asked, noting the bile in Tom's voice and trying to lighten the conversation.

Tom raised his eyebrows and shrugged. "You won't hear it from me," he said coyly.

"So what do they care if we're asking people questions? Isn't what happened to my husband my business?"

"Yes ... and no," said Tom. "Basically, you know all you appar-ently need to know about your husband's death. There was an investigation and a police report. That's supposed to be enough. According to Jackson, certain people are uncomfortable that you're opening up the file again, so to speak."

"What people? You mean someone's been reporting on my activities – so to speak?"

Tom smiled. "Do I sense a little hostility bubbling to the sur-face of the usually calm, dare I say, prim, Mrs. Reynolds?"

Joanna felt herself blushing. It was true, she was definitely annoyed. She didn't like the idea that someone might be watching her or reporting on whom she talked to or, even possibly, what she said.

She found it offensive. It invaded her sense of privacy. And what did Tom mean by prim? Proper, maybe. But prim? That was too much.

"How dare …" she started to say, but Tom stopped her.

"Don't flip out," he said. "I have a plan."

At that moment, Loretta Bradshaw approached them, all smiles, and asked Tom if he would mind getting her another drink. Tom bowed and said, "Certainly, Madame. Your wish is my command."

Loretta laughed. "Ah, chivalry is not dead," she said. "Apparently it was only resting."

Joanna laughed and Tom dutifully retreated to the bar with Loretta's empty glass. When Loretta turned back to Joanna her expression was serious. There was obviously something she wanted to say, but instead she reached over to a potted plant beside Joanna and pulled off a dead leaf.

"What is it Loretta?"

"Joanna," she said, keeping her eyes down and speaking hesitantly, "Jonathon spoke to me tonight about something and I feel it's only right to tell you what people are saying." Loretta raised her eyes and bit her lower lip before continuing. "They say you've been asking a lot of questions about Franklin and people think you don't believe his death was an accident. They're even saying you want to re-open the investigation. Is that true?"

Joanna thought about how she should answer. Obviously Loretta was uncomfortable with the subject and Joanna didn't want to show the anger that was rising in her. Loretta, rather than being one of Bradshaw's spies, appeared to be her husband's messenger. But nevertheless, it was the second time in a few minutes that someone had told her to back off. Loretta's concern seemed genuine, but why was she concerned that Joanna might want to re-open the investigation? Wouldn't she be doing the same thing if she were in Joanna's position? Would Loretta have accepted the verdict of accidental death if it had been her husband? Joanna wanted to ask her, but this wasn't the time or the place to go into it.

"It's only partly true, Loretta," she finally said. "I have been asking a lot of questions about Franklin, but only because I can't live with a big empty space in my mind not knowing what his life was like before he died. I just wanted to meet some of the people who knew him and talk to them and see for myself what he was doing. I just need to know. You understand, don't you?"

"Yes, I understand. I do, really. And I'd probably do the same if I were in your shoes. But we, Jonathon and I, at least Jonathon, really thinks you might be upsetting people more than you realize. We want you to think about getting out of Bangkok for a while. Maybe go to the beach or something for a rest, some peace and quiet. At least until things settle down a bit."

Just then Tom returned with Loretta's drink and handed it to her. She looked at Joanna and said, "Will you think about it?" Joanna nodded her head and said, "Yes, I'll think about it. Really. I appreciate your concern."

"Well, I just hope you'll take some time to see some of this beautiful country." Loretta said thank you to Tom and left.

"Think about what?"

"She told me Jonathan says I've upset a lot of people by asking questions about Franklin. She and Jonathon think I should get out of Bangkok for a while."

"You know, it's possible they think you're in danger. I can't be the only person in the world who thinks Franklin was murdered. Maybe Bradshaw's worried you might attract too much attention and somebody might not like it."

"Has he said anything to you?"

"Well, not directly. But Brucie did ask me to keep your name out of the papers."

"Tom, are you suggesting Bradshaw's afraid I'll find out something I shouldn't and that someone might try to hurt me?" Joanna didn't know where the idea had come from but, between them, Loretta and Tom had succeeded in spooking her.

"I won't say it didn't occur to me," Tom said. "It might be a good time to think about it, you know."

"You don't think somebody might try to kill me, do you?" Her head was starting to ache and she wished she was curled up safely between the soft, clean sheets on her bed at the Oriental Hotel. "I think I'd like to go now," she said.

"It's possible someone might just want to scare you," Tom said, checking the rear-view mirror as he changed lanes. Bangkok traffic at that hour wasn't much different from the traffic at one in the afternoon.

Joanna realized there had been seven people at the party who knew her and knew whom she had been talking to: Bradshaw and Loretta, Art and Ellen Roberts, Linda and Roger Adams and Tom. And apparently, Bruce Jackson.

"You said you had a plan," she said.

"I was thinking," said Tom, "it's as good a time as any for you to go to Pattaya and see what Franklin might have been up to before he died." He seemed a little uncomfortable. She looked at him but he kept his eyes on the road. "I don't like the idea of you going off on your own," he finally said. "How about if I tag along? I could be your driver." He turned and gave her a lopsided smile.

Joanna thought about his offer for a few minutes. She had certainly sensed hostility from people since arriving in Bangkok, but she still found it hard to believe someone might want her out of the way permanently. Joanna wasn't used to being disliked. Ignored, maybe. But not disliked.

"I guess it's not a bad idea," she said, feeling tired and disappointed. Tom had just wheeled the car into the driveway of the hotel. He left the engine running and got out to help her out of the car but the white-gloved doorman beat him to it. Tom told him he'd only be a few minutes and asked him to watch the car for him. He slipped the doorman some money and followed Joanna into the hotel.

"All right," she told Tom as he walked her to the elevator. "Let's do it. What time should I be ready?"

"Is eleven o'clock too early?" he asked, pushing the button to summon the elevator.

"I can be ready," she said. "Would you mind telling the desk I'll be checking out in the morning?"

"Sure," he said. "Will you be all right going up on your own?"

"I'll be fine." She got into the elevator and pushed the button for her floor. "Goodnight, Tom. And thanks." She watched him head for the desk as the elevator doors silently slid closed. Fifteen minutes later she was sound asleep.

Chapter Fifteen

Joanna was ready to go and waiting with her bags in the lobby at eleven the next morning. Her sleep had been deep and dreamless but she had woken up feeling groggy and a little uncertain about what had happened the night before at the Bradshaw's party. Had she imagined the conversation with Tom? Would someone really try and hurt her, or even kill her, to stop her from finding out what happened to Franklin? Was she being paranoid or was it a fact that practically everyone she had talked to in Bangkok had suggested she get out of town? Including Tom. Although, to be fair, he had persuaded her they should go to Pattaya to investigate the scene of Franklin's murder.

Franklin's murder. She still hadn't got used to the idea. Somehow she still wasn't able, even on an intellectual level, to link the concept of murder with the image of Franklin that she had in her mind. It felt like she was walking into the ocean. She could feel the resistance of the water with every step and wondered which step would plunge her in over her head.

And now here she was sitting in the passenger seat of Tom's late model Mercedes-Benz heading east toward Pattaya, and who knew what else? The trip would probably take a couple of hours but the car was air-conditioned so she wasn't uncomfortable. She could feel herself starting to relax. She hadn't mentioned her visit to Franklin's house to Tom and spoke vaguely of shopping when he asked her what she'd been doing the last few days. She took her time telling him about her conversation with Ruth Hendricks. Joanna had decided not to tell him about her "intuition" that Ruth had been Franklin's mistress. It would not be fair to Ruth if she was wrong, she reasoned, and she didn't want to prejudice Tom's opinion or judgment in any future conversations. He hadn't met Ruth and, should the situation arise, Joanna wanted him to form an opinion based on his own instincts, not hers.

"You're right," he said. "It does sound as if she's hiding something, or, if not actually hiding, reluctant to reveal what she knows. You don't suppose she'd be protecting Fred for some reason? Naw," he said, answering his own question. "But maybe, just maybe, she's protecting herself. Did she seem frightened? Was she looking over her shoulder or anything?"

Joanna told him to calm down and stop thinking like an amateur detective. Ruth had been nervous when she talked to her on the telephone, she told Tom, but Joanna suspected that it was because she had been caught unprepared. By the time they met for a drink, Ruth had composed herself considerably. Joanna told him she thought Ruth Hendricks was a very private person who minded her own business and was naturally cautious.

"You're being naïve, Joanna. If Franklin was murdered, she may well know more than she wants to. She's in a position to see and hear things from a number of different sources. If Franklin's murder has political underpinnings, she might well have been privy to events or information leading up to it. If it was a private or personal vendetta, she might know who wanted him dead. In any case, she could be in danger if she lets on to anyone that she knows something."

He was right, of course. The likelihood of Franklin's death being an isolated incident unrelated to some larger series of events was small. If Tom's theory of a cover-up was correct, then there were people out there involved in that very activity. It was entirely plausible they were being apprised of every move Joanna made. She felt a shudder go through her body as she stared dumbly through the windshield of the car. Tom must have noticed because he reached over and took her hand.

"I'm sorry, Joanna" he said. "I didn't mean to frighten you. I just assumed you had thought this through and were prepared for the possibility. This isn't a game of cops and robbers. We could be walking into something very unpleasant, not to mention potentially dangerous. Are you sure you want to keep going?"

Joanna nodded but the look she gave him made him stop talking and squeeze her hand. Who did she think she was kidding? Barging into the American Embassy, demanding to know what had happened to her husband. Barging into people's lives and asking them questions that reminded them of something unpleasant. Unpleasant? Try sinister and frightening. How would she have reacted if she were faced with the widow of a man who had died under mysterious circumstances? Now that the door had been opened a crack, it seemed to throw a lot more light on the situation. Joanna could see it from a different perspective now and realized how foolish her presumptions had been. She had been naïve, as Tom said. She had come to Thailand hoping to find that Franklin had died in some freak accident. She wanted to be told the facts that would convince her and send her home with some peace of mind. But now that she had been presented with the possibility of murder, she had to face the very real and ugly implications that it held. The air-conditioning in the car suddenly felt very cold and she asked Tom to shut it off. She rolled down the window and let the hot, dry air blow over her.

Joanna put her head back and closed her eyes, forcing herself not to think any more. She concentrated on the heat and tried to put herself in the middle of it, letting it surround her like some kind of silky cocoon. It made her feel safe for a few minutes, protected from some cold reality she didn't want to know about. This is why I came here, she thought. To be warm. To be reassured that horrible things don't happen to people who mind their own business.

When her mother had been dying of cancer, Joanna had refused to go to the hospital to see her. She had watched her mother lose weight and strength to the disease over a relatively short period of time and she could not bear to see what further damage it had done to her. She and Franklin had been married about six years then and he had watched her ignore and deny the truth of what was before her. Her grandparents were suffering a terrible pain and she was no comfort to them, choosing to be by herself, burying herself in books. As the end drew closer, Franklin became more forceful in his efforts to persuade her to go and see her mother.

"If you don't deal with it now, you'll regret it for the rest of your life," he said. "You must see her one last time, if only to say goodbye."

And so she went. But when she saw her mother's haunted face, saw the shadows formed by hollows that hadn't been there before, she knew it was already too late. She could not comfort her mother and she herself could not be consoled. After that, the image of her mother's ravaged, dying self replaced the memory of the vibrancy and beauty that Joanna had been holding on to. She never quite forgave Franklin for making her go. She would have preferred to remember her mother living, always young and laughing, but she had died a horrible and ugly death and Joanna had been witness to it. And now here she was, preparing to witness another kind of ugliness. Was Franklin somehow reaching out to her from the grave and once again making her face something she didn't want to see? Would she again be inconsolable? Would she again destroy a memory of something fine and good? She wanted to believe she was doing this for herself. That the old Joanna had grown up and could face whatever hand life dealt her. But still she wondered if this was Franklin's legacy to her. It was his voice that was saying, "If you don't deal with it now, you'll regret it for the rest of your life."

After a while Joanna opened her eyes and looked over at Tom. He was concentrating on the road and handling the car with the kind of easy assurance men always seemed to have behind the wheel. His arms were long and tanned and his hands were well-shaped and strong, the fingers long, the nails trimmed straight across. His all-American profile looked as if it should be stamped on the back of a coin or an Olympic medal. She was glad he was there. She wanted to believe she could rely on him if the going got rough. But she hoped it wouldn't come to that. He glanced over at her and smiled. "Almost there," he said.

They had been working their way south along the eastern seaboard of the Gulf of Thailand. They followed a paved highway that just barely managed to keep at bay the thick growth of ripe vegetation. The richness of the countryside in the fullness of its summer growth created an atmosphere heavy with the fragrance of its fecundity. People had built their houses on stilts to prevent their being overgrown by the vines and stalks that could only grow taller and thicker in the heat of the sun. Occasionally, Joanna caught sight of the glittering blue waters of the Gulf.

"Do you think we could go for a swim when we get there, Tom?" She wanted to submerge herself in cool water and wash away the sticky hotness of the city they had left behind. She suddenly realized she wanted to see Tom in a bathing suit.

"I though we might stay at the Siam Country Club because that's where Franklin stayed the last time he was here. It's a few miles inland, but they have a pool. Or, if you like, we can drive to the beach for a swim." He looked over when she didn't answer and said, "If you don't think you can handle staying at the Club, just say so. There are lots of other places."

"No, you're right. We should stay at the Club. It would be useful to get to know some of the staff. Someone might remember

Franklin or even some of the people he was with. We'll worry about swimming later."

She had been starting to enjoy the heat and the scenery and being with Tom but a little warning bell was ringing in the back of her head. It was all too much, too soon. Was she in charge or was she still allowing herself to be controlled by others? If she wanted to end it now, she thought, she could take the first plane back to Chicago. There was still time. Everything would still be there, just as she had left it. The garden would be full of the hot July sun; the roses would be blooming. She could pick up right where she had left off, as if none of this had happened. And gradually she could get used to the idea that Franklin was never coming back and persuade herself that their life together had been exactly as she remembered it. But there was still the problem of the money. Did it really belong to her? If Franklin had got it by doing bad things or associating with bad people, as Tom had suggested, did she want it? Could she just ignore the fact that the money might be dirty?

"This is it," said Tom, jolting her back to the present. They checked into the Siam Country Club Hotel and chose two single rooms on the same floor. Tom suggested they clean up and meet in the dining room for a strategy session over lunch.

Half an hour later they were sitting in the air-conditioned dining room sipping tall, cool gin and lime drinks and poring over the menu. They decided to share a whole fried snapper that was served with a ginger sauce consisting of Chinese mushrooms and red ginger – preserved ginger slices colored a deep red. Tom seemed to share her enthusiasm for oriental cuisine and they talked about their culinary adventures while they ate. She could feel her sense of purpose slowly returning.

"I want to go and see the Chief of Police," she said, as they were finishing the snapper. Jonathon Bradshaw gave me his name. I have it written down somewhere."

"Prem Panakorn," Tom said. "I made some notes of my own before we left. What are you going to say to the Chief, may I ask?"

"I'm not sure," she said, savoring the last of the pungent ginger sauce. "What do you suggest?"

"Well, I'd be careful choosing a pretence. He's a cop and won't be that easy to fool. So you should be consistent and direct. If there's a cover-up of come kind, he'll be watching you pretty closely. I would try and say as little as possible and keep your eyes and ears open. You could start by asking if the weather had been stormy the day your husband died and if he thought perhaps that had caused the accident. Ask simple, straightforward questions and don't even hint at the possibility of foul play. Let him believe you accept the accident theory but need, for your own peace of mind, to know how it happened. Feel him out; see if you think he's telling the truth."

The waiter brought a fresh pot of tea and she poured some into both their cups. "You know, I still want to believe it was an accident, Tom. I mean, improbable accidents do happen. Why can't you consider the possibility that this might be one of them?"

For a while she thought he wasn't going to answer her. He kept sipping his tea and watching her, trying to decide what to say. "I'd like to believe it too, Joanna," he finally said. "It might restore my faith in my fellow man. It might allow me to hang on to all the notions of goodness and rightness and bravery that I used to cherish. But I've had to develop a lot of instincts in my life, because of my profession and because I wanted to survive. And when my instincts tell me that people aren't behaving like themselves and I think they're shutting me off from something, I have to listen to those instincts. That's how I survive." He stopped and poured some tea into his cup. "I know that's not evidence, it's not proof of anything, but I'm asking you to believe me, to trust me and to accept my conviction that somebody out there murdered your husband and got away with it. And that there was a reason and that reason still exists and is being covered up."

Tom's conviction was unshakeable. And the "who" and "why" of it headed the list of unanswered questions about Franklin's death. What had Franklin been involved in so far from home that could have cost him his life? Was Joanna walking into something equally dangerous? Whoever had decided Franklin's time was up might not appreciate her snooping around and asking questions. Was she prepared to deal with that? Joanna kept waiting to feel outraged, angry, horrified by the injustice of a murderer walking around free while his victim slowly faded into oblivion. She wanted to be Clark Kent, bursting the confines of his three-piece suit and transforming himself into Superman. Instead she felt confused, as if things were closing in on her just when they should be opening up.

Chapter Sixteen

Prem Panakorn looked like a man who could stand to lose thirty pounds. Either his wife was a very good cook or he'd given up the street beat in favor of a desk and chair when he got his promotion to Chief of Police. His greeting was friendly but formal and Joanna could tell he'd rather see Genghis Khan walk into his office.

"Good afternoon, Mrs. Reynolds," he said in English. He had a bit of difficulty with his R's and it made him seem soft-spoken. Her name came out sounding like "Wrenolds."

Good afternoon, Chief Panakorn. It was good of you to see me."

"I'm not sure I can help you, Mrs. Reynolds," Panakorn replied, settling himself into his well-worn chair with an after-lunch sigh. He folded his hands over his ample belly. "The file on your husband's unfortunate accident has been closed for several weeks now."

"I realize that, but I was hoping you would talk to me in a sort of unofficial way, if you understand. It's taken me some time to get up the courage to come to Thailand – my friends tried to talk me out of it – but I couldn't rest easy until I spoke with people myself. I was so far away when all of this happened, I'm still not sure I believe it."

"I see," said Panakorn, measuring five percent on the compassion scale. "What is it you'd like to hear from me?"

"The circumstances surrounding my husband's death have never been clear to me." Joanna plunged ahead trying to remember Tom's advice about not saying too much. "Were you able to determine if he was alone at the time?"

"It would seem that he was. No one came forward to say they had been with him and he left the hotel alone. You must bear in mind, Mrs. Reynolds, this is a resort town and most people here are transient. We were unable to find any eyewitnesses to your husband's activities on that day."

"I'm supposed to believe that my husband went to the beach alone, walked into the water for a swim and drowned without anybody noticing?"

"I agree that seems unlikely," replied Panakorn. "It's more probable he went swimming off the side of a boat. But since there is no record of his having rented a boat that day or of his having been on a boat rented by someone else, we have to assume he was on a private yacht or vessel from another area, since no one known locally came forward to report him missing. Or," he went on, "if he was a strong swimmer, your husband may have swum very far out, got into trouble in the water and drowned without anyone seeing him. That would explain why his body was washed up on shore without attracting any attention."

"When you say 'got into trouble,' Chief Panakorn, what do you mean? Was there a storm or anything that might have caused him to be in trouble?"

"No," the Chief said, "the weather was clear, not even any wind to speak of. It's possible he developed a cramp while swimming. He may have eaten a heavy lunch or the water may have been too cold. There were no marks on the body other than an abrasion on the forehead, which may have occurred after death. The body had been in the water for some hours before being discovered."

Joanna tried to put the image of Franklin's drowned body out of her mind. "Why wouldn't someone report him missing if he had gone swimming off the side of their boat and not come back?"

"I wonder that myself, Mrs. Reynolds," Panakorn replied with a measure of frankness. "Perhaps they were frightened off by the thought of an investigation in a foreign country. Perhaps they were involved in something that couldn't bear investigating or exposure."

"Such as?"

"Such as some sort of smuggling. Works of art say, or national treasures."

"Surely you're not suggesting that my husband had anything to do with a smuggling operation?" What was he getting at?

"Certainly not, Mrs. Reynolds. I'm merely suggesting that the alleged owners of the alleged boat may have been involved in some lucrative, but not quite legal activity quite unknown to your husband. After all, he was a very well-respected individual in this country. I would not for a moment consider the idea that he was involved in such a thing."

Panakorn was starting to sound a little oily and Joanna began to wonder if she had been manipulated into a position where to go any further might open doors to nasty speculation about Franklin's activities in Thailand. Was this subtle pressure a form of blackmail?

"Besides," Panakorn continued, "there's no evidence whatsoever to suggest it. It may simply have been a matter of a sex party and your husband's alleged hosts may have decided discretion was in his best interest, not to mention their own, and therefore decided to say nothing about the incident. I mean, it couldn't bring him back to life, could it? Sometimes it's better to let the dead stay buried."

Panakorn had the decency not to smile. Joanna didn't say anything for a couple of minutes but her teeth and jaw were clenched in anger. She wanted to make her exit quickly and quietly so he would assume he had seen the last of her. She wanted him to think she understood exactly what he was saying and would heed his warning. And she was certain it was a warning. He thought he was appealing to her American middle-class sense of decency and that would be enough to silence her and leave Franklin's memory intact. And maybe it should have been. Who would it benefit to drag Franklin's name through the mud if, in fact, what Panakorn was hinting at was true? Who, besides herself, wanted to know what had really happened? She thought of Claire and knew what she would say if she were there. "Go home, Joanna. Drop it. The man's right. Nothing will bring Franklin back to life. At least let him stay buried in peace."

"Thank you, Chief Panakorn," she said stiffly as she rose from her chair. "I'm sure you have more important things to do than talk to people like me. I appreciate the time you've given me."

"You're welcome, Mrs. Reynolds," replied the Chief, seeing her to the door. It's no trouble. I hope I have set your mind at ease. This is not a pleasant thing, a husband's drowning. Please try and put it behind you. You will only prolong your grief by dwelling on it."

She had agreed to meet Tom at an open-air restaurant a few blocks from the station and as she got closer she noticed the silver-colored Mercedes parked nearby. Tom was hanging around, checking out some of the kiosks loaded with useless items for tourists, when he caught sight of Joanna walking – no, marching – toward him. He headed her into the restaurant and sat her down, ordering two beers before she got her teeth unclenched.

"Tom," she said quietly and with what she thought was incredible control, "that man threatened me, in no uncertain terms."

"Whoa, hold it," said Tom, trying to restrain her. "We're talking about a police officer here. You can't tell me he'd be stupid enough to do a thing like that."

"Dammit, Tom," she said, "he did! I know a threat when I hear one. It may have been veiled, but he as much as told me if I pursued this thing any further I might turn up something scandalous about Franklin. How dare he suggest such a thing to me?"

She was fuming, almost spitting fire, and Tom kept raising and lowering his hands in a "calm down" gesture. Joanna took a deep breath and drank half her beer before she finally started to relax.

"Joanna, he's a police officer. He's been trained to consider every possibility. Couldn't this just be a matter of interpretation?"

"Tom," she almost hissed at him. "It wasn't just what he said, it was how he said it. There was a lot of significance behind the way he spoke. He is definitely not interested in knowing any more about the case."

Joanna finished her beer and ordered another before she told Tom, in detail, about her conversation with Panakorn. She emphasized the fact that no witnesses had been found and that Franklin had apparently left the hotel by himself and no one had ever seen him alive after that.

"No witnesses," said Tom, thinking about what she had said. "I agree that's odd, but not impossible."

"But Tom, if he had been on somebody's boat and not come back from a swim, assuming for a minute it was an accident and not murder, don't you think they would have reported it? I mean, what are the chances they were involved in something illegal? Especially if Franklin knew them. I say practically nil. I know Panakorn was trying to put me off by suggesting that Franklin's reputation might be ruined if I tried to open the case up. I think he was trying to blackmail me into keeping quiet."

"Don't forget, Joanna, people get murdered because they do bad things or they're involved with people who do bad things. And why, have you asked yourself, why wouldn't the police want to solve the case?"

"I don't know, Tom." She was reaching, thinking out loud. "I'm so confused. Maybe there's some kind of official incompetence in this whole thing. Maybe the police bungled the job and are afraid I'll make a stink if I find out. Create an international incident or something."

"Would you?"

"Oh God, I don't know. I really don't know what I'd do. You see, it's not just Franklin I'm concerned about in all this, but myself. I'm the one who's getting the brush-off everywhere I turn. How can I drop it now and just go back to my life? Don't you see? There is no going back, Tom. I have to wipe the slate clean and start over. As for an international incident, I'm no crusader. I'm doing this for myself. I'm not out to change the world."

"You still want to believe it was an accident, don't you?" Tom drank his beer and waited for her to answer.

"Tom," she went on, "I want you to know that I appreciate what you're doing for me. I know I seem uncertain and disbelieving but try and understand what it's like for me. I feel like I've been dropped into someone else's life. You're looking at someone who's developed evasion into a fine art. I'm talking about a lifetime of not stepping on toes, not getting in the way, being what everybody always wanted me to be. I came here with some vague notion that there was a simple explanation for what happened to Franklin. Well, all I've been hearing are simple explanations and they're just not good enough. I'm tired of people pushing me away and trying to make me believe that Franklin, who's the victim, is somehow to blame for everything. I won't have it!" She slapped the table hard with her hand. She was on her third beer but it didn't seem to be helping her cool off.

"Listen, Tom," she continued, putting her hand up to stop him speaking, "I would understand if you decided you didn't want to help me anymore. I mean, you could be putting yourself at risk just by being with me. I wouldn't want that to happen. I wouldn't want to be responsible for it happening."

"Joanna, I told you my suspicions right from the beginning. I was getting the brush-off before you entered the picture. If there is some high-level incompetence or cover-up going on, I want to know what it is and who's giving the orders. I have my own reasons for wanting to get to the bottom of things. I don't especially care about Franklin's reputation or what people say about him. But

I do care if someone got away with murder and has the power to keep the lid on it. Like you, I can't go back now. I have to find out what's going on. And maybe I'm walking into something I should leave alone. I'm not so naïve as to think that this sort of thing doesn't go on. But I don't ever want to be in a position where I have to let it happen because I've got too much to lose."

Joanna wiped the pool of water that had formed under her beer bottle. "So what's our next move?"

"I think we need to be careful and take it one day at a time. Somebody's gone to a lot of trouble to keep all this under wraps. They're not going to be pleased to discover you've been poking around and talking to the police. If the stakes are high, you could be in danger. Make no mistake about it."

They could both be in danger, Tom realized. He hoped Joanna wasn't going to become a loose cannon. She apparently had a lot of baggage from her marriage to Franklin and he might be walking into a messy situation with a woman who was teetering on the edge of some kind of personal crisis. Just what I need, he thought. Every relationship he'd ever had with a woman had been messy and ended badly. Not that this was a relationship, of course. It was a working partnership of sorts but they were each depending on the other for something that could change their lives. Big stuff, thought Tom. Maybe too big.

Chapter Seventeen

They decided to lay low for the first couple of days so it wouldn't look like they were conducting a full-scale investigation. They agreed Panakorn might be keeping an eye on them. There were hotel staff and locals they could get to know without arousing suspicion who might have interesting things to say without being asked. The hotel was a logical place to start and, although they had arrived together and there was some risk of Tom's being identified as a newspaper reporter, they felt it was unlikely Panakorn would bother with them if they appeared to be minding their own business. Joanna wanted the chief of police to think she was on a kind of pilgrimage to expunge her grief, not on a holiday with Tom, so they didn't do a lot of things together. Tom played some golf and tennis while Joanna indulged in some light reading and the occasional swim. Tom joined her in the pool once or twice and swam like the athlete he was while Joanna paddled around to keep afloat and cool off. She caught herself glancing at his long, lean legs once or twice, but only long enough to confirm that they were well-shaped and strong and that his ankles and feet were slim and perfectly formed.

Between these activities, they got to know the hotel staff and some of the local restaurants. They stayed away from the bars and nightclubs, figuring that Franklin probably didn't spend his evenings that way. But try as they would, they couldn't draw any information out of anyone. If the locals knew anything, they were being judiciously silent. The more Joanna thought about it, the more she began to wonder if Franklin hadn't stumbled across some criminal activity and been killed because of what he knew. She also wondered if, by following in his footsteps, they were walking into the same cul-de-sac.

Secretly, Tom was glad they weren't spending too much time together. So far, he had been able to maintain the façade that they were both in this for the same reasons. An injustice had occurred. A man had died under mysterious circumstances and there had been only the most superficial of investigations. The results had been inconclusive and it was apparent a cover-up had been put in place. But by whom, and for what reasons, was not apparent. Also, he found himself starting to like Joanna and that made him uncomfortable. She hadn't had another outburst like the one the other day and, most of the time, she was pretty good company. Despite appearances, she had guts and she had determination. He knew she could lead him to the information he needed. He had to stay focused on the story.

On the fourth day of their stay in Pattaya something happened that was to significantly affect the course of events. Joanna returned to her hotel room around one in the afternoon to change for lunch and found one of the hotel chambermaids waiting for her. She was sitting in a chair in front of the curtained window and jumped to her feet when Joanna entered the room. She was startled by the swiftness of the young woman's sudden movement and spoke to her in an irritated voice. "Who are you? What are you doing here?"

She reminded Joanna of a frightened kitten, her eyes wide and dark, her voice soft and pleading. "Oh please, you are Missus Franklin?" She spoke slowly and carefully as if she were unfamiliar with English.

"Yes. Who are you? What's your name?"

"Your husband name me Malee, Missus Franklin."

"My husband named you? What are you talking about?"

"I am sister of Dinh, houseboy of Mr. Franklin. He bring me and my family from Vietnam. Because he like me, Mr. Franklin keep me here and not make me go to America like other girls. Please Missus Franklin, please go away from here. Bad thing happen here. You must not stay."

"What do you know about my husband's accident? Do you know how it happened? Malee, you must tell me what you know."

"No, no, Missus Franklin, I cannot. Too many bad thing here. You must go very soon. Please." She bolted for the door, looked quickly up and down the hall and was gone before Joanna could say another thing.

Joanna got out of her wet bathing suit and into the shower in record time. Ten minutes later was sitting at a table in the dining room waiting for Tom to come down to lunch. As she sat there waiting for him, she went over and over her conversation with Malee. Why had Franklin "named" her? Why had he kept her at the hotel? Why hadn't he "made" her go to America like the other girls? What other girls? What did she mean by "bad thing?" And how much did she know about Franklin's accident?

"If you're not careful, your face will freeze in that expression," said Tom cheerfully as he sat down beside her. "Why the furrowed brow?"

Joanna repeated her conversation with Malee word for word as she remembered it and then listed her questions for him to think about. When she finished, she noticed he was looking distinctly uncomfortable. This was something Tom hadn't anticipated and he realized it might take them into territory Joanna didn't need to know about.

"What's the matter?"

He took a deep breath and said, "Listen, Joanna, I've been thinking it over and I have a bad feeling about this whole thing. Maybe we should just drop it right now and go back to Bangkok."

"What are you saying? I can't believe my ears. We've come all this way and now, when it looks like someone might know something, you want to quit? Is that what you're saying? I thought we had agreed to keep going."

"I know, I know, but what I'm saying is I'm getting a bad feeling from this girl and it's giving me second thoughts. Joanna, what if you start to find out things about Franklin that, well, that …"

"You mean you think Malee was his mistress, don't you?"

"I mean I don't know what might happen next and I'm not sure, for your sake, we should wait and find out."

"I've gone too far to turn back now, Tom. I've got to know what happened to Franklin even if it turns out to be horrible. If he was murdered, as you say, I want to know. But if you honestly don't want to go any further with this, I'll understand. If you're afraid …"

"I'm not afraid for my sake, Joanna, I'm afraid for yours. My gut feeling is that there's more going on than you bargained for and you may be in danger."

"Tom, the girl was frightened. She's young and probably uneducated and superstitious. Of course she doesn't want us to rock the boat. Let's just talk to her. Find out who she's afraid of."

He looked at her for several minutes before speaking. "Okay," he said. "But promise me, the minute you start to feel you're getting in too deep, tell me and we're out of here. Don't forget, we don't have the authorities on our side here. It's not worth your life to find out the truth."

"Oh, Tom," she said, "that's just healthy American paranoia talking. You need some lunch." But she could tell he didn't appreciate her joking about the matter. She was determined not to let him know how concerned she was herself about the girl's warning. Joanna half believed what she had said to him, but the other half shared his gut feeling of uneasiness. She wasn't going to be frightened off so easily, but she was going to be a little more careful walking down the street. As to Malee possibly being Franklin's mistress, the thought had occurred to her but she was beginning to suspect a little wifely paranoia on her own part. First Ruth Hendricks, now Malee. Was she going to suspect every woman she met of having been her husband's mistress?

The thing that puzzled her most was that Malee said Franklin hadn't "made" her go to America like the other girls. Joanna thought they all wanted to go to America. But then maybe Malee didn't want to go if her family couldn't go. That would be understandable. Maybe the houseboy Dinh, her brother, would be able to explain it. Joanna made a mental note to see him again as soon as they returned to Bangkok.

After lunch Joanna went back to her room for a nap. She didn't like to be out of doors when the sun was at its hottest and, besides, she and Tom had decided to go out to one of the town's popular restaurants for dinner later in the evening. She turned the ceiling fan on low and lay down with a novel she had been reading. But before she finished the chapter, she was asleep.

Joanna awoke feeling less than refreshed to find that the room had become quite hot in spite of the constantly revolving ceiling fan and decided to take a quick swim before dressing for dinner to clear some of the cotton wool from her brain. There wasn't much activity around the pool and she could see the busboys getting the dining room set up for the evening meal. She kept an eye open for Malee but didn't see her or any of the other maids for that matter. She wondered if she could find out what shift Malee was on without arousing suspicion.

After her swim, Joanna took the long way back to her room, looking up and down some of the corridors to see if she could find one of the other maids. She finally located a couple of girls sorting linens and asked them when Malee would be working and if they knew where to find her. One of the girls couldn't speak English so the other one translated for her. She shook her head and said something that the other girl translated as, "No Madame. Sorry. She is not here." "Do you know when she'll be back?" Joanna asked, and they looked at each other nervously and both shook their heads.

"Malee not come to work today, Madam. Boss very angry. She maybe lose job."

Joanna started to say she had seen Malee earlier so she must have come to work, but changed her mind. They both seemed a little frightened so she decided not to push it. If Malee had risked her job to speak to Joanna in her room, these girls were better off not knowing about it.

Joanna thanked them and made her way back to her room. It bothered Joanna that Malee might have lost her job because of her. She wondered if someone had seen Malee leaving her room and reported her to "the boss." He must run a pretty tight ship, Joanna thought, if the staff was afraid to be seen talking to the guests.

The swim had cleared Joanna's head and she showered and dressed at a leisurely pace, going over her conversation with Malee to see if her reference to Franklin's "bad accident" could in any way translate as "murder." She wished she had some standard of reference to help her determine if "bad thing"' and "bad accident" measured low or high on the danger scale. Malee's use of English was halting and unfamiliar and "bad" in her mind could mean anything from "not nice" to "deadly."

When they met for dinner, she told Tom about her encounter with the maids and the fact that Malee had not shown up for work. Tom agreed that they should try and look into it, but at the moment he wasn't sure how to go about it. They decided not to talk about Franklin or Malee or anything to do with the private investigation they were conducting for the rest of the evening. Instead they talked about Thailand and how Tom had got to be there.

He told her he had been a senior at UCLA in the early sixties, studying political science at a time when America was still innocent about the implications of involvement in a war halfway around the world. The assassinations of the Kennedy brothers and Martin Luther King, Jr. hadn't happened yet, nor had the Tet Offensive, the bombing of Hanoi or the My Lai massacre. People still had faith in the authority of their government and still waved the flag in the face of a threat to the free world. Raised in the conservative, patriotic mid-west by a schoolteacher mother and a retired army sergeant who had distinguished himself during the Second World War, Tom joined the army before he was drafted. Two years later he was sent to Saigon, a junior officer assigned to an intelligence unit.

He saw things he could not have imagined happening and he learned the smell of death up close. He learned to hate the fighting and its aftermath but he earnestly believed the job he was doing was somehow shortening the war, saving lives. Information, he thought, was the key. The more they could learn about the country, the VC, the people hiding in the jungles or fleeing to the cities, the better equipped they would be to help the Vietnamese fight their own war.

At the same time, he was learning to love Indo-China, its mysteries, its dangers, its beauty. "There were lots of guys who got hooked on the East," he said. "For every hundred guys who hated the place and the war, there was one who loved the killing and another one who discovered a fascination for the Orient. That was me."

When his tour of active duty ended he tried to transfer to the civilian diplomatic corps but was turned down. Eventually he went to Bangkok on his own, by way of Manila, Singapore and Kuala Lumpur, working as a freelance stringer for some American newspapers. In the intervening years he had only been stateside a few times and each time had felt out of place, anxious to get back to Asia.

They talked their way through lemon shrimp soup, a selection of satay served with a tantalizing peanut sauce, a spicy sweet and sour fish and stir-fried vegetables washed down with buckets of cool beer. Joanna found herself captivated by Tom's history and did not think once of her rose-colored wing chair back home or the book she was currently reading or Franklin.

It was late and Joanna was feeling a little high as they staggered back to the hotel arm in arm. The air was that perfect temperature where it blends with your skin and feels like a gossamer cloak. There, but not a part of your consciousness. Perfect. She said goodnight to Tom at the door to her room and let herself in. She knew that if had tried to kiss her, she would have let him. A week ago she would not have let that thought enter her head but, tonight, she felt giddy and ridiculously girlish, possibly because she had experienced more emotions in the past few days than she had felt in years.

The air inside the room felt hot and close and Joanna realized with some dismay that she hadn't left the fan or the air-conditioning on. She walked over to the balcony and opened the sliding door to let some of the night air in. It was then that she noticed her bed was unmade. It had not been when she left. She distinctly remembered smoothing the sheets and blanket before going to dinner. As she got closer, Joanna noticed that someone was lying on the bed.

Malee's throat had been cut from ear to ear. The look on her face was one of absolute terror, the look of someone who could see her killer and knew there was nothing she could do to stop him. Joanna stared at Malee's fear-ravaged face a full five minutes before she pulled herself away and ran down the hall to Tom's room. She knocked and he called out "Who is it?" from behind the door. Joanna found she couldn't speak and just kept knocking softly and rhythmically on the door. Tom finally opened it and when he saw her stricken face, he led her to a chair and sat her down. Then he ran down the hall to her room to see what had happened.

Chapter Eighteen

Joanna could hear someone whimpering and it took her a while to realize there was no one else in the room, that the sound must be coming from her.

"Are the police coming?" she asked, when Tom returned.

"I didn't call the police. I didn't think it would be too healthy for either of us if we had to explain how she got there. Is it Malee?"

"Yes." Her hands were clenched like fists in her lap. She could feel the muscles in her shoulders tightening. "What are we going to do? How am I going to explain to Panakorn how Malee was murdered in my bed?"

"You won't have to explain, Joanna. She's not in your bed anymore. I moved the body."

She didn't quite grasp what Tom was saying. "How could we possibly get away with that? There's bound to be clues."

"Maybe not. You probably didn't notice, but Malee's body was wrapped in a piece of tarp. If she had been murdered in your room, there would be a lot of blood. But there isn't – just the dried blood on her clothes and on the tarp. I checked very carefully. That means she was probably murdered somewhere else, quite a while before you found her. Someone must have carried her to your room and put her on the bed. I wrapped the body and the tarp in the bed sheets, just to be safe, and went down the back stairs. I didn't want to risk being seen, so I put her body in the bushes about twenty yards from the exit. On my way back I grabbed clean sheets from one of the maid's trolleys and put them on your bed."

"Do you think anybody could have seen you?"

"I don't think so, but I can't be sure. It's pretty late, so I don't think anyone's around. Just the same, it's not a good idea to hang around here much longer. I think we should head back to Bangkok in the morning. If the body's discovered and the police start asking questions, we'll have to play dumb. Hopefully they won't connect Malee to you."

Joanna felt sick about Malee; she was just a kid and she had seemed so frightened. A chill went up Joanna's spine and she couldn't get the image of Malee's dead face out of her mind. Was she the reason Malee had been killed? She suddenly felt cold and started to shake. She told Tom she didn't want to sleep in her room and he told her she could stay with him. He wrapped a blanket around her shoulders and reassured her that whoever had dumped Malee's body was long gone. She got into Tom's bed and he sat with her and held her hand until she went to sleep. Joanna slept as if she were covered with a heavy wet blanket. She kept tossing and struggling to breathe as if there wasn't enough air in the room. When she woke up she could feel the tears behind her eyelids and, when she remembered Malee's face, she felt sick to her stomach.

Tom was sleeping in the chair by the window and he heard her get up and go into the bathroom.

"Are you okay?" he said when she came back out.

"No," she said, sighing deeply. "I've never felt so terrible in my life. I feel as if I'm the reason for that poor girl's death. I feel responsible, Tom."

"It's not your fault, Joanna. You don't know what kind of life she had, what kind of stuff she was involved in. These girls play a dangerous game. Sometimes they get hurt."

"Yes, but why was she in my bed? Somebody put her there to send me a message. I'm sure of it. I think I'm in over my head, Tom, and I'm scared to death."

Tom stood up and walked over to the bed. "Hey," he said, sitting beside her and putting his arm around her. "It'll be all right. Someone just wants us to get out of town and that's what we're going to do. Nothing's going to happen to you. I promise."

He saw the tears that were dampening her cheeks and began to wipe them gently away with his thumb. She looked into his eyes and realized she hadn't experienced this level of intimacy with anyone for a very long time. Then Tom kissed her softly on the lips. She felt herself responding and knew she didn't want him to stop. Her lips parted and she put her arms around him as they lay back on the bed.

Tom was already up and packing his things when Joanna woke up. He heard her groan and said, "I don't think I like the sound of that." She pulled the sheet up over her head and he pulled it down and kissed her. "Time to get up and face the day, lazybones. I'm afraid reality awaits. It's not going to be an easy day for either of us, Joanna. I'm sure the gardener will discover the body at some point and unless we can be gone before the police get here, we'll probably have to answer some questions. It wouldn't look good for us to check out suddenly and take off, so I think we should have some breakfast before we go."

Joanna would have preferred to go back to sleep and wake up at another time, in another place. She wanted to be facing a different reality than the one outside the door. She wanted that reality to include Tom in a very different context than the one the hard light of this day was presenting.

By the time they went down for breakfast, it was clear someone had found Malee's body. There was an unnatural silence to things, punctuated now and then by the buzz of hurriedly whispered comments or a short outburst from an anxious hotel employee dropping a spoon. They ordered breakfast and waited uneasily for it to arrive, not speaking, but all the time knowing what the other was thinking. They had gone over the events of the previous evening so they would be able to answer any questions, carefully eliminating the details concerning Malee. They would say that Joanna had gone straight to bed and slept soundly through the night. Tom had done the same. There would also be no mention of Malee's visit during the afternoon. Joanna was fairly certain no one had seen her since Malee had taken great pains to leave the room unobserved.

They were finishing their coffee as casually as possible, deciding it was time to collect their bags and leave the hotel, when Joanna saw Panakorn enter the dining room and walk straight across the room to their table.

"Mrs. Reynolds," he said, in a voice dripping with false courtesy. "I see you declined to take my advice about leaving Pattaya. Now I find you in the middle of a murder mystery."

"I don't understand, Chief Panakorn. Has someone been murdered?" Stop there, Joanna thought. You're no match for him, especially if you lose your cool.

"Yes, I'm afraid so. A young woman, a Vietnamese. Very sad. Her throat was cut. I don't suppose you or your friend would know anything about it." He kept his eyes on Joanna, waiting to see if she would flinch. When she didn't answer he delivered the kicker. "No, I didn't think you would. Although … she was known to your husband, Mrs. Reynolds. It seems he assisted in her escape from Vietnam and obtained employment for her in this hotel."

"I'm sorry, Chief Panakorn, I know nothing of her." Joanna forced herself not to blink or look away.

"Ah, yes. Well, too bad. At any rate, I hope you won't mind telling me where you were last evening until about two a.m. You and your, uh, friend."

They told Panakorn their story, disagreeing, as planned, over the time of their arrival at the hotel, and said they were just about to depart.

"I hope you are not planning to leave the country just yet, Mrs. Reynolds. It may be necessary to speak with you again if there are any, uh, further developments."

"I have no immediate plans to leave Thailand. But if I should decide to go I'll notify the embassy in Bangkok. I have no desire to hamper your investigation."

"Thank you, Mrs. Reynolds. That is most thoughtful of you. Mr. Thorpe," he turned to Tom, "I shall find you at your address in Bangkok, I trust?" Tom nodded his reply and Panakorn turned to leave.

"Chief Panakorn." He stopped in mid-stride and smiled at her.

"Yes, Mrs. Reynolds?"

"Do you think this woman's death is in any way connected to my husband's?" Joanna knew he was making an effort to remain inscrutable.

"No, Mrs. Reynolds, I do not. Your husband's death was an accident. This is clearly murder." With that he turned and left the room.

Joanna saw the surprised look on Tom's face. She didn't know what had made her do it, but something had forced the words from her mouth. Joanna hoped she hadn't just signed her own death warrant. Tom didn't say anything. That told her he was thinking the same thing.

They drove most of the way to Bangkok in silence, thinking over recent events and trying to decide what to do next. Finally Joanna said, "I want to talk to Dinh, Malee's brother."

She saw Tom's cheek muscle tighten ever so slightly. He didn't answer right away, but after a minute or so he took her hand and said very quietly, "Okay." She still hadn't told him she had been to Franklin's house and met Dinh there. She couldn't see any reason for telling him now.

When they got back to town Tom dropped her off at the Oriental and she went in to re-register. As she approached the desk, Joanna noticed a man with close-cropped hair and big shoulders turn and walk away. She glanced in his direction, thinking he seemed familiar, and caught a glimpse of his profile. She was pretty sure it was Fred Hendricks, although she had never seen him standing up and this man was shorter than she had imagined Hendricks to be. He was obviously in a hurry and he didn't look back.

Joanna gave the desk clerk her name and fished around in her handbag for her credit card. "Ah yes, Mrs. Reynolds. Welcome back." She filled in the registration form and he handed her a long white envelope, the kind with the flap on one end. "Someone left this for you, Mrs. Reynolds." He rang for the bellboy and said, "Please enjoy your stay." Joanna stuck the envelope in her bag and followed the bellboy to the elevator. The only thing she wanted to do was take a nice long shower. She forgot about the envelope until room service brought her lunch. When she went into her handbag looking for a tip she saw the crumpled white paper crammed into the corner.

There was nothing on the front of the envelope to indicate who had sent it so she tore open the flap and pulled out a single sheet of white paper. The message was printed in block letters, all lower case, the way a child might write it. It was unsigned.

"Mrs. Reynolds," it said, '"take my advice and go back where you belong. You don't want to follow in your husband's footsteps."

Joanna shivered and remembered seeing the man she thought was Fred Hendricks in the lobby. She wondered if he had left the message. But why? Why would Fred Hendricks care whether she was in Bangkok or not? He hadn't seemed that interested in her when she had talked to him at the golf club. What connection did he have to Franklin except through Ruth? Had Ruth been protecting her husband after all, as Tom had suggested? Joanna decided it was time to find out more about Fred Hendricks and it was also time to start looking over her shoulder every minute.

Chapter Nineteen

What the hell's going on?" Bruce Jackson yelled into the phone. "I thought I told you to keep that woman out of trouble." Tom Thorpe, on the receiving end of the call, bit his lip and thought carefully about his response.

"Calm down, Bruce. I didn't know it was going to happen. Jesus Christ, we were staying at the Golf Club. How was I supposed to know the girl was working there? You haven't exactly been helpful on the information end. You told me to get her out of Bangkok, so we went to Pattaya for a little sun and sand."

"Don't bullshit me, Thorpe. There's more than sun and sand in Pattaya and you know it. You could have gone to Hua Hin if you just wanted to get a suntan."

Bruce was fuming and Tom knew it was because he'd probably been chewed out himself by Bradshaw over the episode in Pattaya. Bradshaw would know that Joanna had been to see Panakorn. And he would definitely know that Malee had been murdered. It was a nasty business and Bradshaw didn't like to get his hands dirty.

"Just get her the hell out of the goddamn country," said Bruce and hung up.

Joanna telephoned Loretta Bradshaw the next morning and asked if she would join her for tea later in the day. Joanna had discovered the Authors' Lounge in the hotel and thought it would be a perfect spot to meet. When Loretta arrived, precisely at two, Joanna had already spent half an hour browsing through the books, many of them first editions, by some of the hotel's illustrious guests – Conrad, Maugham, Noel Coward and Graham Greene – that were displayed throughout the room. The Authors' Lounge was like a large greenhouse, filled with potted and fresh-cut flowers and white rattan furniture. The tea, served in the traditional English way with little sandwiches, cakes and scones filled with fresh cream and strawberry jam, was set up under a flowered umbrella on a glass table. The dishes were sparkling white and the tray was decorated with a vase of bright pink orchids.

"Oh, this is lovely," said Loretta, taking in the lavish surroundings. "I'd heard about it, you know, but I've never had the occasion to come here. I'm so pleased you invited me."

Joanna was happy to see her again and was looking forward to spending a couple of hours talking and drinking tea, despite the fact that their last meeting had ended on an awkward note. Joanna was sure Loretta's motives in suggesting she leave Bangkok were not sinister, but that she was just delivering her husband's message. It was nice to be sitting opposite a woman she liked and trusted and to be talking in a way that didn't involve pretence or guilt. Perhaps she had let herself get too close to Tom and it might cause her to lose her way. Franklin had dominated her for so long, she wasn't sure how to handle the intimacy that had developed between herself and Tom. She felt foolish for even thinking about it and told herself it probably meant nothing to him. Just something that happened because they were thrown together by circumstances. Now she didn't intend to bare her soul to Loretta, she wasn't the type, but it was time to get another perspective on things, a woman's perspective, and she thought Loretta was someone who would be honest with her. Joanna believed they were alike in some ways and, being married to a powerful man like Jonathon Bradshaw, Loretta would understand things about her that other people might not. If she could have talked to Fay, who still thought she was in Europe, she would have picked up the phone and poured the whole thing out to her. But she knew there were some things Fay would say that Joanna didn't want to hear.

They talked a bit about Loretta's life in Bangkok which seemed to consist of a constant round of social and public appointments quite separate from her social commitments with her husband. Joanna said her life with Franklin had become just the opposite. She had spent most of her time at home, gardening and reading, or taking courses at the university. She hadn't been involved with Franklin's public life for over a decade.

"I envy you in a way, Joanna," said Loretta, taking another cream-filled scone. "I wonder what my life would be like if I could choose not to be part of Jonathon's public life."

"Franklin shut me out of his life, Loretta. He didn't want me to be part of it. That's not the same thing as choosing not to be involved. In a way, though, I suppose there wasn't a place for me in his world. Eventually I would have got tired of sightseeing and shopping and we would have ended up living separate lives anyway, I suppose. It wasn't until after he died that I realized how hurt I was. I never allowed myself to think about it too much while he was alive. I just made a life for myself without him. But you have a role in your husband's life that's part of the diplomatic lifestyle."

"It's true," Loretta said, looking wistful. "Jonathon's the one who gets the salary but I'm expected to work just as hard and, if I say no, it reflects badly on him." Just then, the waiter brought a fresh pot of tea and another plate of sandwiches.

"Tell me," Joanna said, sitting back with her fourth cup of

tea, "why do people like Fred and Ruth Hendricks come to a place like Thailand? I mean, what's the attraction? Surely it's not a career decision."

Loretta pushed herself back from the table and sipped some tea before answering. "Fred and Ruth," she echoed. "Now there's a strange couple. Fred seems so bitter. He was in the Marines, you know, and was injured in one of those awful offensives, so they sent him home to get fixed up. He was in hospital for a long time. I don't know whether he had a breakdown or what but, apparently, when he came out he got his discharge and a pension and decided to come back here. I don't know why Ruth came except that she seems to be a very loyal person. They have no children and I guess they decided they could have a pretty good life here on his pension. But I don't know if it's worked out the way they thought it would. They have a nice little house and he seems to pick up the odd job here and there, but I think she works because there's nothing else to do. They just seem to exist together. I think he may have developed a bit of a drinking problem."

Joanna remembered Fred's sullen manner and the way he drank alone at the golf club and had no trouble believing what Loretta was saying.

"Oh dear," Loretta said, furrowing her brow, "I hope it doesn't sound like I'm putting them down. I really don't know that much about them, just what I think I see. They may have a lovely life together for all I know."

Joanna couldn't help laughing and told Loretta she doubted it. She said she liked Ruth but didn't feel she could get to know her. "It's as if she wants to keep me away. Maybe she doesn't want anyone to get close to her. When I met her, she didn't strike me as being a very happy person. I wonder if her life would have been better if she'd stayed in the States?"

"Who knows?" said Loretta, reaching for the last sandwich. "I'm sure mine would have been." They both laughed and she told Joanna she was actually looking forward to Jonathon's retirement so she could have some permanence in her life. "You get tired of moving around so much and always living in someone else's house. I dream about a place of our own where I can do anything I want, including cook a roast of beef. I miss cooking roast beef on Sundays. Can you believe that?"

Joanna said she could but, when she thought about it, she realized it had been a long time since she'd cooked a roast beef on a Sunday. Or any other day for that matter. Maybe she didn't miss it after all.

"Loretta," she said, "do you think Tom Thorpe's reliable? I mean, does he seem like a fairly down-to-earth guy to you?"

"Yes, I think so," Loretta said, surprised by the sudden change of topic. "I've never known him to be anything but steady and reliable. Why on earth would you ask that?"

There was no way to maneuver the conversation around to it, so Joanna finally decided just to come out with it and get Loretta's reaction. "Well," she finally said, "I don't know how else to say this, but Tom seems to think that Franklin might have been murdered and I wondered if you thought there was any basis for that."

The look on Loretta's face made her answer clear. For a full minute she didn't say anything. Then she reached forward and put her cup and saucer down on the table. "Are you serious? He can't actually believe that!"

"I'm afraid he does."

"Based on what evidence?"

"Well, that's just it. There doesn't seem to be any real evidence. He just feels very strongly about it. He thinks people know more than they're saying and that someone's covering the whole thing up."

"You must be joking," Loretta said, her face still filled with astonishment. "I've never heard anything so ridiculous!"

"Well, that's how I felt at first, but Tom's convinced it's true and there are a number of things that don't add up."

"Like what?" Loretta asked, curious, but still disbelieving.

"Well, like the fact that Franklin was afraid of the water and never went swimming."

"But surely that's no reason to suspect he was murdered. If he was out on a boat, then that's all the more reason to think that he might have drowned accidentally. Tom should be ashamed of himself for telling you such a thing. You must have been beside yourself." Loretta was watching her to see her reaction. "You don't really believe him, do you?"

"Well, I'm not entirely convinced, but there have been some strange things that have happened since I arrived in Thailand." Joanna told her how she had been getting the brush-off from people right from the start and how everyone had been trying to avoid the topic of Franklin's death.

"Why of course it seems that way, my dear," Loretta said, trying to be comforting and reasonable at the same time. "People don't know how to handle that kind of thing. It was a tragic accident and here you are in your grief and nobody knows what to say. They seem rude but it's just because they feel awkward and inadequate."

"Then why was I told, indirectly, by the police and by your own husband, to stop asking questions about Franklin's death? Why wouldn't they want to get to the bottom of it? Even Tom got the brush-off when he tried to get the story." Joanna thought she was sounding pretty unconvincing and knew before she said it what Loretta's answer would be.

"But Joanna, this is a foreign country and Franklin's death is a police matter. Tom knows you can't interfere with that. I can't believe he's being so foolish."

Then Joanna told her about Malee and what she had said before she died.

"Oh, the poor child," Loretta said, genuinely shocked at the news. "How awful. I wonder if Jonathon knows about it."

"Please, Loretta, don't repeat any of this to Jonathon. We were questioned by the police and I told them I knew nothing about her. I wouldn't want to get Tom into trouble and I wouldn't want

Jonathon to be compromised in any way by knowing I'd lied to the police. You understand, don't you?"

Loretta thought about it for a minute and said, "But there's no reason to think it has anything to do with Franklin. Come on, Joanna, you're not one of those people who believes in conspiracy theories are you?"

"No, I'm not. It's just that if you talk to Tom he can be pretty convincing. He says he knows it in his guts. He just doesn't know how to prove it." Joanna realized she might be putting Tom in a very awkward position. "Loretta, promise me what I've told you won't go any further. I don't want to cause trouble between Tom and Jonathon. Tom's just doing his job, in a way."

"Don't worry," Loretta said reassuringly. "Tom won't get into trouble. I'm sure this will all blow over in time. After all, there's no evidence whatsoever. Franklin had no enemies that I'm aware of. And I'm sure if Jonathon had thought anything was amiss with the investigation he wouldn't have allowed them to close the books. I'm sure of that. He and Franklin were friends. He was terribly distressed when Franklin died."

"There's just one other thing," Joanna said, reaching for her handbag. "This message was waiting for me when I got back to the hotel last night. I'm not positive, but I'm pretty sure I saw Fred Hendricks leaving as I was arriving. Do you think he might have left it?"

Loretta read the message a couple of times and turned the paper over to see if there was anything on the other side. She seemed to be thinking about something. Finally she said, "I didn't want to tell you this, but some people seem to think that Fred Hendricks was jealous of Franklin. They say he didn't like Ruth working for him."

She was clearly embarrassed so Joanna didn't press her about it. She had her own suspicions about Ruth and Franklin, based on gut instincts and no evidence, she reminded herself. But it didn't explain why Fred would leave her a message to get out of Thailand.

"I think he may have transferred his dislike of Franklin to you," said Loretta. "You probably remind him of his jealousy and he just wants you to be out of his sight. I don't really think it's a threat, although it looks like he wants to scare you into leaving. If you like, I can show this to Jonathon and have him speak to Fred."

"No. I'd rather you didn't. I don't want Fred to think he's got to me. Besides, I'm not even sure he was the one who left the message. I'd be very embarrassed if I was mistaken. Don't say anything to Jonathon. I'd rather he didn't know about any of this. I'll speak to Tom myself and tell him he's overreacting."

"Yes," said Loretta, smiling, "Tom's just being overzealous. I've always liked that quality of energy and eagerness about him. But sometimes I think his imagination goes into high gear. I think Tom secretly wants to write spy novels. He needs a wife and some children to keep his feet on the ground and his head out of the clouds."

They both laughed, relieved that they had settled the matter between them. Loretta was as convinced of her view as Tom was of his. What Joanna did next would come down to whose instincts she should trust. Tom's, Loretta's or her own.

Chapter Twenty

Bangkok was as steamy as a bowl of hot and sour soup. Despite its sprawling avenues and meandering canals, it felt oppressive to Joanna, closing in on her just when she was feeling the need for more room. She wanted to talk to the houseboy Dinh but she had no idea where to look. Franklin's house would be occupied by someone else by now and she was sure Dinh was gone. He might not even be in the city and, if he was, he might very well be impossible to find. It was a city full of hiding places that she couldn't begin to know in the time she had.

Joanna went through the list of people she had met since coming to Thailand in the hope of finding someone who might be able to help her. Tom might have some ideas, but she doubted the wisdom of his sticking his neck out any further, especially on her behalf. As for the Bradshaws, she didn't want them to know she was still poking around asking questions. The less Jonathon knew about what she was doing, and the less he knew about Tom helping her do it, the better for both of them. She didn't know how much power Jonathon Bradshaw could wield and she didn't want to find out during a complimentary cab ride to the airport. Joanna wasn't finished with Thailand yet and she didn't want to leave until she was ready.

As for Art and Ellen Roberts and their friends, they might know something of the whereabouts of Dinh through their own servants, but Joanna would have to think up a pretty good story to tell them so it wouldn't spread like wildfire through the resident Americans that she was looking for him. On the other hand, if the opportunity presented itself to ask one of them, she would do it. She could probably concoct something about some personal possession of Franklin's she couldn't find or wanted to give to Dinh for his faithful service.

Joanna wondered about Ruth Hendricks. Ruth might be willing to help her on compassionate grounds. If she had been in love with Franklin she might want to help Joanna find out what had happened to him. If she were honest with Ruth and told her she was suspicious of Franklin's death, Ruth might open up and talk to her, woman to woman. On the other hand, if Ruth already knew what had happened to Franklin because she had been involved with him in something that had caused his death, she could be setting herself up for real trouble. When Joanna last talked to her, Ruth Hendricks had been careful and inscrutable. Joanna had felt at the time that nothing short of a piece of hard evidence would cause Ruth to open up. She wondered if she could get Ruth on her side by telling her about Malee's murder. Maybe it would shake her up enough to help Joanna find Dinh. When Joanna called Ruth at her office shortly after 9:30 in the morning, Ruth answered her own phone and didn't seem particularly pleased to hear from her. Joanna jumped on her before she had a chance to beg off.

"Mrs. Hendricks, I have to see you. It's quite urgent and I don't want to discuss it over the phone. Could you come to my hotel room this afternoon when you finish work?"

Joanna could hear her thinking on the other end of the phone. Finally, reluctantly, Ruth answered. "All right. Yes, Mrs. Reynolds. I'll be there about 5:30."

"Thank you," Joanna said and hung up before Ruth had time to reconsider. She didn't know where to contact Tom during the day, so the only way he was going to know she would be seeing Ruth was if he phoned her. She didn't feel like hanging around the hotel all day and decided to do some innocent sightseeing to pass the time. She hadn't yet seen the Grand Palace, the Temple of the Reclining Buddha or the Temple of the Golden Buddha, all absolute must-sees for tourists. If someone was watching her, she wanted to give the right impression.

Joanna went for the Grand Palace first. As she approached the large, square-mile compound surrounded by high white walls, the first thing she noticed was that it was guarded by armed sentries. Inside the compound, however, all was peaceful and pleasant. Green lawns were dotted with flowerbeds and artfully manicured trees and bushes and meandering pathways leading to and around a multitude of buildings combined traditional Thai architecture and Italian Renaissance styling. Cool white marble structures were topped with bright orange tiles and shining gold *prangs*. Gabled roofs were decorated with golden licks that caught the sun and looked like flames. Joanna feasted on the details and contrasts that were endemic to Thailand and tried to forget why she was really there. She knew she might never be back again but, even as she was thinking it, a small voice inside her was saying, Never say never.

The soft tinkling of temple bells drew her toward Wat Phra Kaeo, the temple of the Emerald Buddha. Inside she found the small fourteenth-century statue poised under its own canopy. She learned that the King himself changed the statue's gold costumes three times a year in accordance with the seasons. This was the most sacred Buddha in Thailand. The air inside the Temple was heavy with the scent of jasmine and incense left by Thais who had come to pray and meditate before the statue. It felt so peaceful inside the cool walls of the Temple that Joanna forgot for a moment the awful reason she had come so far. The events of the past few weeks seemed a long way off and, just like the serene statue in front of her, she might not have had a care in the world.

She emerged from the sweet silence of the Temple into the intense sunlight of outdoors and quickly covered her smarting eyes with dark glasses. She located Wat Pho, Temple of the Reclining Buddha, just south of the Grand Palace and entered the compound. Its gravel walkways and gray stone stupas were in direct contrast to the gold and green splendor of the Grand Palace grounds. The temple itself, said to be the oldest in Bangkok, housed the 150-foot reclining Buddha. He appeared to be very comfortable, lying on his right side, his head propped in his hand. The immense gold-plated figure was impossible to view in its entirety and had to be looked at in sections and from various angles. She was especially interested in his feet, inlaid with mother-of-pearl and depicting the 108 auspicious signs. Equally fascinating to her were the silent, saffron-robed monks gazing at the statue, their heads shaved, one shoulder and arm bared.

To round out a three-Buddha day, Joanna made her way to the Wat Traimit Temple of the Golden Buddha and took a good long look at the 10-foot, solid-gold seated statue that weighed in at five-and-a-half tons. She wondered what it was worth in dollars and that made her think of the three million she had sitting in a Swiss bank. Did she have a right to that money? Where had it come from? When, and if, she discovered the truth would it make a difference? For the first time, Joanna wondered if she would be able to keep the money. If it belonged to someone else, would her conscience let her keep it? Whatever spiritual enlightenment she may have glimpsed in the last few hours suddenly evaporated.

Joanna stopped for a spicy noodle concoction on her way back to the hotel and washed it down with a cool beer. She had been keeping one eye open to the people around her as she had toured the temples and now, sitting in the open-air restaurant, she took a long, slow look at the various people eating and drinking beer. She was looking specifically for an ex-Marine with close-cropped hair and big shoulders but couldn't see anyone fitting that description. There were a couple of men with short hair, but one was older and one was younger than she had remembered Fred Hendricks being. And neither of them had big shoulders. The one man who had big shoulders was black and he was making himself conspicuous by his antics with two young Thai girls. However, he could have been an ex-Marine and maybe Fred Hendricks had hired him to follow her. What better cover than to attract attention to himself?

Oh brother, she thought, I've been in the sun too long. Repeat the following: there is no conspiracy. She had to admit she had been rattled by seeing someone she thought was Fred Hendricks in her hotel and by receiving an anonymous message that seemed clear to her in its implications. The fact that Loretta Bradshaw had completely discredited Tom's murder theory, at least to her own satisfaction, had not completely invalidated it for Joanna. If Loretta was like her, and she did feel a certain affinity for her, then Loretta could be as naïve as she once was, a sister in the art of evasion. Loretta hadn't been prepared to consider the possibility and Tom remained unwaveringly certain of his instincts.

Joanna just had time to shower and change before her appointment with Ruth Hendricks who arrived a few minutes after the half hour looking as cool and guarded as Joanna remembered her. She invited Ruth in and ordered drinks from room service.

Joanna got right to the point and told Ruth she wanted her to find Dinh. She said she had real problems believing that Franklin had died accidentally and then she told Ruth about Malee. Ruth listened carefully to everything Joanna said and, when she finished, she got up and walked over to the window overlooking the river. She stood there for what seemed like ten minutes but was probably only two or three. Then she spoke.

"Okay," she said, "I'll help you. I know where he is. But first there's something I want to say to you. I agree with you that something's not right about your husband's death. I knew he didn't like the water and that he never went swimming. But when the police talked to me I told them nothing. First of all, because I didn't really know anything. I mean, I couldn't substantiate any suspicions I had. And second, because I was afraid. I'm still afraid. And I think if you knew what you were dealing with you'd be afraid too. I suspected and worried, I'll admit, for a long time that Franklin, Mr. Reynolds, was involved in some kind of deal. He used to disappear, sometimes for two or three days at a time, and not tell me where he was going. 'Up north,' he'd say – and nobody could get in touch with him. There was no apparent reason that I could see for him to make those trips. He'd never tell me anything about them when he got back and they didn't seem in any way to be connected with what we were doing at A.A.R. I think I would have known if they were. I worked very closely with your husband – I handled his confidential correspondence myself, I screened his phone calls, I knew everyone he dealt with. Those trips of his just didn't fit in any place."

"But I was told he took the occasional trip up north to play golf and relax with a few friends," Joanna said, trying to make some sense of what Ruth was telling her.

"Yes, but that was only a couple of times, and I knew about those trips. In fact, I even made the arrangements for them. But it was the trips I knew nothing about that made me suspicious. Don't you see? Not telling me anything was out of character. It just didn't fit the pattern."

"But why should you be afraid just because your boss slips away for a few days and doesn't tell you. You were his secretary, after all, and maybe this involved something very personal. I'm his wife, for God's sake, and it seems plain to me."

Joanna wondered if Ruth Hendricks was blushing under her even tan. She could feel her discomfort and thought, don't push it.

"Look, Mrs. Reynolds, this is a country where intrigue is part of the daily diet. Sexual and otherwise. Men like Art Roberts, married to that she-wolf, go off for a little oriental *poontang* once in a while. Your husband didn't strike me as someone on the make. Anyway, he lived alone. Why go out of town?"

Either Ruth was trying to protect her or she was very naïve or she couldn't bear the thought of Franklin being her lover and having Thai girls on the side. Joanna was beginning to think him capable of anything, since almost everything she had learned about him from the day of his death was "out of character."

"Okay," Joanna said, "I accept your theory. But that still doesn't explain why you're afraid."

"Look," Ruth said, sounding a little exasperated, "it was all just too secret. Nothing gets by anyone around here. Whatever you do hits the gossip mill before the ink's dry on the hotel registration. But there was never a word about these trips of Franklin's. Nobody knew about them. Nobody went with him. Nobody saw him. I promise you, anything kept that carefully under wraps is pretty serious stuff. I don't even want to think about what he might have been involved in. I can't believe he would compromise his position, but from what you tell me about Malee, maybe he was being forced to do some dealing under the table to get some of those people out."

Joanna hadn't told Ruth her suspicions about Malee being Franklin's mistress and from what Ruth was telling her it hadn't occurred to her. She still believed anything Franklin did was for a noble purpose. But Joanna was beginning to wonder if Malee was just "poontang" and her death had nothing to do with Franklin's. They were going in circles.

"When can you take me to see Dinh?"

"I can take you tonight but it will have to be after dark. I'll come back here and get you at nine o'clock."

Ruth got up to leave and Joanna asked her if she would be coming alone. She said yes and Joanna asked her not to tell anyone she'd been talking to her. Especially, she thought to herself, your husband.

As soon as Ruth was gone, Joanna called Tom at home. He answered on the first ring and sounded a little annoyed when he said, "Joanna, where have you been? I must have called you ten times today. I didn't want to leave messages in case someone was watching you."

Joanna told him what she had done, from calling Ruth Hendricks through her little tourist excursion and her meeting with Ruth. "What do you think?" she asked.

"It sounds like she believes Franklin was some kind of angel," he answered. "I can't believe she doesn't think him capable of anything underhanded. She seems to think he can only have been a victim of evil forces or something."

"There could be reasons for that," Joanna said. "She may not have wanted to be that frank with me. I am his wife, after all. Was, I mean. She doesn't know all the facts. And she may have been very much in love with him. Maybe more than I was." Joanna could tell Tom didn't know how to answer that. "Does that shock you?" She was beginning to come to terms with the fact that Franklin's life was not what she had thought it was. In fact, she was even beginning to believe he was capable of all sorts of things he probably hadn't done.

Tom finally found his voice. "Look, she may have been infatuated with him, especially if her marriage was unhappy – which it probably was and is – but that doesn't mean Franklin reciprocated."

Joanna found Tom's delicacy rather charming but she didn't tell him that nor did she ask him any more stupid questions. "Anyway, do you want to come with me tonight and, if so, do you think it would be a good idea?"

"I think it's a hare-brained idea for you to go at all. Why don't you let me go with her and report back to you? Then if anything happens to us – like we don't come back – you'll know to get out of town quick."

"I appreciate the offer, Tom, but no deal. I'm definitely going. Besides, why would Dinh talk to you? He'd be more inclined to open up to me about Franklin's personal life."

"You have a point there. But I still don't like the idea. Why does it have to be after dark, anyway?"

"Ruth didn't say. She just said it would have to be. I didn't want to antagonize her."

"Okay, then. I'll be there about quarter to nine. You handle it any way you like. But I'd just as soon you didn't say anything about what I do. I don't think Ruth Hendricks knows who I am."

Chapter Twenty-One

Tom and Joanna were waiting when Ruth Hendricks arrived at nine. She looked at Joanna and her eyes said, "What gives?" Joanna introduced Tom as an old family friend who was living in Bangkok and said she would feel better if he came along. Ruth looked him over like an experienced tailor measuring him for a suit of clothes. If she had any objections she kept them to herself.

They went down to the boat landing behind the hotel and got into a longboat with a powerful outboard motor, the kind that were common on the larger canals. Ruth had apparently pre-arranged the trip because she just nodded her head to the boatman and they took off in a southerly direction. Joanna soon lost track of where they were going. The water was black as tar and after a while the canal seemed to get narrower and more twisty. They seemed to leave the main *khlong* at some point and turn onto a lesser canal, but it was impossible for her to tell. She could see Tom straining to make out landmarks that would identify their where-abouts but he didn't seem to be having much luck. After about twenty minutes they entered an intricate system of waterways that could have been going around in circles for all they knew.

Eventually they pulled up to a kind of jetty that was part of a string of shacks built on stilts over the water. What light there was came from candles or dingy oil lamps that made the air smoky. The place was smelly from a combination of charcoal burners, dry fish, urine and a very pungent kind of incense. They followed Ruth on foot along another intricate course that seemed to lead in a zigzag, back-and-forth pattern. Joanna wondered if all this was diversionary or whether it was in fact the only way in.

They finally stopped in front of one of the shacks and Ruth tapped on the door. She turned to Joanna and said, "Please be quick about this. It's not a good idea to hang around too long." Joanna nodded her head just as Dinh opened the door. His face seemed careworn from hard work and worry and his eyes darted fearfully from face to face before stopping at Ruth's with a flicker of recognition.

"Dinh," she said, almost whispering. "I've brought Mr. Franklin's widow. She has asked to see you again. May we come in?" His eyes darted to Joanna's face for an instant and then lowered as he stepped back to let them in. The room was about ten-feet-square and gloomy. It was lit only by a small gas lantern. Joanna noticed a bed in one corner where a young woman sat holding a sleeping baby. In another corner she made out some cooking utensils and a wok on the floor. She didn't know if Dinh had fallen on hard times or if this had always been his lifestyle. Possibly he was saving his money for a new life somewhere else. Or maybe he just didn't have any money.

He didn't introduce them to the young woman, presumably his wife. He just looked directly at Joanna and said, "You wish to ask me something, Mrs. Franklin?"

"Dinh," she said, not really knowing where to begin, "I have just returned from Pattaya where I saw your sister." He didn't comment on this and his expression didn't change. It occurred to her that he might not know Malee was dead. So she told him what had happened as carefully as she could. His eyes widened with a look of pain and he turned to the woman on the bed and spoke to her in a harsh choking voice, in what was probably a Vietnamese dialect. It was hard to see the expression on the woman's face and the only discernible reaction from her was a sharp intake of breath.

"Tell me what you know," he said. So she told him that Malee had come to her room and warned her to leave Pattaya. And that she had told her "bad things" were happening there. Finally, she told him about Franklin's "bad accident," as Malee had referred to it.

"Dinh, the reason I'm here is I do not believe my husband died in an accident. I want to know what really happened. The Embassy won't help me. The police won't help me. I want you to help me by telling me what you know. Was my husband involved in anything that might have led to his death?"

"How can I know this, Mrs. Franklin? I am only houseboy to Mr. Franklin. He not tell me about business. He just say, Dinh, I am home for supper; Dinh, I am not home for supper. Like that."

"But didn't your sister ever say anything to you about Mr. Franklin? Perhaps she knew something and she told you. She was afraid of something, Dinh. She must have told you." The woman on the bed had begun to sob quietly and Dinh turned and said something to her in a low voice. Maybe it only sounded harsh because of the dialect.

"No, Mrs. Franklin, she not say to me. I am not see sister for many months since Mr. Franklin make her job at hotel. I am sorry."

"Okay then, can you tell me who came to see him, who he entertained? Anything might be helpful."

Joanna could see he was trying to remember. The woman on the bed was still sobbing but her sobs had become more rhythmic as if she were humming a sad lullaby to the sleeping baby. "Mr. Franklin very quiet at home," said Dinh at last. "He not entertain – only in restaurant, like that. Sometime Mrs. Ruth come for meeting. Sometime Mr. Roberts. They talk business, make note. I serve drink."

Joanna wanted to ask who left last, Mrs. Ruth or Mr. Roberts, but what was the point? Whatever had happened between Franklin and Ruth was ancient history. She was more useful now as a friend than an enemy.

"Was there anyone else, Dinh? Anyone you know of that he talked to on the phone or maybe went on trips with?"

"He make trip often, Mrs. Franklin. Usually to north he say. He tell me to pack suitcase, that all."

"What kind of clothes did he take on these trips up north, Dinh? Business suits, golf clothes?"

"Mostly not business suit, Mrs. Franklin. He say pack only shirt, pants and jacket. Sometimes cooler at night, he say. Golf clothes maybe only one or two times."

Joanna glanced at Ruth and saw her nod her head slightly in accord. "What about a bathing suit, Dinh. Did Mr. Franklin have a bathing suit? Did he ever ask you to pack it?

"Oh no, Mrs. Franklin. Mr. Franklin not have bathing suit. I think he never go to beach. I think he maybe not like swim."

"But you know that his body was found in the water and he was wearing a bathing suit when he died?"

"Yes, Mrs. Franklin, I know this. It surprise me but who am I to say? Mr. Franklin very important man."

"Did the police question you after Mr. Franklin died? Did you tell them anything you haven't told me?"

"Police ask me question about Mr. Franklin trips and visitor, like that, like you ask. I can not tell what I do not know."

She could see that Dinh was the model houseboy – careful, discreet, turning a blind eye to his employer's private life. Even though he was probably closest to the intimate details of Franklin's life, he chose not to see things.

"Dinh, why do you think your sister was murdered?"

"I do not know, Mrs. Franklin," he said after deliberating for a few minutes. "She work in hotel at Pattaya. Maybe she have trouble with someone there. It is dangerous place. I think since Mr. Franklin die she cannot take good care of herself. She is very young and very beautiful." A look of great sadness came over his face and Joanna realized that this was not the first tragedy of his life, nor, probably, would it be the last.

"I'm sorry, Dinh. I won't bother you any more. I just have one more question. About the telephone. Did Mr. Franklin receive calls from anyone not known to you? I mean, could there have been anyone he talked to on a regular basis that never came to see him?" It was a stab in the dark, but she thought that, if Franklin was involved with something on the side, he probably wasn't doing it solo. There might have been some kind of silent partner that connected him with information or plans or shipments, or who knew what?

Dinh thought about it for a minute before answering. "There was sometime a man who call, American man I think, he call two maybe three time every week. I never see this man."

"Did he ever leave a message for my husband? Did he ever leave his name?"

"No, he only say he call back. But I think Mr. Franklin, he call him 'Jack.' I hear him say sometime, 'Yeah, Jack.'"

At least it was something new. Joanna didn't recall being introduced to anyone called Jack, but maybe Tom would have some ideas. Then again, it was possible that Franklin was using the name "Jack" in a colloquial sense when he said something like "Yeah, Jack" or "Sure, Jack." But whoever this person was, if she could find him, he might be the link to whatever had been happening "up north."

Joanna asked the others to step outside and wait for her. She had taken the time earlier in the evening to change some traveler's checks just in case she needed to grease a few palms. Dinh hadn't asked for anything and Franklin's death had obviously altered his circumstances considerably. She handed him the envelope with the cash in it and said, "Please take this, Dinh. My husband always spoke very highly of you and I know he would have wanted me to give you this. Please take care of yourself."

Dinh took the envelope but didn't open it. She didn't think it mattered to him how much was in it. No amount of money was going to undo what had already happened to him.

When she got outside, Ruth led them back to the longboat presumably by the same route they had taken in. The trip back was as silent as the trip in except for the roar of the huge outboard motor. They might have been going in the wrong direction for all Joanna could tell. Nothing looked familiar except the tarry black water. She was anxious to talk to Tom and see what he thought of her conversation with Dinh. She hoped he'd have an idea who "Jack" might be. She had deliberately avoided showing him the anonymous letter because she was afraid he would never let her out of his sight if he thought Fred Hendricks was stalking her. Tom had become increasingly protective of her ever since Malee's murder. It annoyed her that he didn't think she could take care of herself. On the other hand, she was flattered by his concern. She wanted to believe he liked her and didn't just feel responsible for her.

At any rate, Joanna already knew her next move. She was determined to talk to Art Roberts. Alone.

Chapter Twenty-Two

Ruth Hendricks dropped Tom and Joanna off at the jetty of the Oriental Hotel and headed off in the longboat. She acknowledged Joanna's "Thank you" with a nod of her head but no other words were exchanged between them. It was after eleven o'clock and Joanna needed a drink, so she suggested a nightcap in the bar. Tom agreed readily and was as anxious to talk about the meeting with Dinh as she was.

Joanna was glad the bar was nearly empty. She couldn't tell if they were being watched, but if they were, she thought it would be easier to detect with fewer people around. Ever since they'd returned to Bangkok she'd felt vaguely uneasy and, the deeper she got into things, the more she felt that everybody else knew something she didn't. If she could only pull together all those separate pieces of information, maybe they would tell the whole story. Or was she wrong? Was there only one person who knew the whole story and was his name Jack?

"Well?" she said, after the drinks had been served. "What do you think? Is 'Jack' someone we should know about?"

"Jack," said Tom, rubbing his eyes as if somehow that would release the answer. "I've been wracking my brain since Dinh said it and I can't think of who he might be."

"Maybe it's not his real name. If they were involved in anything illegal they might have used code names for each other."

"It's possible," said Tom, "but a little far-fetched. I mean, they were part of a community where everyone knows everybody else. So you'd have to be sure no one would recognize your voice if you were going to use another name. In other words, it would probably arouse less suspicion if you called on a regular basis using your own name. The fact that this Jack character never left messages would indicate that, first of all, Dinh didn't know him and, second, that Jack didn't want Dinh to know him. It could be any number of people, however, because, as Dinh indicated, Franklin didn't entertain at home and very few people came to see him. So it wouldn't be hard for him to avoid being known by Dinh."

"Very good, Sherlock," said Joanna, trying to absorb the logic behind his explanation. "I'm sure that makes perfect sense. But give me a couple of more drinks on a hot night and the opposite would probably be just as logical."

It was worth the lame joke to see Tom's smile. She liked sharing secrets with him. She realized with some discomfort that it was Franklin's death that had brought them together and, also, that it was the most intimate she'd been with a man for a long time. She had never felt deprived before but she was beginning to realize how much she had missed something as simple as companionship being married to Franklin all those years. Of course the other possibility was that she was feeling bitter over the fact that Franklin had a complex secret life that she had known nothing about. While she had been sitting at home reading books, he had been involved with mistresses and mystery men in faraway exotic places. Joanna was beginning to hate him for getting killed behind her back. She wanted to deny the good things about their relationship because she resented the life he had without her. But who did she have to blame but herself?

"Come on," said Tom, breaking into her mixed-up thoughts. "It's not that complicated. Whoever this Jack is, we know he's American, and it's entirely possible your husband was associated with him professionally or socially. The next thing is, how do we figure out who he is?"

"I haven't a clue, Tom. All I know is that nobody wants to talk to me. I seem to make them all very uncomfortable. Don't you think it's odd that Ruth Hendricks knew where Dinh was? Is it because she knows something rotten was going on, and maybe she and Dinh were part of it and now they're afraid for their lives? Or, they weren't part of it but they're afraid someone thinks they know something. As for the rest of them, they've closed ranks to protect themselves, or they're pretty damn suspicious about what happened and they don't want some outsider prying the lid off their rotten little cesspool."

"Whoa! That's pretty strong language coming from the gentle and restrained Widow Reynolds. What about Franklin's reputation? Do you really want to put it up in front of a firing squad and shoot it full of holes? Because that's what just might happen."

"Damn him for doing this to me, Tom!" she said. "And damn all of them for thinking I'll go away quietly. I'm going to get to the bottom of this if it's the last thing I ever do and I'm going to do it for myself. Me. Joanna. To hell with them all!"

And then she did it. The ultimate female payoff. She burst into tears and sobbed deeply and miserably, holding her face in her hands and wishing she were onstage at the Met playing *Madame Butterfly* or something instead of being a melodramatic fool in real life.

Tom had the decency, or the wisdom, not to say anything. He just put his arm around her shoulders and waited until she came to her senses and closed the floodgates.

"I'm sorry, Tom," she said, wiping away tears and mascara along with her dignity. "Forgive me. I haven't behaved like that in a long, long time."

"That's okay, Joanna. You're entitled. You've had a pretty rough ride lately. I think you've held up remarkably well."

"For a woman?" she said, finishing his thought for him.

"I didn't say that, nor do I think it. I wasn't married to Franklin for sixteen years, so obviously I don't have the same emotional investment you have in the situation. I understand why you have to know what happened to him and I understand that you won't rest easy until you do. I also know that I'm afraid of what we may find out and I'm afraid for our lives if we do find out who killed Franklin. Whoever killed your husband won't hesitate to kill you or me if we get too close."

"So why don't you pull out, Tom? Let me handle it my way and take my chances. Why should you risk your life on something you have no emotional investment in?"

"I can't do that, Joanna. I told you before. I do have an investment, a personal investment, in this thing. If there's a cover-up, I want to know why. I want to know how an American citizen can die under mysterious circumstances in a foreign country and no one wants to do anything about it. Especially other Americans. You're in it for your reasons and I'm in it for mine. Now where do we go from here?"

"I want to see Art Roberts," she said. "Alone. Maybe he'll open up a little more if I talk to him privately."

She could see Tom didn't like the idea, but he agreed reluctantly when she promised to meet Art in a public place. "Okay," she said, "no secret rendezvous where he can strangle me and dump my body into the canal."

"Don't joke about it, Joanna. You can't assume Art won't hurt you. If he's involved, he might do anything to save his own skin."

"I'll be careful, Tom. I promise. I won't overplay my hand. And now," she said, heaving a sigh of exhaustion, "I'll say thank you and goodnight. Especially thank you." She stood up, kissed him on the cheek and exited gracefully. She half hoped he would follow her and when he didn't, she told herself to stop thinking like a lovesick teenager. Besides, she was so tired when she crawled into bed she didn't even turn out the light. It was still on the next morning when she woke up.

Tom watched her walk out of the bar and then he ordered himself another drink. This was what he wanted, wasn't it? She was doing his legwork and asking the questions he couldn't ask. So why did it bother him when she took the lead and decided what to do next? Was he afraid of what might happen to her? Or was he afraid of what she might find out? Tom didn't like not knowing what was going to happen next. And he didn't like the fact that his emotions might be getting in the way of his judgment. Was he starting to like Joanna a little too much? Were his priorities changing and should he tell her? Tell her what? That it wasn't about the story anymore – all that stuff about injustice and cover-ups? That it was about her?

"Shit," he said.

Joanna called Art at his office at A.A.R. right after breakfast and asked if he would meet her sometime during the day at the Siam Center on Rama I Road. He was reluctant at first but, when she told him she would be leaving Bangkok soon and wanted to see him before she left, he acquiesced. She said she'd wait for him outside the American Express office in the Center. That way, she figured, if anyone was watching, it would look like she was getting mail from home and was, therefore, in touch with someone. She might also be able to make the meeting with Art look accidental. She was sure she could persuade him to have a drink at the Siam Intercontinental next door.

They agreed on two o'clock so she decided to do another tourist turn and visit the Jim Thompson house around the corner on Soi Kasemsong II. Joanna was starting to feel the attraction of the Orient that Tom had talked about and she found herself eager to take in more of the mystery of Thailand. The contrasts of the ancient and modern co-existing in an east-west marriage of convenience pulled at her from all sides. She was being seduced on the one hand by brilliant bits of beauty and repelled on the other by their stinking, mucky context. It was like finding a precious and perfect jewel set in a brass ring that turned your finger green.

She wondered if the mystery of Jim Thompson was symbolic of what happened to Americans who tried to put down roots in the fecund Asian soil. Thompson had come to Thailand at the end of the Second World War and breathed life into the Thai silk industry, setting up a factory and taking his unusual gem-colored fabrics straight to the editor of *Vogue* magazine. He became a devoted admirer and collector of Asian art and artifacts, but was to disappear one day for no apparent reason in the Malaysian jungle never to be seen again. His house, a remarkable edifice of ancient teak logs salvaged from former palaces, was now a museum displaying his fabulous collection of Chinese porcelain, Cambodian stone figures and Burmese wood carvings. But, wandering through his house, Joanna could grasp no sense of the missing man; no ghosts reached out to remind her that a real person had once occupied these rooms. She was overcome by an intense feeling of loss as she realized how easily a human being could be swallowed up by the deep, dark throat of Asia. It had happened to Jim Thompson and it had happened to Franklin. Could it happen to someone like Tom Thorpe? Or her?

She didn't have much time to shake off the morbid feelings aroused by her visit to Jim Thompson's house before she was to meet Art Roberts. She forced herself to concentrate on the pamphlets on display in the American Express office while keeping an apparently nonchalant eye out for Art. When she spotted him striding purposefully across the mall in her direction she stepped out and hailed him before he noticed her.

"Art! Hi there," she said as if greeting a long-lost friend. When she got right up to him she stopped and said in a much quieter voice, "Can I interest you in a drink next door?" He bobbed his head once in assent and said, "Okay, sure. Why not?" just like she hoped he would.

The bar was cool and dark, the exact opposite of the real world outside. The drinks were tall and cool, the exact opposite of how she felt. Art wasn't saying anything. It was her show.

"Art, I'm going to ask you some straight questions and I hope you'll give me some straight answers." She wasn't going to beat about the bush. "First of all," she said, trying to keep the quaver out of her voice and trying to remember her promise to Tom, "do you think Franklin killed himself?"

Art was very still for a moment. Then he raised his eyes from his drink to her face just slowly enough to make her aware of the nuances of his performance. "No Joanna, I don't."

"Do you think he might have been involved – either inadvertently or knowingly – in anything that was maybe, well, unsavory or uh, quasi-legal?"

"Such as what?" he asked, with just the right note of indignation.

"Well, I don't know, Art. That's why I'm asking you."

"Listen Joanna," he replied, seasoning his speech with concern and a touch of masculine worldliness frustrated by female obtuseness. "Franklin's death was an accident. The sooner you accept that, the better off you'll be."

"Don't patronize me, Art. I'm getting tired of being treated like Rebecca of Sunnybrook Farm. I know my husband well enough to know he wouldn't put on a bathing suit and go out swimming alone. And I think you knew that about him too. That's why I want you to level with me, Art. Just tell me what you thought when it happened. Tell me what you think now."

"Joanna, whatever it is you want me to tell you, I'm not going to say it. I'll admit I was a little, shall we say, disconcerted by the official version of things. I had hoped there would be a more definite account of what happened. Dammit, I liked the man. He was my friend. But I had to accept what they told me. You don't expect me to believe there's some kind of conspiracy to cover up the facts of Franklin's death, surely? Because I won't believe that. Not for a minute."

Joanna didn't know anymore if she was getting Art's version of Theater 101 or whether he was sincere. On the one hand, she couldn't believe he was so naïve. On the other hand, she didn't think he would insult her by stating so vehemently that he was Franklin's friend if he wasn't. Of course, there was always the possibility he was a consummate liar and she was the perfect sucker. If he were a bad guy he'd sell his mother up the Chao Phraya before he'd let himself get caught. She remembered the old woman she'd seen selling bunches of garlic in the market and wondered if she had a son like Art.

Joanna was facing the entrance to the bar and, as she looked over Art's shoulder and tried to focus in the gloomy darkness, a moving figure caught her eye and she half-raised herself from her chair, letting out a tiny gasp of surprise. She thought of the expression "she nearly jumped out of her skin" as if she were reading it in a book, but, before she could identify Fred Hendricks, the stocky, broad-shouldered man with a very short haircut had disappeared.

"What is it?" asked Art, obviously bewildered by her skittish behavior.

"For a minute I thought I saw Fred Hendricks," she blurted out. "I think he's been following me."

"I'm sure you're mistaken," said Art, without turning around. "Why would Fred Hendricks be following you?"

"I don't know, Art," she said, trying to hide her nervousness. "I just keep seeing him." That wasn't entirely true, she realized as soon as she'd said it. She kept seeing him in her mind's eye because she was always looking out for him. But she had only actually seen Fred Hendricks once, when she was certain it was him, in the bar at the golf club. The other times she had only thought it was him.

"What do you know about him?" she asked, hoping Art would be frank, but at the same time doubting he would be.

"Well, I only know what I've heard," Art said, choosing his words carefully. "He was with the Marines, commando I believe, and his unit was wiped out in Nam. People say he's very bitter about it and some people think he may be a little unbalanced because of it. I don't know the man, so I can't say one way or the other."

Unbalanced, she thought, that's a pretty damning remark about someone you don't know. Even if Hendricks wasn't unhinged, the fact that people believed he was could have a pretty disagreeable effect on his life. If he was unbalanced, as Art was suggesting, then maybe he had been jealous of Franklin's close association with Ruth. So jealous he might have killed him? She looked at Art and wondered if he was trying to plant ideas in her head or if he was just trying to figure out what she knew.

"Did Franklin have anything to do with him?"

"Well, his wife was Franklin's secretary, but I'm sure you already know that. Other than that, I'm sure they never associated with each other. You know you could get yourself in trouble if you keep looking for needles in haystacks." She could see Art was beginning to lose patience with her.

Now it was Joanna's turn to be the thespian. "Okay Art," she said, trying to sound defeated. "I believe you. I'm sorry to do this to you, but I'm having a hard time accepting this whole 'accident' thing. I mean, there just seem to be so many unanswered questions."

"I know Joanna. Believe me, I understand. But you've got to let it go. It's not going to bring him back."

"Yes, I know. I'll try. Don't worry. I'll be out of your hair soon. I was just in the American Express office figuring out my flight plans," she lied.

They finished their drinks, discussing ways Joanna could fly back to Chicago with a couple of stopovers going either east or west. Art pretended to be friendly and helpful and she pretended to be interested in his suggestions.

When they got up to leave she said, "Oh, by the way, Art, did Franklin ever mention anyone named Jack to you? He mentioned him in one of his letters and I was hoping I might get to meet him."

"Mmmnno," said Art, as if trying to remember. "I can't say he ever did."

"Oh well. Too bad. I guess if he was a close friend he'd have turned up by now." She reached out and shook his hand. "Thanks Art, and if I don't see you again before I leave, goodbye."

"Goodbye Joanna. I'm glad to have met you. Franklin spoke of you many times. I know how much you meant to him."

Joanna had been prepared for almost anything but Art's parting words caught her off guard. He saw the look of surprise on her face. If he had meant to shock her, he had succeeded. If he had meant it sincerely, it only served to further unnerve her.

Chapter Twenty-Three

Joanna hadn't even bothered to ask Art some of the questions she really wanted answers to. What did he know about Franklin's trips up north, especially the unscheduled ones that Ruth Hendricks had professed ignorance of? Were they just the guys getting together for a little whoopee or were those secret trips for a more sinister purpose? She had read that the girls from Chiang Mai, which was in the north of Thailand, were reputedly the most beautiful in the world. She had no trouble picturing Art seeking a little diversion from the Dragon Lady and she couldn't blame Franklin for taking the occasional side trip. If he was having an affair with Ruth, that would explain why he didn't want her to know about those trips. But if that was the case, why did she know about some of them and not others?

None of it was making any sense. Joanna wanted to believe that Franklin was as straight as an arrow, the victim of an unfortunate set of circumstances, but she still didn't know where the three million dollars had come from or why Malee was murdered or who

Jack was. She wanted very badly to see Tom and talk things over with him but he had told her he would be attending some embassy function that night and would be unavailable. Besides, he had suggested they shouldn't spend so much time together because it might look like he was using her to get information. His words, not hers.

Joanna felt all alone that night knowing nobody wanted to see her or be with her. She felt very far from home and wondered if anybody was thinking of her. She was sure everyone would be worrying by now, not having heard a word since she'd left Switzerland over two weeks ago. She had a sudden impulse to call Fay and tell her everything, but she didn't. She was afraid Fay would jump on the next flight and try to persuade her to come home. It might have been the wisest thing to do but it wasn't what Joanna wanted. She had lied to Art Roberts about leaving soon; she wasn't going anywhere without a few more answers. She wasn't sure how far she was prepared to go to get them but she wasn't ready to give up yet. Her visa was good for another two weeks and, when that ran out, she could go to Kuala Lumpur or Singapore and get another one.

Joanna spent the evening in her room and tried to think things through. Whoever was watching her must have had a pretty boring time sitting in the lobby or the bar or wherever he had decided to post himself. If he could have seen what was going on in her head he might have thought his time could be better spent. Her thoughts ranged from her courtship and marriage to Franklin, right up to the events of the last few hours, and still she was no closer to the truth. She fell asleep with her thoughts in a jumble and dreamed that she hadn't been married to Franklin after all, she had been married to Tom. She was so relieved to find this out that she rushed over to tell Fay, but Fay wasn't Fay, she was Ellen Roberts. "You're a fool Joanna," Ellen said. "Tom doesn't love you, he loves me. We've been going to Chiang Mai together for the last three years." Joanna was so devastated by this news that she woke up with a start, shouting "No!" and scared herself half to death.

She drank a glass of water to calm herself down and saw by the clock it was four a.m. She knew it was useless to try and go back to sleep when she was feeling so agitated, so she read for a bit and finally dozed off around six.

It was almost nine o'clock when she got out of bed feeling like a piece of dirty laundry. She looked out the window and saw the sun glinting on the Chao Phraya and the longboats loaded with produce and wares maneuvering their way through the muddy water. I'm a long way from home, she thought.

When the phone rang she figured it was Tom calling for a report on her conversation with Art. She was surprised to hear a rather husky female voice saying, "Hello Joanna, this is Ellen Roberts. Can we meet at your hotel in an hour?"

"Sure," Joanna said, trying to sound casual as she sorted out her thoughts. "How about the Verandah for breakfast?"

"Fine," Ellen said. "See you in an hour."

Joanna hung up the phone thinking she must still be dreaming. Ellen was coming over to tell her she was having an affair with Tom and not to follow them to Chiang Mai. Right? She shook her head to clear it and desperately wished she could talk to Tom. But then she decided she could handle Ellen on her own.

She showered and dressed in the most casually chic outfit she had – a black linen slim skirt and box jacket with a white linen sleeveless top. She accessorized with jade green beads and earrings. She wasn't crazy about the freckles the hot sun had been giving her so she applied more powder to her face than she normally would. It lent a mask-like quality that wouldn't be a disadvantage facing Ellen Roberts. Women sometimes used their wardrobes the way men used to use six-guns. If this was going to be a showdown, she wanted all the ammunition she could muster.

Joanna knew her instincts had been right when she saw Ellen walk into the dining room at precisely ten o'clock. She was wearing a slim yellow sheath that accentuated the knife-like thinness of her figure. Her accessories were jet black like her hair (dyed,

Joanna was sure) and she was immaculately coiffed and made up as if she'd just come from an appointment at the hotel beauty parlor. Air-conditioning suited her. Joanna couldn't imagine her outside in the sun or tramping through the street markets in search of a little local color.

They exchanged greetings with fake sincerity and ordered breakfast right away. Ellen dined on cigarettes and coffee and Joanna had her usual platter of fresh fruit hoping it might disarm Ellen a bit or even nauseate her with its healthiness. Joanna told herself this was Ellen's show and she was prepared to let her do the talking. Eating a pile of fruit would keep her occupied, so maybe she'd be less tempted to interrupt and ask a lot of questions. Joanna had learned that if you listened hard to people, they kept talking long after they had intended to stop and said much more than they had intended to say. She hoped Ellen Roberts was like that.

Ellen got right to the point. "You've been asking a lot of questions, Joanna," she said, lighting her second cigarette. "People are beginning to think you don't like the answers." Joanna took another bite of pineapple and didn't respond. After all, Ellen hadn't asked her a question yet, had she?

Ellen watched her eat for a while and when she saw Joanna wasn't going to volunteer anything she said, "Just why did you come here?" Her tone was part accusing, part demanding, but Joanna wasn't going to let Ellen put her on the defensive. She wiped her fingers on her napkin and took a sip of coffee before answering.

"I wanted to find out what really happened to my husband. Is that so unreasonable?" Answer one question with another; make her do most of the talking.

"In certain circumstances it might be," Ellen answered.

"What circumstances?"

"Circumstances that are none of your business and which might, shall we say, be disruptive to other people's lives."

"Oh? Are you saying my husband's death is none of my business?"

"No, I'm not suggesting that, Joanna. But you've been told the facts. His death was an accident. Why don't you accept that?"

"What if I told you I don't believe his death was an accident? That I'll never believe it as long as I live."

"You're mistaken," said Ellen, looking her straight in the eye and butting out her cigarette. "Your husband's death was an accident and nothing's going to change that."

"You mean nothing's going to change the official version. I want to know what circumstances you're talking about. I think I have a right to know."

Ellen wasn't prepared for the severity of her tone. Women like Ellen either backed down when you confronted them or else they just froze up a little more. Ellen Roberts was the second kind. Joanna felt an icy tingle go up her spine.

"Let's not play games, Joanna. If you're not prepared to believe Franklin's death was an accident, then believe this. Stirring up the ashes can only lead to two things, trouble and heartbreak. Trouble because a few people are going to be very upset with you – and I don't mean the hotel manager and the headwaiter. And heartbreak because you might just learn a few things you'll wish you hadn't. Take my advice, go back to Chicago and get on with your life."

So there *was* some kind of cover-up. Joanna wondered how high up it went and how deeply Ellen was involved. She tried to keep the look of triumph out of her eyes. Ellen Roberts didn't know it, but she had just confirmed Joanna's suspicions. Two weeks ago, Ellen had met a recently widowed matron fresh from the suburbs of Chicago. Now she was dealing with a woman scorned. What Joanna had learned in the last couple of weeks about human nature and how to handle it could have filled a file cabinet. What she was learning about herself spoke volumes. She realized with a twinge that the woman she was becoming through Franklin's death probably would have been a better companion and mate to him than the woman he had been married to for sixteen years. You never seemed to get one thing without losing another.

Joanna kept her eyes fixed on Ellen Roberts's face as she put her cigarettes and shiny black lighter back in her shiny black handbag. Ellen pushed back her chair, but before she stood up she said one more thing.

"I mean it, Joanna. Quit trying to be Sherlock Holmes. It doesn't suit you." Ellen's eyes were cold when she said this and her movements careful as she stood up and walked out. Joanna watched her go, but her mind was still trying to grasp the significance of Ellen's parting words. Had someone sent her to deliver this warning or had she thought of it all by herself? Had Art told her about their meeting? If so, Ellen couldn't have thought Joanna was after him. She was very clearly after information, not a man. Or was Ellen afraid the information would lead her to a man, maybe Art, maybe someone else, and she didn't want that to happen.

Joanna looked down at what remained of her breakfast with Ellen. An ashtray full of cigarette butts and the mushy leavings of a tropical fruit platter. Waste and rot. Even the lingering fragrance of Ellen's Chanel No. 5 couldn't eradicate Joanna's sense that those two elements pervaded everything she had discovered since coming to Thailand. She was more determined than ever to get at the truth and wash away the stink of lies she'd been told.

Joanna couldn't make the time go fast enough before she could speak to Tom. She tried wandering around the shops near the hotel but she was so well dressed that the merchants quoted her exorbitant prices for everything. She finally found an air-conditioned movie theater and sat through a terribly depressing film called *Desperate Characters* about hopelessness and decay in New York City. By the time she talked to Tom she was feeling pretty grim.

"Jesus, not Art Roberts," he said. "I can't believe he has anything to do with this. I mean, I don't like the guy a whole lot, but I'm sure he's straight. He's in a pretty important position, Joanna."

"Well so was Franklin. Maybe the fact that they're both above suspicion lets them get away with …" she almost said "murder" but stopped herself before it got out.

"Well, it's a little far-fetched. We'll need pretty strong proof before we go out on a limb with that one."

"Then that's what we'll have to get, Tom. Pretty strong proof. If there's a connection, I want to find it. And if there isn't, well, then it's just another dead end. We'll look somewhere else."

She heard the long inhale and exhale of Tom's sigh on the other end of the phone. "Let me sleep on it, okay? I need to think it through a bit more."

Joanna hesitated before she spoke. "There's something I haven't told you, Tom." And she explained in detail about the letter Franklin had written to her before he died and the subsequent discovery of three million dollars in a Swiss bank account. It was a risk, but one she had to take. If she was wrong about Tom, then she was wrong about everything. If she was right, she needed his help more than ever and she needed him to trust her.

"That does throw a different light on things, doesn't it?" he said, sounding tired. "Okay. I'll call you tomorrow. I still want to think about it."

Jesus, he thought, as he hung up the phone. Where was this thing going? He wasn't surprised there had been money involved – money was a big motive for murder – but it had never occurred to him that Joanna might be the one who'd ended up with the cash. Did anyone else know about the Swiss account? And, if so, were they just waiting for her to make a mistake? Jesus. Three million bucks. It was more than enough to kill for.

Chapter Twenty-Four

The next day was Saturday. Joanna was just stepping out of the shower when she heard the phone ring, so she grabbed a towel and ran to answer it.

"Hello," she said a little breathlessly. The chill from the air-conditioning felt like ice water on her wet skin and she was covered in goose bumps.

"Joanna, it's me, Tom." He sounded grim and very far away, as if he were calling from a phone booth. "They just fished Fred Hendricks's body out of the canal. First indications are that his neck was broken."

Now the chill she felt wasn't from the air-conditioning. She sat down on the bed still holding the phone to her ear.

"Joanna? Are you there?" She heard Tom's voice and realized she hadn't said anything for about a minute. For some reason she was thinking about how the man from the State Department had come to the house to tell her Franklin's body had been pulled from the sea. She wondered how Ruth Hendricks was taking it.

"I'm sorry. Yes, I'm here, Tom. Do they have any idea who did it?"

"Apparently not. But they think it might have happened sometime last night. According to Ruth he hasn't been home since yesterday afternoon."

The night of the embassy party at Bradshaw's that Tom had attended. She had no idea why that had popped into her head, except that it accounted for a lot of people's whereabouts if he was killed that night. But then, she thought, why would those people need alibis? Fred didn't associate with them. He probably had his own circle of friends and enemies, even if he did like to drink alone.

"Listen, I feel like getting out of this town for a few hours." It was Tom again, interrupting her thoughts. "There's a little tourist attraction called the Ancient City we can get to by bus. You can pick up the bus at your hotel in an hour. I'll pick it up at an earlier stop. I want to make sure we're not being followed."

Joanna ordered some toast and coffee from room service and plundered the ever-present fruit bowl that the staff refilled in her room every day. She thought the food would dispel the hollow feeling of nausea that was creeping over her. She wanted to feel warm and nourished instead of cold and empty. She dressed quickly and, as soon as the room service waiter left, she picked up the phone and dialed Ruth's home number. Ruth had given it to her the night they had gone to see Dinh. They both understood she was only to use it in case of emergency.

The phone rang five times before she heard a man's voice say hello. She asked for Mrs. Hendricks.

"Who wants to talk to her?" the voice said.

"This is Joanna Reynolds," she replied, annoyed at the man's brusque manner. "Who am I talking to?"

"Joanna, this is Art Roberts. I'm sorry, Mrs. Hendricks can't come to the phone right now. She's had a terrible shock and she's not taking any calls."

Did that mean Art Roberts was a friend of the family? Art told her that Fred had met with an accident and was dead and that the police had been questioning Ruth all morning.

Another accident, she thought. She wanted to ask Art if Hendricks had been practicing his swan dive in the canal and that's how his neck had been broken, but she didn't let on that she already knew he was dead.

"How terrible," she said instead. "Please tell Ruth I called and give her my deepest sympathy. I understand how she must feel."

"I'm sure you do, Joanna. And I'll convey your sympathy to her. Thank you for calling."

Art hung up the phone the way they do in the movies. Without saying goodbye. Poor Ruth, she thought. Joanna had read somewhere once that people in unhappy marriages often had a harder time dealing with the death of their spouse than people whose marriages had been happy. Ruth must have loved Fred when she married him, just as Joanna had loved Franklin, but things hadn't worked out the way she thought they would. Joanna wondered if Ruth would leave Thailand now and go back to the life she'd had before.

Joanna caught the bus for the Ancient City at ten o'clock and saw Tom sitting at the back, watching to see who got on with her. A French couple and their teenage daughter were the only ones who boarded so she relaxed and tried to put her suspicions out of her mind. If Fred Hendricks had been following her, he certainly wouldn't be doing it today. But if someone had hired Fred to watch her, then that someone may have hired other people as well. Maybe if Fred had been looking over his own shoulder instead of watching her, he wouldn't be dead.

They didn't talk much on the twenty-mile ride to Samut Prakan. They waited till they were off the bus and away from everybody before rehashing all the things that had happened to date. Fred Hendricks's death might or might not be another piece of the puzzle. There had to be some missing link that would hook everything together, some person who was running the show. So far, Franklin, Malee and Fred Hendricks all appeared to be players – losers – in a game that somebody had to be running.

"One of the things I don't understand in all this," said Tom, when they finally decided to sit down and have a cold beer, "is why Ellen Roberts would be delivering her husband's messages."

"Maybe she has a lover and that's who she's trying to protect." Joanna realized she was becoming obsessed with illicit liaisons and secret rendezvous but, what the heck, she couldn't be wrong every time.

"We can't rule out the possibility." Tom was sitting hunched over his drink, both hands wrapped around the glass.

"Tell me about the embassy party last night," she said. The party, or function as they liked to call them, had been at Bradshaw's place and had something to do with a trade delegation from Hong Kong. "Were Ellen and Art there?"

"Yeah, they were there," said Tom, taking a long swig of cold beer. He pressed the side of the bottle against his forehead. "God it's hot!" It was well into the nineties and steaming. They had already done a fair bit of walking through the outdoor museum that covered some 200 acres and was filled with small replicas of monuments and temples from all over the country. After about an hour-and-a-half, they looked at each other and wordlessly decided they had had enough and headed for the first place that sold cold beer. Joanna hadn't really been in the mood for sightseeing anyway. She had too much on her mind.

Tom seemed to be trying to remember the events of the previous evening so she quietly sipped her beer and waited for him to speak. After a couple of minutes he looked at her and said, "You know, I just remembered something that didn't mean too much to me at the time, but now I wonder if it has any significance. I had already put away a couple of drinks and was circulating, looking for an interesting conversation to eavesdrop on. Most of the Hong

Kong contingent had moved on to another reception and the party was just starting to cook. Anyway, as I was drifting around the room, I spotted Ellen having an intense conversation with Bradshaw. I really didn't think too much of it because I'm used to seeing Ellen nail people and lay into them for one reason or another. I figured she was just giving him a piece of her mind about some stupid thing. It's no secret Ellen's not crazy about Bangkok and its citizens. Anyway, just as I came into earshot of them I heard her say, 'It's your ass if you don't, Jack.' Funny, I'd never heard anyone call him Jack before, but I can't say any warning bells went off in my head. Until just now when you told me Ellen called to see you."

They discussed the connection between Franklin and Bradshaw. They had been friends, Loretta told her, and Jonathon had been very upset when Franklin had died. Even if he was the mysterious Jack who had phoned Franklin, what of it? He was probably just keeping in touch on an informal basis with the activities of the A.A.R. As far as Tom knew, they had never golfed together; he was pretty certain Bradshaw didn't golf. They would have met socially on several occasions but, according to Tom, he could only remember having seen Franklin at maybe two or three official functions connected with the embassy. Tom wasn't convinced that Bradshaw was the Jack they were looking for and, if he was, then maybe Jack wasn't anyone they needed to worry about.

"I don't think there's any way we can approach him directly and ask him," said Tom, finally, sitting back in his chair and stretching his long legs under the table. "If he's not involved in anything, he'll be outraged that we – I mean you, of course – are asking him about it. And that could put an end to any more unofficial investigating, at least within these borders. Bradshaw's got a long reach, even if he isn't top man at the embassy. If you think you're persona non grata now, just wait. And if he is involved, he'll lie about it and that might be the end of everything forever."

"You mean I'll end up wearing cement shoes at the bottom of the Chao Phraya?" Joanna asked, thinking of Fred Hendricks.

"In a word, something like that."

"That's three words," she said. "Come on. Let's get back to town. This heat's killing me and I can't think anymore." On the way back she asked Tom if he thought Ellen might have been protecting Bradshaw rather than Art when she came to warn her off. He said they couldn't afford to discount any possibility, but at this point he couldn't see what course of action they could take to prove anything. Asking questions wasn't getting them anywhere. Hell, he said, they didn't even know if Jack was a resident American. He could be someone who came into town once a month and called Franklin for any number of reasons. Finding out who Jack was might turn out to be a big waste of time.

When the bus got back to the hotel, Joanna got off and went straight upstairs to her room and took a cool shower. Tom had got off at a previous stop with the agreement that they would talk on the phone the next day to see if either of them had come up with some brilliant plan of action. Her stomach was a little off from the heat and the beer, so she ordered some tea and biscuits from room service and settled back to read a few more Somerset Maugham stories. She was halfway through the second one when the phone rang. She picked it up expecting it to be Tom with a brilliant idea, but it wasn't.

"Joanna?" She recognized the deep mahogany voice immediately. "This is Jonathon Bradshaw. I wonder if you'd have a drink with me tonight? There's something I think we should discuss."

Joanna's brain was racing a mile a minute trying to think of what to say. Finally she just said, "Certainly, Jonathon. I'd be delighted."

"Fine. I'll pick you up at your hotel in an hour."

"Yes. See you then."

She dialed Tom's number immediately but there was no answer. Damn, she thought, where can he be? Bradshaw had said he would pick her up, which meant he intended to take her someplace. She was very reluctant to leave the hotel without Tom knowing. Joanna kept ringing Tom's number while she changed her clothes and once more after she received Bradshaw's call from the lobby to say he would wait for her to come down, but there was still no answer. If she couldn't persuade Bradshaw to have a drink in the hotel she would have to go with him and take her chances. Joanna asked herself what she was afraid of but she couldn't really define anything more than a strong sense of anxiety. She felt very nervous all the way down in the elevator and made herself take three deep breaths to calm down. She was almost hyperventilating.

Bradshaw was waiting for her in one of the large beige armchairs in the lobby. He saw her get off the elevator and stood up to greet her. "Good evening, Joanna. It's good to see you again." His voice oozed charm but his blue eyes glittered hard.

"I have to admit," she said, sounding too chatty in her own ears, "that I was a little surprised when you called, Jonathon. I can't imagine what you want to see me about."

His only reply to that was a throaty chuckle of the who-are-you-trying-to-kid variety. There was no convincing him they should have a drink in the hotel bar. He very definitely had other plans and Joanna very definitely wanted to hear what he had to say.

He had his own car and they drove east through the downtown Bangkok night to a district she knew to be Patpong, the notorious strip that was home to bars, discos, restaurants, luxury hotels and bordellos. This was the heart of the Bangkok sleaze trade where the red-light district was open for business twenty-four hours a day, where drug deals took place on every street corner and where pimping took on new meaning. Everything was for sale at any price. She wondered why Bradshaw had brought her here.

"I wanted you to see this part of town," he said, as if reading her mind, "because it's important that you understand what goes on in a city like Bangkok. This is all very serious business and it's easy to be fooled into thinking it's just a game you play for fun and profit. Too many people get into serious trouble when they don't play by the rules."

He drove very slowly, cruising the strip to give her lots of time to take in the action. The street was filled with people strolling leisurely up and down as if it were a hot sunny Sunday instead of the neon bright night. Everybody, men and women, girls and boys, wore tight, garishly colored clothes in fabrics that either shone satiny smooth or sparkled with a hard glitter. Rock music blasted from loudspeakers mounted in front of every doorway, each one playing a different tune. The thumping cacophony drowned out the murmured conversations and the deal making. People seemed to glance over their shoulders a lot and, as slow and deliberate as their body moves were, their eyes never stopped moving, glancing left and right, forward and back, never missing a thing. Joanna wondered if Bradshaw was trying to shock or frighten her, or both. She tried not to show any reaction, but her muscles were rigid and she could feel the veins on the backs of her hands pulsing because she was holding onto her bag so tightly.

Joanna wondered if Loretta knew Jonathon was with her and, if so, what he had told her. Had he said, "I'll show that woman something she'll never forget," or, "I'm going to give her the scare of her life?" He couldn't possibly have told her he was bringing me here, she thought. Loretta's my friend. She would never have allowed him to do this to me. It was insulting, humiliating and frightening. No, she was sure Loretta didn't know her husband was taking her friend into the heart of Bangkok's red-light district. Loretta would not have stood for it.

Bradshaw finally pulled over and maneuvered the car into a solitary parking space that seemed to appear out of nowhere. He got out of the car and came around and opened her door, offering her his hand as she stepped onto the street. She felt as if all eyes were on her, examining her for her worth and preparing to make an offer. She kept her mouth tightly shut as the first of a series of pimps approached them and asked Bradshaw in very low tones if they were looking for a good time. In the minute or so it took them to walk the fifty feet to their destination, a bar as raunchy-looking on the outside as any of them, they were approached by no fewer than six of these gentlemen of the night. Bradshaw didn't say a word to any of them; in fact he appeared not to notice them any more than he might notice flies buzzing.

The bar they entered was darker than the street and it took her eyes a few minutes to adjust. They could still hear rock music but it was slightly muffled by the dark red, plush chairs and thick black and red carpeting. They were led to a table by a shapely Thai hostess in a tight silver satin gown slit up to her waist. Joanna heard herself order a gin and tonic and Bradshaw ordered J&B on the rocks. She waited until the drinks arrived before she spoke.

"What's this all about, Jonathon?" The whole thing was too obviously a ploy to get a reaction out of her to let it go without comment.

"Joanna," he began, fixing her with a hard blue stare that said: This time I mean business. "The first time we met, I advised you not to interfere in what was a local police matter and a closed case. It has come to my attention that you ignored that advice and have been going around saying you thought your husband's death was not an accident. Now, we are in a sensitive position in this country and we need all the good will we can get from these people to do what we have to do here." He offered her an American brand cigarette. She shook her head and he lit one for himself, deliberately, giving her time to think about what he was saying. If she had thought Art Roberts was into theatrics, this guy had him beat hands down. Besides looking the part, Jonathon had all the right moves. Even in the dim light of the bar she could see that his clothes were expensive and well cut. When he lit his cigarette, he did it with a gold cigarette lighter at an angle that revealed a wafer-thin gold watch on his wrist. Everything about him said, "Yes, I have money, but I also have taste." He was as smooth as silk and as hard as steel. So far he had told her nothing she didn't already know.

"I'm afraid you've put me in a very uncomfortable position, Joanna." She could sense the subtle shifting of gears as Bradshaw took another sip of his scotch. "I had hoped I wouldn't have to tell you this but, in a way, you've forced my hand."

What was he getting at? Was this going to be some kind of confession? Was he about to throw himself at her mercy and plead with her to leave the country? She wished he would just get on with it.

"Joanna," he started, giving the impression he was reluctant to go on, "it came to our attention some time ago that your late husband was involved – uh, to what extent we didn't know at the time – in some kind of drug trafficking that was paying him huge sums of money." Bradshaw's eyes hadn't left her face. She wondered if he could tell she wasn't breathing. She could feel the expression on her face change in a sickening way as if a hot lamp was slowly melting her flesh. "I'm sorry to have to tell you this, but you leave me no choice." His voice sounded like he was shouting at her through the windows of a car as she was driving through the Holland Tunnel. She wanted to be sick but forced herself to swallow hard.

"I know this must be painful for you and I want you to know that we have no intention of letting this information become public. Your husband was quite probably killed by one of his suppliers or customers, someone who didn't like the way he did business, but the official record says 'accident' and we're quite prepared to let it stand." A mixture of blood and loud music was pounding in her ears and she felt so hot she thought she might explode like a homemade bomb. Get yourself under control, she thought. Don't let this man see how you feel. Just calm down until you get out of this place. It'll be over soon. Bradshaw's lips were moving but she had tuned him out. She was concentrating hard on keeping herself in one piece. She caught things like "highly confidential," "national interest" and "public humiliation."

She waited until his lips stopped moving and then she spoke, very carefully, very deliberately. "Can we leave now?" She could barely hear her own voice, but he must have heard her because he answered, "Of course."

He put an American twenty-dollar bill on the table, stood up and took her arm. She didn't know how she managed to walk out of the place, but the next thing she knew she was in the passenger seat of his car and they were headed back to the hotel. The car was air-conditioned but she had opened the window wide to let the hot night air blow on her face.

"Are you all right?" she heard him say. "I'm sorry it had to be this way. It must be like having him die all over again." In a way he was right, but it had been much more brutal than that. It was like seeing him murdered before her eyes, a much more violent death than the first one. But she had got what she came for. She had got the truth.

Bradshaw insisted on walking her up to her room when they got back to the hotel and, above her protests, he rang for the maid to help her get ready for bed. He told the maid Joanna wasn't feeling well and asked her to look in on her during the night. Before he left he told Joanna he would be going out of town for a couple of days with his family to escape the heat, but if there was anything she needed before she left Thailand she could contact his assistant Bruce Jackson at the embassy.

That's the last thing she remembered until she woke up several hours later feeling very cold and very small in the large white bed.

Chapter Twenty-Five

Joanna couldn't bring herself to leave her hotel room so she called Tom and asked him if he would come up to the room for coffee. She said she wasn't feeling very well but that she had something important to tell him. He asked her if she wanted a doctor and she said no, just to come as quickly as possible. He said he'd be there in half-an-hour. She had bathed and dressed before she called Tom, so she spent the half hour fidgeting. She was in an agony of nerves, unable to think, unable even to cry. She just kept wringing her hands, pacing back and forth, counting the minutes until Tom arrived. When he finally did arrive he took one look at her and called room service for some Scotch. Then he made her sit down and stop wringing her hands. She drank the Scotch, fast, in big gulps. It gave her a real jolt and seemed to snap her out of her anguish. She started to tell him what had happened the night before and pretty soon it was spilling out of her along with the tears she had been holding back all night.

"Tom, it's what I came for," she said, still sobbing, but starting to slow down from sheer exhaustion. "I wanted the truth and now I've got it. I can't deny that's what I came for."

"What makes you so sure it's the truth, Joanna?" Was he kidding? It all made perfect sense. It explained why no one had wanted to talk to her. They must have suspected Franklin had been involved in something deplorable and were trying to spare her and themselves the gory details.

"Yes, I know it ties things up very neatly, and I'm not saying it might not be part of the truth, but I'm not sure it's the whole truth." Now Tom was the one pacing up and down, but he was doing it to help himself think. "I don't suppose you asked Bradshaw any questions last night or tried to get more details?" he asked, already knowing the answer.

"No, I was nearly paralyzed with – with what? I don't even know. All I know is I was in a kind of semi-conscious state. I couldn't have asked for a drink of water."

"Yeah, I know. That's what makes me suspicious. It's an old trick, Joanna. Sensory overload. He deliberately took you to a place that would shock and stun you and then he delivered the most unpleasant news he could have given you when you were least able to cope with it. Why did he go to so much trouble to traumatize you? Why didn't he tell you in a quiet, more private way? Let you down gently?"

"You mean he was trying to terrorize me?"

"Yes. It was a deliberate, calculated course of action to intimidate you and lower your resistance."

"I was very nervous about going with him," she said, recalling how she had felt going down in the elevator. "I tried to call you several times but there was no answer. Where were you last night?"

"Well," he said, smiling ruefully, "I was having a rather interesting evening of my own." He poured himself another cup of coffee from the silver-plated carafe before going on. "There's a young woman at the embassy I dated a few times, but she stopped seeing me after a while because all I was interested in was gossip for my column. It occurred to me last night it might not be a bad idea to take her out for a drink and see if she had anything interesting to say. Luckily she didn't have a date so she agreed to see me, for old times sake.'"

"Did she say anything?"

"She did," Tom said, savoring her obvious impatience. "We started talking about Bradshaw," he continued. "She told me he had quite a reputation as a ladies' man. She said he had movie star looks that drove the girls around the office crazy. I asked her if she knew who any of his conquests were and she said the big rumor was that he was having an affair with the wife of someone high up at A.A.R."

"Ellen Roberts?"

He nodded. "She also mentioned something else I didn't know. She said both Bradshaw and his lady friend were reputed to have very expensive tastes. Hadn't I noticed, she asked, what expensive clothes he'd started wearing? I had to confess I hadn't."

"I did," said Joanna, and described the cigarette lighter and gold watch Bradshaw had been flashing the night before.

"Kind of makes you wonder, doesn't it?" asked Tom, a smile twisting out of the corner of his mouth. "Where he's getting the money, I mean."

"You think he might have been involved in this whole thing?" Joanna would have been less shocked if Tom had told her Bradshaw was a double agent. Then she could have imagined some high-minded political motivation for crossing to the other side.

"Joanna," said Tom, interrupting her mental wanderings and catching her with her mouth open, "you seem to have got your whole life's education from reading fiction. Let me give you a crash course in reality in just two words: anything's possible."

Yes, of course, she thought. If a man like Franklin could fall into the trap, why not a man like Bradshaw? It shouldn't have surprised her. She hadn't trusted him the first time she met him in his office at the embassy. The events of the previous evening really had traumatized her. She was thinking like a child.

"Okay, okay," she said. "I'm catching up fast. But even if Bradshaw was involved, why should we care? I mean, I know what happened to Franklin. That's really what I came to find out. There isn't anything I could do about it anyway."

"Don't you see, Joanna? If Bradshaw is involved in some scam, drugs or whatever, he might have lied to you, using those scare tactics just to get you the hell out of the county."

"You mean it's possible Franklin wasn't involved in a drug ring?" Now she really was confused. In spite of everything, she had been convinced that Bradshaw had told her the truth about Franklin.

"Have you forgotten lesson number one already? Anything's possible. Bradshaw intended to scramble your brains last night. Now I'm trying to unscramble them." Exasperation was starting to creep into his voice.

"Well, you don't have to talk to me like I'm an imbecile." He looked at her with a stunned expression that made her laugh out loud.

"Okay," he said, smiling. "I guess we're even now." He poured himself another cup of coffee and poured her one too.

"Even if Bradshaw is involved in some scam, what can I do about it? I've already made a nuisance of myself over Franklin. If I start pointing a finger in Bradshaw's direction, I could be in real trouble. Chances are I've come too close for comfort already."

"I'm sure of it," said Tom. "That's why he laid such a heavy number on you last night. If he had just taken you someplace quiet and told you privately, I might not have given it a second thought. But there was no need for him to do what he did unless he wanted to scare you real bad."

"Well, he did. I was ready to get on a plane today."

"There's got to be some kind of evidence in existence," he went on. "Something on paper somewhere. If this scam was bringing in millions – let's not forget, Franklin got hold of a great deal of money in a very short time – they must have kept records of some kind."

"So Franklin was involved in the drug ring," she said, more to herself than to Tom.

"He had to be involved in something to get that kind of money. Whether it was drugs is still not certain. All we have is Bradshaw's story and if he's involved in the same scheme then what he says is highly suspect."

"Well," she said, trying to keep up with Tom's reasoning, "it makes sense they would keep some kind of records. But I'm sure there was nothing in Franklin's papers or his attorney would have noticed. He went through everything that was sent back to us."

"It could mean Bradshaw kept the books or it could mean there are other people involved and someone else has them. Whoever has them, they would have to be kept in a very safe place."

"What about Bradshaw's home? We've both been there. Do you think he might keep something hidden there?"

"It's possible," said Tom, turning the idea over in his mind. "Either there or his boat," he said, stopping in mid-thought with a look of instant recognition that matched her own.

"His boat? You mean he has a boat?" She could feel her excitement mounting and fought against a sense of horror at the unexpected coincidence.

"Yeah, he does," said Tom, with a faraway look in his eyes, like a mathematician figuring out a problem. "But I don't know where he keeps it."

"So we should start with the house. He told me he was going out of town for a couple of days with his family. To escape the heat. It's the perfect opportunity."

"Yeah," said Tom, sounding dubious, "we should start with the house if we decide to go ahead with this. You know we could be making a terrible mistake. Bradshaw could be setting us up."

"I know, Tom, but I want to do it. There's no other way that I can see to get some hard evidence."

He looked at her for a long minute, as if he were trying to figure out where she'd suddenly got all the courage. "Okay. Let's do it," he said. "I think I know the place to look, if we can figure a way in."

Joanna's heart was racing and her palms were sweating. She thought, I'm afraid. This time I'm really afraid. But she couldn't let on to Tom or she knew he'd end it right there.

"There's an office or library in one wing of the house," he continued, "that's sort of off limits. It's the obvious place to keep private papers and things, though they're probably locked up in a safe or a drawer or something."

"What about an alarm system? D'you think he'd have one?"

"Doubtful," said Tom. "The place is surrounded by a high wall and there's probably always someone there. He's got a servant and a full-time cook. The servant lives in. We're not going to get in by the front door so we'll have to figure a way over that wall."

"Can't we climb it?"

"There's the small problem of broken glass embedded in the top of it."

They decided to go that night. Tom knew that Bradshaw and Loretta were probably on the boat somewhere if they were trying to escape the heat. They agreed there wouldn't be a better opportunity. Joanna would wear dark clothes and slip out of the hotel through the kitchen. Tom would be waiting out back with a van equipped with a ladder and a couple of big cushions covered in some kind of thick material.

Bradshaw's house was completely dark and the street itself poorly lit, as were most residential streets they had driven through to get there. Joanna's big fear was Bradshaw would have some kind of guard dog but Tom was pretty sure there wasn't one. They found the darkest spot and scaled the wall using the ladder and laying the cushions across the glass shards. Tom pulled the ladder over the top and laid it against the inside of the wall so they could climb down.

They waited a minute before approaching the house but there was no sign of anything or anybody having detected them.

In the dark, the front of the house looked low and sprawling. The back fanned out on three levels in a modified U-shape. The library was on ground level at one end. Tom took some kind of tool out of the pouch attached to his belt and proceeded to jimmy the sliding patio door that faced the inside of the U. There were a lot of windows in the place and they appeared to be heavily curtained. All the drapes in the library were drawn, including the ones over the patio doors. There was a sinister silence about the place, broken only by the occasional shrill sound of the cicadas. Joanna wasn't thinking at all about the consequences of what they were doing. She was relying totally on Tom's commando training to get them in and get them out again.

When they got inside, Tom switched on a small flashlight and handed her one just like it. "Try to keep the light aimed at the floor, not the windows," he whispered. He swept the lower half of the room with his light and she saw that it contained a desk, a couple of free-standing bookcases, a cabinet with knickknacks and trophies in it, three chairs including the one behind the desk and a sofa against the far wall. There were no file cabinets or anything that looked like a safe. There was a framed map of the world hanging on the wall behind the desk, but there was no hidden opening behind it, just a nail in the wall holding the map. Nothing was concealed behind the Chinese silk print hanging over the sofa.

"I'll check the desk," whispered Tom. "There must be a file drawer." He crouched down behind the desk while she shone the flashlight over his shoulder onto a locked drawer. He worked quickly with a small pointed instrument, something like a dentist's toothpick. In a few minutes she heard the soft twang of the spring lock giving way. He pulled open the drawer and she pointed the light at its contents.

The files were arranged by a number system that meant nothing to her but was probably decoded in a card file somewhere.

She couldn't see one on top of the desk so she figured it was probably locked in one of the other drawers. Joanna started leafing through the files. Tom reached into his pocket and pulled out a camera no bigger than a pocket calculator.

"I'll check out the rest of the room more carefully," he said. "If you see anything interesting, lay it flat and hold the camera up like this and straight over the page. If you aim at the center it should get the whole thing. It has a wide angle lens."

The first few files didn't look too interesting to her. They were mostly lists of names, birth dates and places of birth, along with vital statistics referring to height, weight, eye and hair color. The first three files were all Thai and Vietnamese names. She couldn't tell if they were male or female but, from a random selection, they appeared to be between the ages of 18 and 30 and none of them weighed more than 110 pounds.

The next few files contained the names and ranks of American servicemen with corresponding birth dates and places, height, weight, eye and hair color. Also included on the lists were their service discharge dates and current addresses. Under each set of statistics was a series of code numbers of various lengths and groupings. A random check told her that most of these ex-servicemen were residing in New York, Pennsylvania, Florida and California.

The next set of files contained photocopies of documents that, on closer inspection, turned out to be birth certificates, passport front pieces and marriage certificates. The names on the marriage certificates were always one Vietnamese or Thai and one American. The American name was always the male. She was beginning to get the picture. But she didn't see how a marriage racket could be particularly lucrative even if the documents were forgeries. And why would they be when it wasn't illegal for U.S. servicemen to marry Vietnamese brides? Unless perhaps these servicemen didn't know they were married to Vietnamese girls. She was starting to get a bigger picture, but not necessarily a clearer one.

In among the files of birth and marriage certificates she found a thin, unlabeled file that contained only three sheets of paper. Each was a copy of an official death certificate and all three were young Vietnamese females. She didn't have time to speculate on what they could mean. She wanted to see some columns of figures, a list of bank accounts and deposit slips. She kept looking through the files systematically, trying not to miss anything. There had to be a connection to the three million dollars in Zurich.

Joanna hit pay dirt somewhere around the middle of the file drawer. Bank statements documenting deposits and withdrawals on numbered accounts dating back over the last six months. The amounts were high, usually in the 100,000 figures. Most of the deposits were cash and there were transfers to other numbered accounts, including the one that she had access to in Switzerland. Other files contained information about safety deposit boxes in both Thai and Swiss banks.

Joanna started photographing sample pages from each of the files, carefully laying each page flat the way Tom had told her. She still wasn't sure how valuable they were as evidence, but she wasn't going to take the time to analyze the situation. She wanted to get out of there in one piece and do the paperwork later. She worked quickly and carefully for the next ten minutes or so but, just as she was putting the bank account file back in the drawer, she heard a soft click as the room filled with light. Her heart froze in mid-beat and her breathing stopped.

Chapter Twenty-Six

I've been expecting a farewell visit from you, Joanna." He was standing in the doorway wearing a T-shirt and an old pair of jeans. She almost didn't recognize him. His left hand was still on the light switch and his right hand held a gun that was pointed at her face. Oh Jesus, she thought. This is it. She wanted to yell Tom's name – where the hell was he anyway – but her face muscles were paralyzed, as if her mind were telling them one twitch and that gun would go off.

"Find what you were looking for?" he asked. His cold eyes told her he was prepared to kill her. She managed to swallow the large amount of sawdust in her mouth and her breathing kicked in again. The way her heart and head were pounding, she was afraid she might have a stroke and spoil all his fun.

"What were they carrying?" she asked. Her voice sounded dry and cracked, like she hadn't used it in a year.

"You mean the war brides?" He smiled when he said it, amused at his little joke. "Whatever we could conceal on those lovely little bodies, darling. You'd be amazed how many hiding places there are in the female form. Personally, I preferred Burmese sapphires and heroin. Pound for pound and dollar for dollar your best return on investment."

"What happened to the girls?" She was desperately trying to buy some time. Where the hell was Tom?

"Oh, we invested them too," he said. "There's a big demand for oriental pussy all over the world. A hungry market just waiting to be fed." His deep voice had acquired a hard edge of hate she hadn't heard before. "We had a sense of mission, Franklin and I. We couldn't stand by and watch people starve, now could we?" He laughed in one harsh burst and she wanted to throw up.

"What was Franklin's part in all this?" If she was going to die, she was going to die knowing everything. And if Tom was listening, maybe he could use it to nail Bradshaw to the cross.

"Your late husband, my dear, supplied the girls and the contraband and I supplied the documents. It was the perfect partnership, don't you think? Franklin had a lot of very good connections."

"Then why did you kill him?"

"Oh, I didn't kill him, Joanna. Franklin's death was an accident. He accidentally drank a Mickey Finn and fell off the side of my boat." His smile was like a grimace but she could tell he was really enjoying himself. "Unfortunately, Franklin's fatal flaw reared its ugly little head. He didn't know when to stop. The whole thing was his idea. Did you know that? No, I suppose you didn't. Well, then he wanted to expand. He wanted to set Art Roberts up in a Hong Kong operation and I would help expedite matters of shipping and documentation through my diplomatic connections. Very dangerous, I told him. Why take the additional risk? The more people we involve, the more chance of something going wrong. But things started going wrong anyway."

"The death certificates?" It was a wild guess.

"Yeah, the death certificates. Franklin's fatal flaw again. He kept getting carried away satisfying his sexual appetites. Something was coming out of him that I hadn't realized was there. Maybe I should have seen it coming. Your husband seemed to have no limits, Joanna. He was becoming a dangerous man and he was a real danger to the operation. I had to do something before he made any more mistakes, before he had any more 'ultimate experiences' as he called them." Jonathon was leaning against the door frame still pointing the gun at her. He wasn't smiling anymore. "So we went for a little boat ride. Just like you and I are going to do, Joanna. It's a pity nobody back home knows where you are. You were foolish not to keep in touch."

"How do you know that?" she whispered, feeling time running out, feeling the blood draining from her head. What difference did it make anyway? Nobody was going to help her now. She was all alone.

"I made a few discreet calls. They think you're in Switzerland. But they wish you'd write. They're starting to get worried. Pity. They're never going to hear from you again."

Poor Claire, she thought. If only I'd called her. She was never going to know what had happened to Franklin or to her.

"I also know you're not doing this cloak and dagger stunt on your own, Joanna. Thorpe! Get out here! I know you're in here somewhere."

She saw his eyes move away from her face to look around the room and then she heard the ping-ping as two shots were fired. Her own voice was yelling "Tom! No!" as Bradshaw spun back against the door frame and slumped to the floor. She was still on her knees in front of the file drawer listening to the dead silence. The sound of movement drew her eyes in the direction of the sofa and she saw Tom slip a small gun into the pouch on his belt. He walked over to Bradshaw's hunched-up form and pressed his fingers against the still throat.

"You killed him," she said in a half-whispered choke.

"I had to. He was prepared to kill us both. A man in his position can't afford to leave any survivors."

"What are we going to do?" Her voice was barely audible and she wasn't even sure she had spoken aloud.

"We'll leave the same way we came in. If there was somebody else in the house, they'd have been here by now. So pick up everything you were using and give it to me. Make sure there's nothing left here that could connect you to this place. You didn't take the gloves off, did you?" She shook her head. Tom had made them both wear surgical rubber gloves and her hands were sweating and itchy.

"Good," he said. "Now give me the flashlight and the camera. Leave the file drawer open. If the police decide to investigate, which I doubt, I want them to see those files."

"Tom." She was whispering even though he had spoken in a normal voice, "I want to take the bank account file. It has the number of the Swiss account in it and some deposit slips."

"Okay," he said. "Put it in here." He handed her a nylon drawstring sack that he had pulled from one of his pockets.

"Boy," she said, her hand shaking as she filled the sack, "you think of everything."

"Is there anything else that might connect you or Franklin to Bradshaw?"

"I don't think so. But I can't be sure." She gave him the gist of what was in the files and he nodded and said they'd have to take the chance that there was nothing personally incriminating on paper. "Better grab the file with the death certificates, just in case," he said.

The ladder and van were just as they had left them and Joanna's body went through the motions of following Tom as he retraced their steps swiftly and silently. In her mind she kept hearing the ping-ping of the two shots Tom had fired. She didn't think she would ever stop hearing them. She couldn't believe they were just walking away from it all. No one came after them. Apparently no one saw them; no lights went on, no traffic passed them on the street. It was as if the whole thing had taken place in a time warp – like an episode of *The Twilight Zone*. Except Bradshaw had walked in on them and now his life was over. Ping. Ping. Just like that.

And Franklin was a killer. Bradshaw was a killer. Now even Tom was a killer. She had lost track of how many people were dead, some because of Franklin, some because of her.

Joanna was sure now that she had been watched all along. How else could Bradshaw have known where they were? He had probably known everything she had done, everyone she had seen. Was he responsible for Malee's death? And Fred Hendricks? Had Fred been working for Bradshaw and been set up so they'd think he killed Franklin? The jealous husband? The bagman for the drug deals? Had Bradshaw been prepared systematically to murder anyone who got close to her? Had Tom been on his list? What about Ruth Hendricks? And what had Loretta unwittingly told her husband that had put people's lives in jeopardy? Joanna was glad Jonathon Bradshaw was dead. She hoped there was no one left to carry on the business.

She had no idea what was going to happen next. Her stomach was in knots; her head was aching. Were the police going to arrest Tom and her? Would there be a trial? She had a million questions shooting through her brain and in the middle of it all was Bradshaw's voice saying, "The whole thing was his idea. Did you know that?" How was she going to live with that terrible knowledge?

Tom didn't say a word all the way back to the hotel. Whether he was shaken up by what had happened she couldn't tell. She was too preoccupied to notice. But he must have known that she was in shock. He pulled the van over about a block from the hotel.

"Are you going to be okay?" he asked. She nodded her head but she wasn't convinced and she didn't think Tom was, either. "Look," he said, "if the police ask, tell them you never left the hotel. No matter what they say to you, no matter what anybody else says, stick to your story. There's nobody who can prove otherwise. Now go up to your room and order a brandy from room service. Take a bath, drink the brandy and go to bed. Call me for any reason, any time tonight. I'm going to work tomorrow and I'll call you later in the day. Okay?" She nodded again, just as unconvincingly. After a minute or so she turned to look at him. She was very tired. "It'll be all right," he said. "In time." Then he kissed her, softly at first, then more intensely, as if for the last time.

Joanna got out of the van and walked the block to the hotel. She kept her head down and walked through the lobby as far from the desk as she could. When she got back to her room she did exactly as Tom had told her. She tried not to think too much. She knew that would come later. For now she concentrated on the pain – the one behind her eyes and the one deep inside her. She thought, If I get right inside this pain I won't have to do anything else. It'll take care of everything. I'll just wrap it around me like a blanket. Because nothing that happens now could be worse than this. Except the thinking.

She didn't sleep at all that night. Even though she kept her eyes closed for hours and didn't move around in the bed much, it wasn't anything you could call sleep. When she finally did open her eyes, the pain was still there. But not as bad. Now it was more like a dull ache. It took all the energy she had to get out of bed and get dressed. Then with what felt like her last ounce of strength she lay down on the bed again and waited for Tom to call.

"Your husband had no conscience, Joanna. Human life meant nothing to him." Those words just wouldn't go away. How could he do it? What had gone wrong? Had Franklin become so disillusioned with the world that he wanted to strike back in the most vicious and brutal way he could think of? Or had he always been ripping off the system, ripping off humanity in his own way, getting exactly what he wanted out of it – power, gratitude, money, and now something far too horrible to contemplate?

Would he have done it if she had been closer to him, she had to ask herself? Could she have made a difference? Could she have seen some dark side of his nature coming to life and maybe done something to stop it? The easy answer was no; her effect on anybody, anything, was not great enough. It would have happened anyway. But it was too late to know the real answer. She could go through the whole of their life together and still not find enough clues. Because half the time he hadn't been there. Or she hadn't been there, depending on which way you looked at it. In a way, she had done the same thing he had done. She had made up a life. Taking only what she wanted and conveniently ignoring the rest. Except her life had been benign. His had had a black cancer growing at the center of it. Growing undetected. He had used hundreds of unwitting and desperate people to get what he wanted. She had used only one. Franklin. Maybe it didn't matter how many people you betrayed. One was enough to condemn you. She would suffer more for that one than Franklin had suffered over those hundreds.

Joanna knew only one thing for sure. She had hung on to her innocence longer than most people, but she had lost it more brutally and irrevocably. She could never go back. She didn't want to go back. Everything she knew and loved was tainted. Even her friendship with Claire, in a way. If she went back she would have to live a lie for the sake of those who had loved Franklin. And that, she believed, was out of the question. She lay there for hours until the phone rang. She reached over and picked it up to hear Tom's voice as if in a dream.

"Are you all right?" he said. "You sound awful."

She didn't want him to be kind to her. She didn't want to be treated like Little Miss Muffet. "Do me a favor, Tom," she said. "Don't ever ask me again if I'm all right. I'm not all right. But I'll be all right. Okay? Just believe me. I'll survive in spite of myself."

"Okay," he said. "I'll take your word for it."

"Now, how about you," she said, feeling a bit guilty. "Are you all right?"

His laugh was touched with relief and he said, "Yeah, I'm all right, tough guy. Now, do you want to hear what happened today or would you rather engage in some more witty repartee?"

"Okay, okay. Don't be cute. Yes, I want to know what happened today. But can you tell me over dinner? I think I'd better have something to eat."

Chapter Twenty-Seven

In less than an hour they were on their way to a Chinese seafood house that featured live fish tanks at the front where you could meet your dinner before you ate it. Tom had taken one look at her and decided she needed air as well as food, so they had made a trip in a *tuk tuk*, an open air scooter taxi that sounded like its name and got them from point A to point B in the straightest possible line. Once they had something in their stomachs, and Joanna had a good stiff drink in her hand, Tom began to relay what had happened that day at the embassy. He had called repeatedly and asked to talk to Bradshaw. But they kept saying Bradshaw wasn't in and they would give him the message when he arrived. He couldn't get through to Bruce Jackson, either. So Tom had gone to the embassy and sat outside Bradshaw's office, ostensibly to wait for him.

"Apparently," he went on, "Bradshaw's houseboy arrived early this morning expecting the family to be away and found the body. Surprise, surprise. There was a lot of stuff going on behind closed doors and then an official announcement was made saying that he had died suddenly of a heart attack. Nobody asked any questions. Nobody so much as said 'shit.'"

"I don't believe it," Joanna said. "We murdered that man!" She had the sense to whisper, but Tom winced at the vehemence of her statement.

"That's right, Joanna. Just like he murdered your husband. Now you've seen it twice. That's how things get done sometimes. And I'm not just talking about Thailand. This cover-up will extend all the way to Washington."

"I wonder how Loretta feels," she said.

"I'm sure you know how she feels. If anybody knows, you do, Joanna. But I promise you she's not going to do anything about it. Ninety-nine people out of a hundred wouldn't do anything. You're the exception that breaks the rule.

"What's she going to do now? I should at least call her but what could I possibly say to her? I don't think I could face her."

"You won't have to. She's already flown home. With Bradshaw's ashes, I might add. He was cremated this afternoon. His papers and files, including the ones at his house, have already been cleaned out by a U.S. agent and, by this time tomorrow, there won't be a trace of him left in Thailand. You can count on it."

The waiter brought a platter of steaming, pungent-smelling crab. The sharp aroma of ginger hit Joanna like a dose of smelling salts. She wasn't dreaming it. This was really happening.

"Art and Ellen Roberts will be going home in the next couple of days," Tom continued. "I'm not sure how deeply they were involved in all this. I suspect Ellen knew a lot more than Art, but I guess it's something we'll never know for sure." Tom ate mechanically. Joanna was taking in the details but not quite comprehending the larger picture. Was this really the way things happened? "Someone will be coming in from the States to head up A.A.R. within a week," Tom continued, "and then it will be business as usual."

They had eaten half of the crab and she had hardly tasted it. This is nuts, she thought. Isn't anyone accountable for what happened?

Do all the widows and survivors just bury their questions along with their dead and quietly go back to wherever they came from?

"What are you going to do now?" she asked Tom.

Tom signaled the waiter for more beer before he answered her question.

"I think I'll probably move on," he finally said. "Get out of Thailand." She tried to ignore the nervous flutter in her stomach.

"Are you sure that's what you want?"

"Yes. I've given it a lot of thought. It's been coming for a long time now. I just needed a couple of murders to put it all in perspective," he said, wryly. "I want to get away from all this for a while. Maybe travel a bit. I think I might go to India and lose myself for a few months."

"That sounds like a good plan. I wouldn't mind getting lost myself for awhile."

He laughed. "I'm not sure that 'getting lost' and 'losing yourself' are quite the same thing, Joanna."

"You know what I mean," she said, smiling and feeling foolish at the same time. "I'd like to disappear for a while. I don't quite know how to handle all this. I can't go back and face Franklin's family and friends knowing what I know. I don't really want to go back. Not yet anyway." They drifted into silence again. After a little while she asked him if he had any money. "I don't mean to pry, Tom, but I feel I owe you something for all you've done for me."

"You don't owe me anything, Joanna. I have some money I've been saving up. Besides, what did I do for you except bring you more unhappiness than you had before?"

"That's not true. You helped me do what I came here to do. You believed me when nobody else would. I couldn't have done it without you. You became a friend when I needed one very badly."

"That was the easiest part of all," he said. "I hope we'll always be friends."

His saying that made her realize they were probably saying

goodbye. But she couldn't deal with that either, so she just said, "I hope so" and left it at that.

They finished eating and then took a stroll along the busy downtown street and watched the goings-on. She didn't feel as much like a stranger as she might have a month or two earlier. In fact, there was something comforting in all the noise and activity on the street. Joanna didn't much care what kinds of deals were being made. She told herself it was none of her business.

None of her business. That was ironic. She had told Ellen Roberts that her husband's death was her business. But she hadn't really considered his life her business. She wondered how Ellen was taking the news of Bradshaw's death, if she would ever know how he really died. It was frightening how Franklin's death reached out and touched so many lives. Three more people had died because of it. Would it end there? What of Loretta Bradshaw? Would she just go back to her old life of cooking roast beef on Sundays? Or would her entire reality be changed as profoundly as Joanna's? And what of Dinh? Would there ever be a time when he would feel safe and content?

"Tom," she said, breaking the silence between them, "there's one more thing I have to do. I want to talk to Ruth Hendricks. I never told you, but I think she was Franklin's mistress."

She should have known better than to expect Tom to be surprised. "What was your first clue?"

She ignored the sarcasm. "Call it an instinct, female intuition. But I just know she cared for him in a big way."

"Yeah, well, he certainly had a way with women, didn't he?"

"That's not fair," she said. "Maybe I was stupid and blind for sixteen years, but I don't think so. I can't believe that the man I married was like that. Something must have happened to him to make him do those things."

"Maybe it was just a logical extension of his personality. Greedy, power-hungry, cruel and calculating. He used people to get what he wanted. It's not so uncommon, you know. Maybe you just didn't want to know about it, so you never saw it."

"That's a pretty harsh scenario for me to live with, Tom. I'm not sure I could forgive myself for being so unaware. So deluded."

"Did you love him?"

She was surprised he was asking her that. "Yes, I did. Do you think less of me for it?"

"No. Is it wrong to love a bad person?"

"No one's all bad, Tom. I refuse to believe it. People are people. Sometimes they're wonderful and sometimes they're horrible. Period."

"Yeah? I think that's now considered a mental illness."

"Hey, don't be so technical. It's either the wonderful side of me or the horrible side of me that wants to talk to Ruth Hendricks. Which is how we got into this whole conversation in the first place."

"I'm not sure I understand why you want to talk to her. Unless it's to get back at her for stealing your husband."

"But she didn't steal him, Tom. She loved him. And she was a bigger fool than I was. Did either one of us know or love the real Franklin? Don't you see that, by knowing the worst, she can finally get on with her life. I have to. I don't have that nice illusion any more and I can't get it back. Ruth Hendricks still does. And she'll be miserable because of it for the rest of her life. She might hate me for telling her but I don't care."

"There's a very clear and specific word for what you're about to do, Joanna. Meddling. Sticking your nose into other people's lives."

"You're right. I agree with you. I've caused a lot of damage since I came to this country. I feel as if there's a trail of dead bodies behind me. Correction. There is a trail of dead bodies behind me. And one of them is the old Joanna. It's just … I know now that, if I were in her position, I'd want someone to tell me. That's all."

"Okay. I'm not going to try and talk you out of it. But just remember, not everyone's like you. She may be one of those shoot-the-messenger types."

"She's got guts, Tom. I know she has."

"Guts enough to hear the ugly truth about the guy she loved, so soon after her husband's body has been fished out of the canal? Don't count on it."

"I know you think Franklin was some kind of monster and that Bradshaw says he saw the dark side of Franklin coming out, but he wasn't always like that. He couldn't have been. I would have seen it, wouldn't I?" She didn't know whose case she was pleading – Franklin's or her own.

"Joanna, you keep saying you want to know, you have to know, you'd want someone to tell you. But I'm telling you that you just can't admit to yourself that Franklin fooled you, just like he fooled everyone else. He was a bad man. He was manipulative, self-serving, clever and cold. Franklin was a sociopath, Joanna. He was dangerous and he was a killer.

"How can you be so sure he was the one who killed those girls?" she asked. "We only have Bradshaw's word that it was Franklin."

Tom was looking at her with a curiously sad and helpless expression on his face. "I knew about the girls," he said quietly.

"What?" she asked, not sure she had heard him.

"I knew about the girls before I met you," he repeated, watching for her reaction.

"You knew?" she said, disbelief rising in her like nausea. "Why didn't you tell me?"

"I couldn't tell you," he said. "You wouldn't have believed me. And I needed someone to ask the questions I couldn't ask. A buddy of mine is married to a Vietnamese woman and they live near the border where the camps are. There were rumors about the three girls who disappeared. I won't repeat the story he told me but there was no doubt in my mind he was talking about Franklin. I didn't have any proof, then. Now I do."

Joanna stared at him. It was like looking at the face of a stranger. "Don't shoot the messenger," he said. She didn't know whether to laugh or to cry.

"You used me," she said, feeling sick at heart, angry and outraged all at the same time. "You knew the most despicable things about my husband and you let me find them out from his own murderer. I can't believe you did that to me, Tom. I trusted you." She was backing away from him on the crowded street, suddenly wanting to be out of there, needing to get away before she heard some other horrible admission.

"Joanna, wait. I didn't know how it was going to turn out. I didn't plan it this way." Joanna had started to run, pushing past people, unable to see for the tears in her eyes. She barely heard his last words.

"Joanna, please. I'm sorry – "

She ran as fast as she could, crying out loud the way she had when she was five years old and she realized her father was never going to come back. One more betrayal in a life filled with lies and deception. Self-delusion. Horrible, stupid and gullible. Poor, stupid, trusting Joanna. When was she going to learn? When was she going to see things and people for what they were? Deceitful, selfish and contemptible. She ran until she couldn't breathe anymore because the pain in her side was too excruciating. She was bent over double, trying to catch her breath and stop her crying. She took deep breaths and tried to pull herself together. Nobody went near her. Nobody tried to help her. Tom was nowhere in sight.

She finally hailed a taxi and gave the driver the name of the hotel. It took twenty minutes to get there. She must have run a long way.

Back in her room, Joanna ran a bath as hot as she could stand it and watched her skin turn an angry red as she soaked herself. She heard the phone ringing in the other room but she didn't answer it. She just lay there and let the anger and humiliation work their way out through her pores and evaporate with the steam that filled the marble bathroom. Finally the phone stopped ringing and she felt exhaustion take over her body, as if it were being injected into her bloodstream. She dragged herself out of the tub and crawled soaking wet into the large cool bed. As she listened to the water drain from the tub, she felt herself letting go of a long skein of lies, like a sweater unraveling when you pulled on the right thread. For the first time in her life she was free of illusion, sure of her past and her present. Her sleep was heavy and dark and dreamless.

Chapter Twenty-Eight

She called Ruth Hendricks the next day and said she wanted to speak to her one last time. Ruth agreed to meet her in the bar of the Siam Intercontinental, the same place she'd had her conversation with Art Roberts. Ruth was waiting for her when she got there and Joanna ordered a gin and tonic because it was a hot day and she needed a cool drink. She told Ruth she didn't have to say anything, just listen. Then she told her everything. She told her about Franklin's childhood and family and about their marriage. She even told her about the memorial service. She explained why she'd come to Thailand and what she'd hoped to find out. And then she told her what she had really found out. She didn't spare Ruth's feelings but she tried not to be deliberately cruel. The only detail she left out was how Bradshaw had actually died. She didn't think it would be fair to Tom.

Ruth didn't say a word the whole time she was talking, but somewhere near the end her eyes filled with tears. She didn't actually weep, but she let the tears run slowly down her cheeks, as if she didn't notice them.

"I'm not asking you to like me and I wouldn't blame you for hating me," Joanna told her. "If you have to ask me why I'm doing this, there's no point explaining. I think you know why. I loved a man without knowing him very well. Or maybe I did know him once, but just hadn't bothered to see how he'd changed. Maybe it didn't really matter to him, but it matters to me. I'll never know how he felt or whether he thought about me before he died. It's too late now. It's over and I'm not going to spend the rest of my life torturing myself over it. I can't.

"I met your husband, Ruth, and I could see he was deeply unhappy. I know it's none of my business, but I don't care what you think. I'm just going to say it and then I'll get out of your life for good."

By this time, Ruth had reached into her cheap straw handbag, pulled out a handkerchief and was wiping her face. Joanna felt awful, but she only had one more thing to say.

"I'm sorry for all the horrible things that have happened to you and that maybe they happened because of the men you loved. But don't spend the next ten years making the same mistakes you made in the last ten. Leave it behind you. Make a new life. And don't blame yourself."

Joanna stopped talking and Ruth stopped wiping away her tears. After a few minutes, she put her handkerchief back in her handbag – it really was an awful bag, Joanna thought – and stood up.

"Goodbye, Joanna," she said. It was the only time she ever called her by name.

"Goodbye, Ruth."

Joanna sat in the bar for a long time and nursed another gin and tonic. She thought about the things she'd said to Ruth Hendricks. She had taken a sixteen-year chunk of her life and tied it into a neat little package that could go on a shelf somewhere and never be looked at again. And she had advised Ruth to do the same. In the few short weeks since Franklin's death, she had seen all her illusions destroyed and discovered that her version of events bore little resemblance to reality. She had a lot of nerve telling Ruth Hendricks what to do with her life when she hadn't even thought about what to do with her own. She knew there were things she would never speak of to anyone. The only other person who knew about them had shattered her trust in him, breaking the one tenuous thread she had been hanging on to as she watched her life story going through the shredder, chapter by chapter. She had told Tom she couldn't go back and face Franklin's family and the people who had known him and cared about him if it meant living a lie. But these people were her family, her friends, and they cared about her too.

She realized that when a person finds out halfway through life that everything she's believed in has been a fraud, she has two choices. She can ignore the facts and carry on as if everything were fine and slowly go to pieces or she can accept the facts and try to make a new life for herself with the few shreds of self respect she has left. Did she really want to live her life without the love and support of the people she cared about? Did what she now knew about Franklin mean she would have to live a lie for the rest of her life? Or would her knowledge free her in some way by releasing her from pretence and illusion? Franklin was dead and she could bury his secrets with him. But she had chosen to go after the truth. She had tracked it down and forced it out for her own reasons and now she would have to live with it. There was only one way to find out if she could do that. Better to know, she thought as she paid the bar bill.

The American Express office was still open. She walked in, remembering the day she had lied to Art Roberts about booking her flight home. She went directly to the travel agent and gave her destination.

"I can get you connecting flights to Chicago tomorrow, Thursday or Sunday, Mrs. Reynolds," the agent said. "When would you like to leave?"

"Sunday," she said. "I have a few things to take care of before I go."

Tom's story was front-page news. Joanna saw the headlines in the *Herald Tribune* and the *Bangkok Post* on every newsstand she passed between the American Express office and the hotel:

U.S. Gov't Hid Drug-Sex-Murder Scandal In Thai Embassy

It was all there. Tom hadn't left anything out. There were even pictures of the three death certificates, pictures of Franklin and of Bradshaw. Bruce Jackson, official spokesperson for the embassy, was quoted as saying, "We knew nothing of this. There was no embassy involvement, no cover-up. This was the work of individuals and has nothing to do with the United States Embassy in Thailand." Except Tom had somehow acquired copies of the forged marriage certificates and immigration documents of some of the "war brides," as Bradshaw had referred to them. Tom must have gone back to the house after he dropped her off and cleaned out the files, thought Joanna. Then she remembered the photographs she'd snapped with Tom's camera. The only things she'd actually removed from the drawer were the death certificates and the Swiss bank account files. Joanna read the entire story twice in both papers. There was no mention of the bank accounts. According to Tom's story, all records of the financial transactions had apparently been destroyed. There was no paper trail leading to the money.

Tom had promised her he wouldn't print the story without her approval. He'd told her the story would be about Franklin's killers, not about Franklin. But that had been a lie. There was even a paragraph about Fred Hendricks and his connection to the scheme. Tom had known all along that Fred was working for Bradshaw as a kind of henchman-errand boy-assassin. It was Fred who had sliced open Malee's throat and, when Fred had become too unstable to trust, another equally dispensable ex-marine had taken care of Fred. But there was nothing about the money. Nothing about Joanna. Nothing about Joanna ever having been in Thailand.

Joanna had made up her mind before Tom's story hit the headlines. It was easier than she thought it would be to make the anonymous donations: one and a half million to Americans Aid Refugees, 250,000 to fund orphanages in Thailand, 200,000 to UNICEF, and 50,000 dollars to Ruth Hendricks. She kept a million for herself because she believed she was entitled to it. It's what she would have inherited, based on their existing assets, at the time of Franklin's death.

She knew she shouldn't feel responsible or guilty about what had happened. Tom had intended to write the story all along. She knew that now. It would have come out eventually, with or without her help. The part she found hardest to bear was the callous disregard for the feelings of those people whose lives would be forever altered because of the exposure of their family members. People like Claire, and Loretta, and herself. Did that mean she approved of the cover-up? That she didn't believe it was important to expose corruption and injustice wherever it happened? No, she didn't believe that. Was Tom really the hero in all of this? A crusader who had sacrificed everything and everybody to get at the truth? Or was he nothing more than a son-of-a-bitch who had betrayed her and robbed her of the chance to bury Franklin's secrets with him? She honestly didn't know. The truth, as usual, was probably somewhere in the middle.

She knew she was ready to go home now, to offer comfort and to be comforted. But home was going to be a place of her own choosing, not the house in Oak Park she had shared with Franklin with the beautiful garden and the rose-colored wing chair.

The End